Evidence

of the

Vampire

BRETTE O'CONNELL

To Diane —
Write your own
happy ending.

Brette O'Connell

This book is a work of fiction.
Any resemblance to actual events or persons, living
or dead, is entirely coincidental.

Crime Scene Publishing
Carson City, NV
Copyright 2016
All rights reserved.
ISBN-13: 978-1523788385
ISBN-10: 1523788380

Book cover by Laura Gordon
bookcovermachine@gmail.com

Book cover photos
www.depositphotos.com

For Simon, Arlene, Kim,
and my Forensic Science Professor, Tina Young, MFS

Many thanks to my betas for their
comments and constructive criticism
Diane Arkell
Santie Erasmus
Sheryl Etter
Matt Ewert
Carol Fontani
Jamie Frandsen
Virginia Grant
Kim Harnes
Arlene Jenkins
Debbie Lessord
Judy Moropoulos
and
Ciel Yogis

In Memoriam
Wacil Anne
My little black panther

The greatest trick the Devil ever pulled was
convincing the world he didn't exist.
Charles Baudelaire

The same can be said for vampires.

NOTES

Nevada Police Codes

10-00: Officer down

406: Burglary

407: Robbery

411: Stolen vehicle

415: Assault

419: Dead body

420: Homicide

425: Suspicious circumstances

426: Rape

Abbreviations

APB: All Points Bulletin

AFIS: Automated Fingerprint Identification System

B & E: Breaking and Entering

BOLO: Be on the Lookout

COD: Cause of Death

CODIS: Combined DNA Indexing System

CPS: Child Protective Services

CSI: Crime Scene Investigator

CSU: Crime Scene Unit

IED: Improvised Explosive Device

mtDNA: Mitochondrial DNA

RDO: Routine Day Off

TITO: Ticket in, Ticket out: Winnings claim voucher for a slot machine

VICAP: Violent Criminal Apprehension Program

"Come on, Baker. Time to rock and roll. We have two new assignments, and you're coming with me tonight," Orlando West said as he good-naturedly swung Sarah's feet off the break room coffee table.

Sarah smiled and nodded at her supervisor.

Tall, well built and exceedingly intelligent, Orlando West was the only African-American CSI in Nevada to have a doctorate in Forensic Science. He'd been shift leader for six years now and was probably the best CSI in the Western United States.

Thomas Grayson, Sarah's usual night shift partner, grabbed his assignment sheet, a B & E, from West's hand and was out the door and headed to the opposite end of the county.

It was Saturday and a traditionally busy night. But by midnight and four hours into a twelve-hour shift no calls had come in, so Sarah had been enjoying a brief break from paperwork. She was reading one of her favorite novels and had just gotten to the good part but would now have to wait until her next day off to see what happened to the attractive, glittering, adolescent vampire. In truth it was a silly novel, but that's just what she needed sometimes to take her mind off the reality of her job.

Sarah had worked for the Las Vegas Metropolitan Police Department as a forensic tech since graduating from the prestigious John Jay College of Criminal

Justice. It was her first real job after graduation that didn't involve waiting tables or working retail. After a particularly gruesome case involving two murdered children, aged three and five, and their mother, Sarah was ready to leave Las Vegas. She accepted a position at the County Sheriff's Department in the state capital, Carson City, where the crime rate and the cost of living were both low.

The native New Yorker was small, but strong, and had a quick wit and a temper that matched, thanks to her Irish roots. Her dark auburn-colored hair was cropped short in a pixie cut because of the job, and the style accentuated her delicate features and big blue eyes. But much to her chagrin, every man Sarah met wanted her to have long hair. She always told them if they didn't like her the way she was now, they wouldn't like her any better with long hair.

That never seemed to appease the men she dated, and subsequently no relationship ever lasted for long. Obviously, there was more to it than that, but this was one of the many easy excuses men used to get out of a relationship with her. The other excuse topping the list was Sarah's ardent desire to get married and have children.

She was thirty years old, and like most women her age Sarah wanted a permanent relationship and a family. What was wrong with that? Maybe it was just the men she chose. In her line of work, Sarah met cops, attorneys, other CSIs, criminals, and dead men. In the big picture that wasn't exactly a large or necessarily great dating pool. Most cops she'd met over the years were sweet but married; the attorneys always ended up being jerks, and CSIs generally didn't make good partners because they tended to be CSIs on and off the job. Never getting a break from work was just too much for any relationship to bear.

As Sarah and West pulled up to their latest scene, a 420, Detective Sean Maguire greeted them. From day one Maguire had had a bit of a crush on Sarah, and she knew it. She felt the same way about him. However, Maguire was a good Catholic boy from a fine Boston family with a devoted wife and five little Maguires at home. Scratch him from the pool of potential mates.

"Evening, folks," the detective said politely.

Sarah and West nodded their hellos.

"What do we have tonight?" Sarah asked.

"Frankly, Baker, I really don't know how to answer that. I'm sure Parker will know. It's major case. I can say that much. The vic's name is Evelyn Dalton. Single. Twenty-eight years old.

The CSIs followed the detective into the ground-level apartment on Rand Avenue. The living room cum dining area was small and fairly ordinary with an easy chair, a couple of tables, a dinette, and a flat screen TV that was a bit too large for the room. Just off the living room, there was a small efficiency kitchen. A short hallway led past the bathroom and into the one and only bedroom.

Sarah and West instantly stopped when they reached the threshold of the tiny room, their eyes slowly scanning the incredible scene. It looked like an animal had been butchered in there. Bright red arterial spray and castoff drenched the walls and ceiling. Swipes of blood, most likely made by a blood-covered hand, ran the length of the far wall and across the sliding glass door that led to the patio.

In the middle of the blood-soaked bed, a naked woman lay face up. Her dark, glassy eyes stared at the ceiling, vacant and unblinking. Her once sensuous mouth gaped open in a permanent scream, and her long golden hair was matted with blood and a mucus-like substance. The gash in her throat was rough and irregular and certainly made by something other than a weapon.

Sarah took out her notepad and began documenting the scene while West prepped his camera equipment. Neither said anything as they began their work. Maguire excused himself and went to interview the neighbors. Surely, someone had heard what must have been horrific screaming coming from this apartment earlier in the evening.

"What do you make of this?" Sarah asked, pointing to a small, white-colored fragment on the woman's neck.

West swallowed hard and then replied, "If I didn't know any better, I'd say it was part of a tooth."

Chapter 2

"A tooth? You've got to be kidding!" Sarah exclaimed.

"Then you tell me. What does it look like to you?"

She blushed and offered an apology. "I wasn't questioning your expertise. I was just surprised." Sarah leaned closer to the body and then quickly pulled back, knowing her boss was right.

"Parker's going to have a field day with this one," West said, shaking his head.

"Somebody call my name?"

Eliot Parker smiled as he greeted the CSIs. Parker was the Medical Examiner for Carson City as well as neighboring Douglas County. If ever there was a man who needed a break, it was Parker. The poor man was buried under with work.

"Oh, my," he said, bending over the body. "Do you have pictures already?"

"Overall, midrange and close-ups," West replied matter-of-factly.

"Okay then. Go ahead and collect this evidence and take fluid samples as usual."

"Yes, sir," Sarah replied in her usual no-nonsense manner.

"How long has she been dead?" West asked.

"I'd say approximately three hours."

"That puts time of death around 2140. Maguire should find someone in this building who heard something around that time. But we'll see. It's funny how deaf people become when they hear someone screaming bloody murder," Sarah replied, a little too sarcastically.

West gave her a knowing look.

"I'll get this young lady out of your way, and you guys can finish up here," Parker said as he motioned for his two assistants to enter the bedroom.

"Thanks, Parker," West replied and backed away from the bed.

Five and a half hours passed and the entire scene had been notated, sketched, photographed, and videotaped. The bed sheets and pillowcases had each been placed into separate, individual brown paper bags, as well as the blood-spattered drapes, and then properly documented. Several hairs of various colors and lengths had also been collected. It appeared someone besides Ms. Dalton, a few someones was more like it, had been sleeping in the queen-sized bed.

"That was one hell of a way to end the shift," West said with a shiver as he packed the last bit of equipment into the back of the SUV.

It was mid-October and fall had definitely arrived in Northern Nevada. The nights got down well into the low 40s despite the days remaining in the spring-like 70s. Sarah was too tired to do more than sigh and jump into the passenger side of the vehicle, turning on the heat before West could slide into the driver's seat. When they had returned to base, Grayson was back from his call as well. For the remainder of the shift, the team filled out crime scene reconstruction reports.

"Who's up for something to eat?" Grayson asked as he signed off on his last case file. "How about the Nugget?"

"Sounds great!" Sarah and West replied in unison.

As the three CSIs left the building, a man dressed in black slacks and a black pullover sweater approached them.

"Excuse me," the man said politely with a soft, slightly British-sounding accent. "Could you please tell me where I can find the Crime Scene Unit?"

"You're looking at it," West replied with a grin.

Sarah eyed the man, wondering why he was inquiring about the unit, especially at this hour of the morning. This gorgeous hunk of man with dark blond curls and eyes the color of green sea glass must have a warm bed with an even warmer wife or girlfriend waiting for him back home.

"I wanted to speak with you about your case tonight."

The smile on West's face promptly twisted into a grimace.

"And which case is that, sir? Why don't you come inside, and we can discuss the matter with Detective Maguire," West stated.

"No! That's impossible. If I tell the detective what I know, he'll lock me up for being a—"

"A murderer," Grayson blurted out.

"No. A lunatic."

West didn't miss a beat. "As I was saying, which case in particular were you interested in and could you please tell me how you're involved with it?"

"I think we both know which case, Mr.—"

"West. Dr. Orlando West," the night shift supervisor replied, extending his hand. "And you are?"

"Please forgive me. My name is Patrick Martin. Father Patrick Martin."

A priest? Good God! I'm having lustful thoughts about a priest, Sarah frantically thought.

As West began to speak, his cell phone rang. Several awkward minutes passed before he swiped his finger across the cell phone screen, ending the conversation. "That was the Reno PD. We've been asked to assist in a triple homicide at Damonte Ranch. Grayson, you'll need to come with me."

The stocky, tightly wound, Iraqi war veteran was eager to go. It seemed the man never needed to sleep. "You got it, boss," he replied as he ran his hand over his closely cropped brown hair.

"Ms. Baker will be glad to assist you in any way," West offered.

"Yes, sir," Sarah replied unenthusiastically.

West shook hands with Father Martin then spoke briefly with Sarah before heading out to Reno with Grayson.

Sarah stood staring at the priest, not knowing what to say. She hadn't felt this uncomfortable with a member of the clergy since her first confession.

"I realize this is a very awkward situation. I do apologize for approaching you like this, but I didn't have any other option."

"I see," she replied, somewhat coolly. "I was just going to get something to eat. Would you care to join me, and we can discuss the situation?"

"That would be lovely."

Sarah asked Father Martin to join her in the Crime Scene Unit SUV. He gratefully accepted, and they drove the few blocks across town to the Nugget Casino. It was a short but pretty drive. For the most part, the quiet tree-lined streets were still empty except for small flocks of Canadian geese that dotted the grassy yards here and there. The trees had not yet lost their green leaves of summer, and Father Martin felt a blissful moment of peace as he took in the sites.

Reno may be the biggest little city in the world, but Carson City was still very much a small town. Provincial with a quaint downtown and capital center, it was an interesting mix of professional, government and blue-collar workers.

"The casinos have the best food at the best prices," Sarah said, breaking the silence as she whipped the SUV into a parking space near the casino's back entrance. "Oh, is there any rule against you going into a casino?"

The priest just smiled.

Blanche, Sarah's favorite waitress at the Eatery, was her usual jovial self as she placed two glasses of water and two menus in front of the couple.

"Good morning! What are you fine folks hungry for today?"

"A Coke to start please," Sarah answered as she folded her hands and placed them atop the table.

"And what would you like, handsome?" Blanche asked unabashedly.

Father Martin colored fiercely as if he'd never heard himself described in such a manner.

"Ah, tea would be nice. Thank you."

"Be back in a flash," Blanche replied with a wink.

"Where would you like to begin, Father?"

"I suppose at the beginning."

"Fair enough."

"To begin with, I want to assure you I'm not a mad man, although you may think otherwise after you hear what I have to say."

"Believe me, I've been around enough crazy people to know crazy, and I highly doubt you're mentally unbalanced. However, I'm concerned you may be involved in something over your head."

"My dear, you have no idea."

Patrick Kennedy Martin was forty-two, although he looked a good decade younger. Tall, slender and athletic, the priest was originally from Ballina, New South Wales, Australia. He preferred surfing to running and beer over wine. His father Adam McFadden Martin had been a minor diplomat in the Australian Foreign Service. During Mr. Martin's tour of duty, he and his family had been stationed throughout Southeast Asia and Western Europe, finally settling down in Rome for his final assignment. After retiring from the Foreign Service, Mr. and Mrs. Martin relocated to Tuscany where Patrick unfortunately had little chance to visit.

Young Patrick attended prep school at St. Stephen's School before going on to college at the University of Udine where he studied Linguistics and Modern Languages. During his last year at university, he decided to enter the priesthood, much to the dismay of his many female friends and his college sweetheart.

Once ordained, Father Martin became the assistant parish priest of a small congregation in Kenilworth, England. After three years at St. Francis of Assisi, the Vatican-sanctioned International Association of Exorcists secretly recruited him. This autonomous organization founded by Pauline priest Father Gabriele Amorth, a well-known demon hunter, sought out the newly ordained priest because of his language skills. Father Martin soon found himself back in Rome training with an elite group of clergymen and laypeople whose mission would be to seek out and destroy vampires all over the world.

Sarah didn't know whether to be enthralled or incredulous. She hadn't expected such a bizarre story and was reconsidering her initial assessment of Father Martin's mental health.

Chapter 4

Anton Krulak closed his eyes and ran his cold, slender fingers through the cool, rich soil. Originally from Ukraine, the Krulak family had lived in the shadow of the Carpathian Mountains since before medieval times, working as farmers, silversmiths and traders. In the mid-1800s Krulak's family migrated to the Transylvanian Alps. The soil in which Krulak now rested each day from the time the sun rose until the time it slipped beneath the horizon was the soil of his Romanian homeland. The soil was as old as time itself. It was eternal and so was Anton Krulak.

The coffin lid gradually covered the last remnant of darkness Krulak would see until night fell again. Sebastian would see to it that nothing disturbed his master. He was fiercely loyal and would give his life for the one he served. Sebastian was the seventh generation of his family to care for Anton Krulak. Over the years Krulak had amassed a vast fortune, and the Dragan family had shared in that wealth, being well rewarded for their vigilance and fidelity. Although their immortal souls would be damned, their earthly lives would be richly blessed.

Now that his master was settled, it was time for Sebastian to take a meal before he began his day. He left the St. Charles Hotel and walked leisurely north, passing the Capitol and State Senate, various quaint shops, a coffee house, and small businesses before stopping in front of the Nugget Casino. He decided to go in and try his luck at the slot machines before eating.

A few dozen senior citizens populated the chairs in front of the colorful, noisy slot machines, gambling away their Social Security checks with abandon. Each new ding, ding of bells and flashing lights renewed their gambling fervor.

Sebastian smirked, feeling almost sorry for these old folks. He stopped in front of an end row slot machine called the Double Dragon. Thinking this was an omen, he slid a dollar bill into the money slot. Within seconds five blue number sevens appeared in a straight row across the screen followed by the sound of bells and the obligatory flashing lights.

Expecting silver coins to fill the metal tray beneath, Sebastian was taken aback when a TITO voucher popped from the machine. He grabbed it in his brawny hand and stuffed it into his pants pockets. Feeling lucky, he slid another dollar bill into the slot machine. Again, a row of matching icons appeared, and the machine's bells and lights went off. Not one to push his luck, Sebastian was satisfied with his bounty and headed to the casino restaurant before cashing out.

The Eatery was packed, and Sebastian followed the hostess to a cushy booth at the back of the room. As he looked about the restaurant, his gaze was instantly stopped by the handsome couple a few feet from where he sat. An icy chill engulfed him, and a cold sweat formed on his brow. Sebastian recognized the blond man. He had seen him in New Orleans and Las Vegas.

Perhaps it was merely a coincidence. Both were gambling towns like Carson City, but he had never seen the beautiful woman who sat next to the familiar man. Despite her shorn locks, she looked like an angel. Desire stirred within him, and the coldness in his heart turned into a flame.

Chapter 5

You do realize I can't discuss an ongoing case? However, if you have any information about criminal activity, it's your civic duty to disclose it," Sarah said matter-of-factly.

"Please, Ms. Baker. This is far too serious a matter to waste time playing games and pretend you don't know why I'm here."

Sarah leaned back into the booth, blue eyes searching green. She didn't like to play games either, but she'd never been in such an odd situation.

"I'm not a detective, and—"

"I understand that, but you were the CSI on duty tonight, and you saw what happened to that young woman."

Sarah could feel her heart thumping hard against her chest. She wasn't sure which frightened her more at the moment, this handsome man or the events of the past night.

"I need to go," she said abruptly, tossing her napkin onto the table.

A strong, soft hand grabbed hers, halting her retreat. "Don't be afraid. I didn't kill her."

"But you know who did."

"I do."

"Tell me, and I'll tell Detective Maguire."

"His name is Anton Krulak. I know you doubt my story and profession, which at one time I would have too. Like you, I've seen terrible things people shouldn't see. The things of nightmares."

"Then you need to speak with Detective Maguire. He can take all your information. As I said, I'm not a detective. I just process crime scenes and collect evidence."

"But aren't all CSIs detectives at heart?" Father Martin asked with a disarming smile.

Sarah couldn't help it and found herself smiling back.

"Tell me what you know," she replied, switching back to a more professionally concerned, but detached, demeanor.

"I've hunted Krulak for over eight years. He's left a trail of butchered men, women and children from New York to Chicago and from New Orleans to Las Vegas."

Sarah jumped slightly when she heard the words *Las Vegas*. "I used to work in Las Vegas."

"And you were on the Blakely case."

"How did you know?"

"Why do you think I sought you out this morning?"

Sarah opened her mouth to speak but then shut it before any words could slip out.

"That murdered young mother and her two children and all the other cases I've investigated are the same. Even though I can't prove it in a court of law, I'm certain Krulak was responsible."

"And you believe Krulak is a vampire?" Sarah asked, hardly able to believe she was asking the question with a straight face.

"I don't believe it. I know it."

"You're obviously an intelligent and educated man. How can you believe in such superstitious nonsense?"

"Do you believe in God, Ms. Baker?"

"Of course, I do."

"Some people would say God is nothing but superstitious nonsense."

"That's not the same thing."

"Isn't it? If you believe in God, then you have to believe in the Devil and his many minions."

"But vampires? They're not real."

"I assure you vampires are quite real. They are the damned who've sold their souls to the Devil himself, and they walk this earth as immortal, corporeal beings, feeding and killing in the night to sustain their evil lives. I can also assure you they look nothing like those handsome young men and women you read about in popular novels or see in movies these days. Think Nosferatu, Ms. Baker, and then you have a small idea what these damned creatures look like. What the vampire Anton Krulak looks like."

A bright scarlet hue eased over Sarah's cheeks as she dropped her eyes and slid down into the booth.

Chapter 6

"Holy God!" West exclaimed as he entered the living room of the Damonte Ranch split-level home.

Grayson, who had seen his fill of gore and guts on and off the battlefield, stood frozen. Not one to be sentimental, he felt tears well up in his eyes as he surveyed the well-appointed room. Every wall and every piece of furniture was spattered with blood. Two small children lay end to end on the couch, their throats torn apart. Their mother lay on the floor beside them, a butcher knife in her hand.

"I can't believe a mother would do this to her own children," said a young, uniformed police officer.

"She didn't kill them," West replied softly.

"How do you know that?"

"She was defending them."

"I believe you're right, Dr. West," came a Latin-accented voice from behind.

West turned to find his counterpart Sonia Garcia of the Washoe County Sheriff's Department Crime Scene Unit right behind him.

"Thanks for coming."

"It's always a pleasure to help Reno's finest."

A slight smile tugged at Garcia's full lips.

"I've never seen anything like this. The entire living room is covered in blood, but there aren't any footprints in or out. The doors and windows were locked, and nothing else in the house was disturbed. It's like the perp appeared out of thin air, committed the murders and then disappeared again."

West tried to process this improbable information.

"We'll have to keep this scene tightly under wraps and make sure no information gets leaked to the press. The adult vic is Governor Sandoval's niece Linda Sandoval-Ross."

As if there wasn't enough pressure on the police and CSIs already, the victims had to be related to the governor, and he'd want answers quicker than immediately. But West didn't have a logical explanation for this crime scene or the one on Rand Avenue. It looked like an animal had killed the victims, but there was no evidence of an animal attack other than the manner in which the victims' throats were torn apart. Plus, the bodies of Evelyn Dalton and Linda Sandoval-Ross and her children were laid out in a ritualistic manner. An animal couldn't have done that. But the principle of parsimony, which stated that one should not make more assumptions than the minimum needed, didn't fit these two scenarios. That left West with nothing, zip, nada, zero.

Hopefully, the autopsies would shed some light on who may have committed these atrocious murders. It was obvious the same perp had committed them, which in itself was difficult enough to grasp since the two crime scenes were twenty-two miles apart, and, according to the initial assessment by the Assistant Medical Examiner of Washoe County, the deaths had occurred less than an hour apart. And for now there didn't seem to be any connection between Evelyn Dalton and Linda Sandoval-Ross, but Detective Maguire would investigate every aspect of their lives, as would his Reno PD counterpart Detective Jason Gaffney.

"When the lab runs the blood and mucus samples for DNA, let me know the results as soon as possible," West said to Garcia as he packed up his field kit. "I have no doubt the results will be the same in both cases, but for some reason I don't think we'll have a hit in CODIS."

Garcia shot West a curious look. "Why are you so pessimistic, my friend?"

"I'm not being pessimistic just realistic."

West had now been up for over twenty-four hours and was ready to go home and get at least eight hours of solid, undisturbed sleep. Luckily, he didn't have to go into work tonight, and he counted this as one of his many blessings. Grayson, however, was not so lucky, but that didn't seem to faze him in the least. He'd sleep an hour or so and be ready to go out in the field again. Combat training proved to be a definite asset for a CSI.

* * *

"I appreciate you taking time to speak with me this morning, Ms. Baker," Father Martin said politely.

"It was enlightening to say the least."

"I'd like to meet with you again if that's possible."

Sarah considered the offer, and even though she was still skeptical about the man's entire story, she found herself wanting to know more. If anything he said or knew could contribute to finding Evelyn Dalton's killer, then it was her responsibility to use that knowledge to the fullest.

"Let's plan on meeting my next day off," she offered, yawning.

"Very well. And when would that be?" the priest asked eagerly.

"Tuesday. I'm off Tuesday."

Sarah dug into her messenger bag and grabbed the silver business card case. An ex-boyfriend had given it to her for a birthday present. That was the first and last present the jerk had ever given her.

"Here's my card," Sarah said as she scribbled her home phone number on the back. "Call me at home Tuesday morning after nine, and we'll arrange a meeting for later in the day if that's all right with you."

"It's more than all right with me," Father Martin replied with a dazzling smile. *Thank God! She doesn't think I'm a lunatic after all.*

Chapter 7

The golden rays slanted through the bright white clouds in the brilliant blue sky, coming to rest warmly and soothingly on Sarah's naked skin. She sighed with satisfaction. It was the first time she'd felt relaxed in days. The glistening waters of South Lake Tahoe lapped at the white sandy shore, and the soft, rhythmic sound drew her deeper into sleep with each gentle wave.

A cold drop of water hit Sarah's face. Annoyed, she wiped at it, but the drop was followed by several others and then by a light shower.

"Ah, come on. I'm sleeping!"

"But it's not time to sleep. It's time to play," the man replied as he shook his wet head over her face once more.

"No! Let me sleep!" came the adamant reply.

Soft, warm lips came down gently upon hers.

Sarah acquiesced and slipped her fingers through the dark blond curls, pulling his face closer to her own. Her lips devoured his sensuous mouth as she ran her hands down the length of his strong back. Her fingers came to rest on the waistband of his swim trunks. Gently, she curled a finger beneath the elastic and playfully tugged on it.

"Woman! Are you going to have your way with me right out here in the open and in front of God and everyone?" he asked with a laugh.

Sarah couldn't repress her own laughter and giggled as she nuzzled the man's neck.

"You are a little devil, aren't you?" he rasped, enjoying the moment.

Sarah pulled away and opened her eyes to find Father Martin gazing at her with profound love. The intensity and sincerity filled her soul with absolute contentment.

"Hey, Baker," Grayson said as he dropped a pile of case files next to her head.

Sarah woke with a start. Groggily, she raised her head from her desk and wiped the corners of her mouth where spittle had collected during her brief nap.

"Are you okay?" her partner asked.

"Ah, yeah. Why do you ask?"

"Your face is all flushed."

"Is it?" Sarah asked, placing a small hand against her cheek.

"If you're coming down with something, you can keep it," Grayson ordered.

"I don't think so. It's just a little warm in here is all," she replied quickly, trying to regain her composure. The dream had been so real, so wonderful. *Oh, Baker! You really need a boyfriend.* "What are all these files?"

"They're cold cases. Some are homicides and some are undetermined death cases. I thought maybe we could find a similar case to our Dalton homicide in one of these files. It couldn't hurt. There's not much else going on at the moment."

Sarah took a couple of folders from the top of the pile and began looking through them. One particular case caught her attention. "Did you see this one?" she asked, handing Grayson the file.

The cold case dated back to 1944. A middle-aged, Caucasian man was discovered dead in his bed at the St. Charles Hotel in downtown Carson. At that time Carson City had a coroner who determined the cause of death was exsanguination. Although the autopsy was inconclusive as to what had caused the gash across the man's jugular, the manner of his death was deemed homicide. However, the subsequent investigation yielded no suspects and no motive for the man's demise.

The crime scene photos were quite similar to the ones in the Dalton case. Blood spattered the walls and ceiling of the tiny hotel room, but unlike Dalton the victim lay in a cadaveric spasm, his arms tossed over his head, his hands clenched as if in a final desperate attempt to fend off his attacker.

"This couldn't be the same perp," Sarah said confidently. "Even if he were twenty years old at the time of the murder that would make him over ninety now. How many nonagenarians do you know out in the middle of the night committing crimes, especially capital murder?"

"Stranger things have happened," Grayson replied with a huge smile.

"You're such an optimist."

"Damn straight."

"Did you know the St. Charles Hotel is haunted?" Sarah asked as she closed the case file and grabbed another.

"Who told you that?"

"No one. I read it. When I was getting ready to transfer here, I bought several books on the area. One of them was called, *Haunted Carson City*. Apparently, all Northern Nevada is chucked full of ghosts."

"What? Come on! You know better than to believe in ghosts."

"Maybe I do, and maybe I don't."

"Seriously, Baker?"

"It's not like I'm the only one who believes in this sort of thing. Ghosts and the supernatural are a multi-million-dollar industry in this country. There are movies, TV shows and tons of books on the subject. The Carson City library has dozens of books by local authors compiled from true-life ghost stories. Most of them from around here."

"When I can conduct an experiment in the lab on a ghost and then replicate that experiment, I'll believe in ghosts as well."

Fat chance of that, Sarah thought. "Touché," she said aloud.

"What's in the next file?" Grayson asked.

"A questionable suicide. Apparently, this woman killed herself by cutting her own throat."

"Let me see that one. Hmm. Looks like she had to try more than a few times to seal the deal. Shit! Look at those gashes! That must've hurt like a son-of-a-bitch. She had to be on something to do that and not stop until she was dead."

"No. Her tox screens were clean," Sarah replied.

"What's the date on the case?"

"Fifteen years ago. Well before you, West or I worked here, but definitely within the timeframe for good forensic test results."

"Let's keep this file out. Evidence should still be in the property room. I'll see what I can find. Wouldn't that be a kick if the DNA from that evidence matched the DNA in the Dalton case?"

"It sure would," Sarah replied and then set about making mental notes on the case to share with good Father Martin when they met tomorrow afternoon.

Chapter 8

Krulak opened his eyes and saw nothing but blessed darkness. He had rested well after gorging himself, and he had not dreamt of his former life or of his homeland as he so often did.

Sebastian checked his antique pocket watch, a gift from his master, and knew the vampire would be rising soon. With a grunt he pushed the heavy coffin lid aside and gazed at the man before him, a man in his prime.

"You look well, sir."

"Do I?" Krulak replied, stretching as he rose.

"Never better."

It was not thirst that had awakened Krulak tonight but invigoration, the invigoration that comes with transformation. For the next month he would be as he was before being cursed; before he sold his soul; before he lost everything to gain the one thing he most desired and now despised—immortality. How vain and foolish is man, and Krulak had been no exception. He had not wanted to grow old, to lose his lust for life, to see the parties and beautiful women come to an end, only to become a useless, senile, bedridden old man like his father.

When the transformation was complete, Krulak would forget the price he'd paid for each new life. Instead, he enjoyed his time, his money and whatever lovely companion graced his arm. He'd spend his nights drinking champagne, gambling and making love. The old wives' tales about vampires consuming only blood amused him. Krulak feasted. He favored lobster with drawn butter, rare filet mignon, truffles, and asparagus, and he enjoyed every mouthful of each delectable morsel.

His curse had not only brought him immortality but extraordinary good luck at the gaming tables. That gift had bankrolled his lifestyle and his travels. Usually, Krulak stayed at luxury five-star hotels, but when he was in Carson City, he always stayed at the St. Charles Hotel. Call it sentimental folly, but Krulak was a romantic.

His first kill in Carson was in 1944. He often reminisced how he had lured the egotistical Dr. Harold Nenn to his room. The man had boasted to Krulak for hours on end how he had met a vampire while an Army surgeon serving on the German front. Nenn had been wounded when the enemy shelled the field hospital where he was stationed and just before being sent back to the States, he supposedly encountered the famous Count of St. Germaine. What nonsense! An American serviceman meeting the famous vampire count! The man deserved to die for such blasphemy.

Krulak stood before the cheval mirror, admiring his handsome form. Tall, slender and pale with coal black hair and eyes that sparkled like blue diamonds, he was perfection incarnate.

"Where shall we go tonight, Sebastian?"

"I suggest the Casino Fandango if we're staying in town."

"I would like that," Krulak replied with one last look in the mirror.

* * *

Dressed in a black Valentino suit and a white Brioni dress shirt, Krulak entered the casino like a crown prince on tour. He surveyed the room, his gaze scanning each gaming table for the best position in the casino and of its patrons. The appreciative glances of the women he passed made his libido awaken and his ego swell.

A vacant seat next to a buxom blonde beckoned him, and Krulak slid easily into it. The blackjack dealer nodded a welcome to the new player, and another game began. After several rounds of play, Krulak had a crowd of gamblers cheering him on. He hadn't lost one hand since sitting down at the table. With each triumph over the house, the cheering increased in volume and enthusiasm.

The blonde leaned close to Krulak and whispered in his ear, "I must be your lucky charm."

"I believe you are," he replied as he took her hand and kissed it.

The woman, unaccustomed to such continental gallantry, blushed and giggled.

Krulak smiled with satisfaction, knowing what the evening ahead had in store.

Chapter 9

"I want to thank you for meeting with me again, Ms. Baker," Father Martin said as he slid into the passenger seat of her bright yellow 2001 BMW Z3.

Sarah smiled but didn't reply. She shifted the car into gear and pulled away from the parking lot of the Hardman House where Father Martin was staying.

"This roadster's a real classic. I've always loved the lines of this model," he said with a hint of envy.

"Are you a car buff?"

"Sort of. Where are we going today?"

"I thought you might like to take a drive out to Genoa. It's beautiful there, and it would be nice to get out of town for a while."

"Sounds like a plan."

Genoa, nestled at the base of the eastern slope of the Sierra Nevadas, was only fifteen miles from Carson City but a world away. Genoa had the prestige of being named Nevada's first permanent settlement, although the residents of Dayton, Nevada hotly contested that honor. All the buildings in Genoa, historic and modern, were well maintained, and the town center was charming, filled with small shops, restaurants and museums. The new homes in and around the town were large with vast acreage, most of which was used for cattle ranching.

Genoa was reputed to be haunted. Every year the town hosted a *ghost walk*, and members of the Carson

Valley Museum and Cultural Center would take visitors on a guided tour of the area, which featured haunted sites and historic landmarks.

"Do you come here often?" the priest asked, breaking the comfortable silence that had settled on them during their journey.

"Not that much, but I do like it here. The last time I came, I had a paranormal encounter in the museum. I swear I heard someone calling to me. When I turned around there was a faint figure of a woman standing by the window. She was nearly transparent in various shades of gray and dressed in what looked like clothes from the 19th century."

"Let me get this straight. You believe in ghosts but not vampires," Father Martin replied and then added, "That seems rather contradictory, doesn't it?"

"Having been a science major, I know the body gives off radiation, and the nervous system sends signals to the body when the brain's synapses fire. That's how our muscles move. Energy creates electricity. Electricity is what carries the messages in our bodies between point A and point B, and it's what keeps our hearts beating. Energy can't be created or destroyed. It can only change form. The energy has to go somewhere when the body dies, so maybe it remains in some humanlike form in the immediate area of the deceased."

"Where does the soul figure into this hypothesis?"

"I'm a science geek, not a theologian. That's your realm of expertise."

"I asked you once before if you believed in God and the Devil."

"Are you trying to pick a fight with me, Father?" Sarah asked abruptly. "Because if you are, you can get out of this car right now and walk back to Carson."

Father Martin was taken aback by the speed at which the relaxed ambience of their trip had changed.

Sarah was proud, especially of her intelligence and her integrity. She bristled when someone questioned them. No doubt Father Martin would have something to say about pride. He probably had an entire volume of homilies devoted to the subject. And it wasn't like he was the first of his kind to think she was proud. Sister Mary Margaret's favorite proverb was "Pride goes before destruction, a haughty spirit before the fall." Sister Mary Margaret had often quoted it over the few years Sarah had attended catechism.

The priest studied Sarah for some time. He'd never met anyone like her. When he said nothing further, Sarah turned to look at him. His eyes were soft and kind, and his mouth looked like an angel who was about to sing the praises of the Lord. Heaven be damned! She wanted to kiss that mouth, and she wanted this man.

Chapter 10

"It's beautiful here," Father Martin said as they arrived at Mormon Station State Park.

Sarah's hot temper had finally cooled. "I think so, and it's the perfect place for a picnic," she replied, pulling a cooler from the roadster's trunk. "We can talk business after we eat."

Father Martin knew Sarah was trying to apologize, and he accepted her apology without reservation and no further comment. They enjoyed a luncheon of French baguettes and Irish butter, cheese, grapes, and salami with a Foster's Lager to wash down the meal. The priest was touched by Sarah's thoughtfulness.

"Now down to business," Sarah said as she crumpled her napkin and tossed it into the metal trashcan next to their picnic table. "I want to know more about vampires and more about you," she managed to say without blushing.

"Good deal. Shoot away, my dear sheila."

"Sheila?" Sarah asked, her face scrunching up like a question mark.

"A sheila is what Aussies call a fair dinkum woman."

"And the definition of fair dinkum, please?"

"Genuine. You're a genuine woman, Ms. Baker."

"I would hope so. Since we're going to be working together, well, at least consulting with one another, why don't you call me Sarah, or Baker would be fine too."

"Only if you call me Patrick."

"Agreed."

"How and why did you become a vampire hunter?" Sarah asked, although she actually wanted to ask Patrick why he became a priest.

"It was never my intention to become a vampire hunter. I was recruited."

"There are headhunters for people in your line of work?" Sarah asked with a laugh.

"So to speak."

"How long have you been hunting vampires?"

"A little over sixteen years. After my ordination I was assigned to a small parish in England. That's where I was recruited by Father Francois Diderot of the International Association of Exorcists."

Patrick went on to explain that he first trained as an exorcist and had been part of several successful exorcisms in Europe and North America. High-ranking members of the association then sought him out for the covert vampire branch. Only a select few members of the association ever ascended to the rank of vampire hunter, and if and when they did, their lives were often cut short.

Vampire hunting was a dangerous profession. Not only did the vampires' caretakers protect their masters and mistresses, they also killed anyone who sought to harm their patrons, that is, if the vampires themselves didn't kill the hunters first. But Father Martin was young and strong and incredibly brave and intelligent. He had all the qualifications needed to be a vampire hunter plus the most essential element of all: he was pure of heart.

During training the young priest learned all about vampire folklore and vampire reality. So much of what the world knew about vampires was gleaned from B rate Hollywood movies and from cheap pulp fiction. Vampires didn't feed on their prey by biting them on the neck, making two perfect puncture marks with their fangs to suck out enough blood to sustain their damnable lives. No. Vampires went into a feeding frenzy, tearing their victims' throats apart without pity or remorse. Every drop of blood was drained from the bodies and what blood wasn't ingested was used to mark the vampires' territories. The blood was spewed from the mouth, causing the spattering effect on the walls and ceilings. That explained the condition of each crime scene where vampire victims had been discovered.

Contrary to popular myth, vampires flew not because they turned into bats but because they were fallen creatures, servants of the Devil himself, and they were accorded certain privileges such as wings and invisibility. And vampires had the ability to dematerialize and rematerialize at will, but doing so completely exhausted them. Vampires could also see themselves in mirrors. Like demons they had superhuman strength, and they had no mortal enemy save the vampire hunter.

The vampire hunter had to be as merciless as the one he or she sought. Great cunning, fearlessness, perseverance, and strength were among the vampire hunter's greatest assets. It was one thing to track a vampire but another thing entirely to destroy him, especially when the vampire was in human form.

One fact true to legend was that vampires did fear the sun. Their skin would burn at the slightest touch of a sunbeam. This was because the light was pure and the place where angels dwelled. There was nothing more loathsome to a vampire than purity. That's why they sought out mothers and their children. These innocents sustained the body while the fallen ones like Dalton and her kind sustained their black souls.

Sarah's cell phone rang, interrupting Father Martin's incredible narrative.

"Baker," she rasped into the phone. Her mouth had gone dry. "That's incredible. I don't know what to say. Thanks for the update."

"Who was that?" the priest politely inquired.

"That was my partner Thomas Grayson. The autopsy results on Evelyn Dalton just came back."

"And?"

"There was no blood in her body. Do you know how much blood the average human body contains?"

"Yes. 4.7318 liters."

"That's ten pints. Now I understand why the crime scene looked like a slaughterhouse."

"Did you have a good RDO, Baker?" West asked as he walked into his subordinate's office.

"As a matter of fact, I did. I met with Father Martin."

"I was hoping to speak with you about him. What's your take on the guy?"

"If you're asking me if he's a nutball, he isn't. He's a real priest who works for a Vatican-sanctioned organization. I know it's incredible, especially if you're a non-believer, but the man is genuine." *Fair dinkum*, Sarah thought.

"That's a relief. So what's his story, and how did he know about Dalton?"

"He has a police scanner. He's followed similar murder cases across the country. He knew about the Blakely case too. That's why he came here to find me."

"And he thinks the perp in both cases is a vampire," West said and then burst out laughing.

"It's a ridiculous theory, but he means well, and he's perfectly harmless."

"As long as he stays out of our cases, I don't care what Father Martin believes in or does for a living. However, if he does have any information on Dalton's murder, or any other, he needs to tell Maguire what he knows. Is that understood?"

"I already told him that. But what about Dalton's autopsy report?"

"Parker's been overworked and underfunded for years. It was only a matter of time until he made a mistake. I'm sure he'll rectify the blood loss discrepancy and issue a new report very soon. Besides, it doesn't alter the cause of death, which was exsanguination due to sharp force trauma."

"What about Father Martin?"

"He's all yours, Baker," West replied and exited the office.

How could a vampire be brought to justice? Even if one were captured, how could he be prosecuted, sentenced and imprisoned for his crimes? Any possible answer was far too implausible to entertain. Besides, no one except Father Martin, his colleagues and like-minded people believed in such creatures.

Sarah had to admit she would be a laughing stock and most likely dismissed from her position if she pursued this angle or a relationship with the priest any further. As much as she wanted justice for the Blakelys and Dalton, blaming their murders on a mythological creature wasn't the answer. But there was still that one unsettling element of the Dalton case. All the blood in the woman's body had been drained perimortem. How could forensics explain that? It couldn't.

If a person sustained a Class IV hemorrhage, a blood loss of 40% or more, he or she would go into shock. The person would then pass the point of aggressive resuscitation and subsequently die. If the heart discontinued pumping blood, the body could no longer lose blood volume. Therefore, it was impossible for the body to be drained of all blood unless it was done by mechanical means such as what occurs during the embalming process. But that's not what happened.

Sarah's favorite Sherlock Holmes quote came instantly to mind. *When you have eliminated the impossible, whatever remains, however improbable, must be the truth.* She felt a chill creep up her arms and across her back.

Vampires did exist!

Chapter 12

Sebastian Dragan had served Anton Krulak for nineteen years. In his youth Sebastian had wanted to become a writer. But he was the firstborn son, and every firstborn son before him for seven generations had cared for Krulak.

Sebastian had gone into service on his eighteenth birthday just like his nephew, Marius, would do when he came of age. Tall, strong and heavy set with dark brown hair and even darker brown eyes, Sebastian looked every bit the bodyguard and not much like the poet he'd dreamt of becoming.

Fortunately for Sebastian, he was the firstborn son but not the firstborn in a family of ten children. He had five older sisters, and Diana, who was eleven years older than he, was the first sister to give birth to a son. Marius was now sixteen, and when he became Krulak's caretaker Sebastian would retire a relatively young man. Perhaps after his service ended, he could dedicate the remainder of his life to writing and perhaps even redemption.

When his master was sleeping, Sebastian would take up his pen and jot down notes in his journal. Most of his journal entries chronicled his travels with Krulak. In nineteen years, Sebastian had toured all the great capitals of the world from Paris to Tokyo and Moscow to Bangkok. For the last thirteen, they'd traveled throughout Canada and the United States. He'd met many beautiful women but never had the opportunity to get to know any of them well. Sebastian would just get comfortable in one spot, and then Krulak would be eager to set off to a new destination.

Anton Krulak was enjoying his time in Northern Nevada and deliberated about staying over the winter. There was plenty of prey here and in the nearby mountains of California—both excellent hunting grounds for his kind.

Sebastian supported his master's idea wholeheartedly. Not only would it give them both a much-needed rest; it may give him time to find the woman who had stolen his heart at first sight.

* * *

"I need to speak with you, Baker," West said softly as he entered her office. "Is Grayson around?"

Sarah shook her head and wondered what was up. Was she in trouble? It felt like it even though she was sure she hadn't done anything wrong or had broken any rules, at least not to her knowledge.

"What do you need?"

West closed the door and pulled up a chair, setting it down on the opposite side of Sarah's desk. He dropped his lanky form into the cold aluminum and then tossed a case file onto her desk.

"I can hardly believe what I'm about to say to you..." He paused before trying to speak again.

Sarah's stomach clenched into knots, and her Spidey sense kicked in. Whatever West was about to say wasn't going to be good.

"Sonia Garcia sent me a copy of her case file on the triple homicide out at Damonte Ranch."

Sarah took the file and began reading it. If she didn't know any better she could have sworn she was reading the Blakelys' case file. Carefully, she scanned the crime scene notes and photos, stopping abruptly when she came to the autopsy report. All three victims had died in the same manner as the Blakelys, and every drop of blood had been drained from their bodies.

"By the way, we got back the lab results on that white fragment we found on Dalton's neck." West said.

"And?"

"It's a fragment of a human tooth. But it gets even weirder."

"I can't see how."

"The fragment is over one hundred years old."

Sarah sucked in another shallow breath as she contemplated the ramifications of the test results.

"I think it's time we asked for Father Martin's help," West said in almost a whisper.

"I think you're right."

Chapter 13

"When will we have the DNA results back on the Dalton and Sandoval-Ross cases?" Sarah asked.

"Not for another week," West replied. "I want you to know I've requested the case file on the Blakelys from the Vegas Crime Lab. I'd like your input from that case to compare with our new ones."

"Sure."

"I'm curious what Father Martin will add. Do you know?"

"He's tracked Krulak for over eight years, so I imagine his notes will be extensive," Sarah replied with hopeful optimism.

"Fingers crossed."

"Mine too."

* * *

Father Martin met with Sarah and Dr. West after the night shift ended, this time in West's office.

"You understand that we'll have to keep the findings of these cases to ourselves," West said, looking back and forth between Sarah and the priest. "I'm not even sure if we'll be able to tell Detective Maguire."

"I understand perfectly," Father Martin replied.

"This puts us all in a very unenviable position," Sarah added.

"Indeed it does," Father Martin intoned.

"I suppose the main concern I have is this. If we can prove Anton Krulak committed the murders, as you believe he did, then how can he be brought to justice?" West asked.

"That's the difficulty of our position, and I'm afraid the answer won't please you."

"It won't be legal is what you're saying," West stated matter-of-factly.

"That's correct."

The nightshift supervisor shifted uncomfortably in his chair, trying to grasp the enormity of this incredible situation. Not only was he a man of science, he was a man of the law. His moral imperative was quite clear. As he silently debated his course of action, West remembered something he had once read. *The dead cannot cry out for justice. It is the duty of the living to do so for them.*

Deep in his heart, he knew dealing with this murderer would be accomplished outside the law. West also knew he would have to bury any forensic evidence regarding the ultimate death of Anton Krulak at the hands of Father Patrick Martin.

"This may come as a silly question at this point in our conversation, but can one actually kill a vampire, and if so how?" West asked.

"Yes, a vampire can be killed, but not like you see in the movies," Father Martin replied.

"No stake through the heart then?" West asked, trying not to laugh from nervous anxiety.

"I'm afraid not. It's rather more gruesome than that and vastly more complicated."

Sarah swallowed hard and waited for the details.

"A vampire can only be killed by plunging a special dagger into his heart and then beheading him immediately thereafter with the same dagger. Ideally, he should be killed while in his corrupted form, but while in that state his strength is superhuman."

"What makes the dagger special?" Sarah asked, almost childlike.

"The dagger must be made of tempered steel to withstand the vampire's incredible strength, but it must also be coated with sterling silver that has been blessed and fashioned in a particular way," Father Martin said as he grabbed a notepad and pen from West's desk.

Both Sarah and West waited patiently as the priest sketched a picture of a vampire dagger. He'd not attempted to bring the actual weapon into the station since he knew he'd be unable to get it past the metal detectors.

"I'm not an artist, but I think you get the idea," he said, handing them the picture.

The dagger was nine inches in length; double edged with a fine, sharp point. The Vatican seal decorated the pommel. At the base of the quillon—the two transverse projecting members forming the cross of the dagger—a smaller dagger approximately three inches in length protruded from each side at a 240 and 300-degree angle respectively. The smaller blades when joined with the main blade symbolized the Trinity. The blade itself was inscribed with the words: *Uero stipendium mors est Satanae. Vita aeterna est donum Christi*: Death is the reward of

Satan. Eternal life is the gift of Christ.

The CSIs studied the sketch.

"What if the vampire can't be found and killed while in his corrupted form?" Sarah asked.

"Then he must be killed while in human form, and I assure you that is just as difficult."

"Just as difficult?" West asked skeptically.

"Yes," Father Martin replied.

"Why so?"

"Have you ever killed a man, Dr. West? I assure you it's more difficult than one would imagine."

Chapter 14

"I appreciate your candor, Father. We have a monumental task before us, but I assure you both Sarah and I will do what we can to assist you in your quest and its eventual resolution."

"I have no doubt," Father Martin replied, shaking the nightshift supervisor's hand. "Thank you, Sarah," he added.

West nodded and Sarah and Father Martin departed.

"I imagine you're quite tired. I apologize for keeping you so long after your shift ended."

"No worries."

"I suppose I should let you go then," the priest said.

"I'm not ready for bed quite yet. I still need to eat dinner. It's weird saying dinner, isn't it? But my dinner is everyone else's breakfast," Sarah said with a smile. "Have you eaten yet?"

"No, I haven't. I could use a cup of tea and a bite."

"Would you like to come to Grandma Hattie's with me?"

"Your grandmother wouldn't mind if you brought along company?"

Sarah burst out laughing. "It's a restaurant, silly!"

Father Martin grinned like a Cheshire Cat.

"Oh, you knew that, didn't you?" Sarah replied, giving him a playful swat on the arm.

"Do you want to drive or shall I?" he asked.

"You can drive today."

"That's ace with me."

"Huh?"

"It's *good* with me."

"Okay then. Let's go."

* * *

They had barely sat down in the comfortable booth when a middle-aged waitress with a youthful face, a multitude of tattoos and long, blonde braids came up to the table with menus and two glasses of water.

"Mornin' folks," she said cheerfully.

Patrick looked up at the waitress and sucked in a surprised breath as she rattled off the daily specials. He stifled his laughter and tried to keep a straight face as he asked whether the sausage was links or patties.

Sarah looked at Patrick then up at the waitress and realized why the priest had nearly lost his composure. The waitress, who Sarah knew was a bit on the weird side, recently had fangs implanted where her upper right and left canines should be. The fangs not only looked like they were difficult to talk with but looked ridiculous as well, especially in light of what Sarah now knew about vampires.

Sebastian Dragan had chosen the same restaurant this morning and had walked into the parking lot in time to see the couple disappear through the restaurant's glass double doors.

He debated for a moment about going in, but he wanted to see the beautiful woman again. And he wanted to know if the man with her was her husband. He waited for a few minutes and then entered the restaurant.

The main dining room was small, and Sebastian managed to get a table near the couple where he could see and hear them without being noticed.

"Do you always eat out?" Father Martin asked after the waitress served them their drinks.

"I like to eat out after shift. The last thing I want to do when I get off work is go home and cook. Unlike my friend Kim, who's a wonderful cook, I'm terrible. Believe me, I can burn water," Sarah replied. "But I'm a good eater."

A smile as bright as the dawn lit up the priest's entire face, and Sarah thought he looked like an angel.

Perhaps he was.

"May I ask you a personal question?"

"Sure."

"Why don't you dress like a priest? I mean, why don't you wear your cleric's collar?"

Father Martin contemplated the question for a moment and then said, "I try not to draw attention to myself. I find it's better to blend in wherever I am. A priest is rather hard to miss if he's dressed like one, don't you think?"

"I don't think you're very successful at it," Sarah said abruptly.

"At what?" he asked, puzzled. "Being a priest?"

"At blending in. I'm afraid you were born to stand out in more ways than one, Patrick."

"Meh? I'm just an average bloke," he replied, feeling an odd sense of bliss as he tried to maintain a humble posture.

Sebastian didn't know if he should be thrilled or incensed. The man wasn't the woman's husband, but he was a priest. Sebastian thought he had seen this man before, and now he was sure of it. He'd been in Las Vegas, and now he was here in Carson City. That was too much of a coincidence for Sebastian's liking. Why would the priest be in both cities and what was this woman to him? He sensed his master was in danger and wondered if the woman was also. He had to devise a plan to meet her, to see what she knew about the priest and if he, she or they knew anything about him or Anton Krulak.

Chapter 15

Anton Krulak had rested well again. Northern Nevada was good for him. Perhaps it had to do with all the spirits that haunted the area. So many of the spirits were those of the damned from the Wild West of years gone by—gunfighters, thieves, harlots, gamblers, and drunkards—who upon their deaths had not been granted the privilege of going into the light. Instead, they remained trapped between the worlds, not in heaven but not quite in hell.

"I need to speak with you, master," Sebastian said as he helped Krulak finish dressing.

"What do you wish to say?" the vampire asked.

Sebastian paused, trying to arrange his words so Krulak wouldn't fly into a rage. He had seen that far too many times, and he didn't want to be the brunt of the creature's anger ever again.

"I've seen one of them."

"One of them?" Krulak asked.

"A vampire hunter."

The vampire's eyes blazed from ice cold blue to searing red like burning coals as he stared at Sebastian with amazement and fury. "Are you sure?"

"Quite sure. I saw him this morning. I thought I'd seen him before, and now I know I have. The priest was in Las Vegas, and I believe he was in New Orleans as well."

"Perhaps he is a missionary, and his being in the same cities as us is merely a coincidence. You know those sanctimonious types," Krulak said dismissively as he brushed aside the antique lace curtain and peered out the window. "Out to save the world and every soul in it. They travel the globe, spreading their fairy tales of a heavenly reward in return for a life of suffering, poverty and chastity. The fools!"

"Nevertheless, I'll remain vigilant during our stay here. If there's even a hint of danger, we must leave at once."

The vampire placed a cold hand against Sebastian's cheek. "You have always been a faithful servant."

"And you have always been a faithful master."

"Let us not talk of grave matters any further. The night is young, Sebastian, and so are you."

Sebastian handed Krulak his overcoat, asking, "Where are we going tonight?"

"I am going to the symphony in Reno."

"What about me, master?"

"I suggest you find some company for the evening. It has been a long time since you indulged yourself in carnal pleasures. Far too long. After all, a man cannot live by bread alone," Krulak said with a mocking laugh.

Chapter 16

After taking Krulak to Reno, Sebastian immediately returned to Carson City. He wasn't in the mood to gamble or visit a brothel, as his master had suggested, so he decided to return to the St. Charles and have a quiet evening with a drink and a good book.

Sebastian pulled up to the convenience store gas station and began refueling Krulak's new, black Cadillac Escalade, an ideal vehicle for their needs. Krulak had won the luxury SUV in a poker game at the Wynn Casino in Las Vegas.

Just as he returned the hose to the gas pump, a bright yellow sports car pulled up to the pump behind him. Sebastian's knees nearly buckled beneath him and his heart pounded to his throat as the woman he desired emerged from the little car. Should he say something to her? Why shouldn't he? It was perfectly natural to engage in casual conversation with a stranger.

"She's beautiful," Sebastian said, his accent still heavy after all the years traveling the world.

"Excuse me?" Sarah said.

"Your car. It's beautiful. A true classic."

"Thank you. It's my favorite model. You can keep the Z4s and 5s as far as I'm concerned."

"I agree. The new Zs look more like spaceships than roadsters," Sebastian replied confidently.

Sarah giggled. She had thought the very same thing the first time she'd seen the new Z4.

"My name is Sebastian," he said, extending his hand.

Sarah eyed the stranger. He was built like a lumberjack, 6'4" and a good 290 pounds, but he was strikingly attractive. His dark, straight brown hair was nicely coiffed, and his nails looked manicured. His brown eyes were soft and unguarded and somewhat sad as if he had seen far too much for one lifetime.

"I'm Sarah. Nice to meet you."

"My pleasure. I recently arrived in town, and I'm here for the season."

"Season?"

"The ski season, although I'm a bit early for it."

"That may not necessarily be true. Mount Rose had snow on it just last week. By the way, you have a great accent. Where are you from?" Sarah asked as the pump clicked off.

"From Hungary," he replied, wishing he didn't have to lie. But he needed to remain vigilant in order to keep his master safe.

"You're a long way from home."

"Yes, but I consider America my home now."

"It's a good place to call home," Sarah said.

"I know this may seem very forward, but would you care to have a drink with me?" Sebastian asked.

Sarah blushed. She wasn't accustomed to being asked out by strangers.

"Forgive me. I'm being forward," Sebastian said, taking a step back. "A beautiful lady such as yourself must have a husband and family waiting at home."

"No husband. No family."

"Well then, that's good news for me," he said with a wink.

"Perhaps, but not tonight."

"I'm sorry to hear that," Sebastian said, the disappointment evident in his voice.

"I have to work."

"Oh, I see," he said, his face brightening.

"Are you free tomorrow night? We could meet for a drink then."

"That would be lovely."

Sarah grabbed her messenger bag from the car. "Here's my card. Call me later tonight, and we'll make plans for tomorrow."

"I'd like that," Sebastian replied.

"Okay. Talk to you later." Sarah slid into the roadster, waved and then pulled away from the gas pumps.

Sebastian smiled as he watched her drive away, but his smile dissolved as he gazed at the small, white card he held. *Sarah Baker, CSI. Carson City Sheriff's Department.*

Chapter 17

Sarah sat hunched over her desk, reviewing case files. Carefully, she compared the crime scene photos from the Blakely case to those of the Sandoval-Ross case. In each case the children had been laid out on a couch, a clear indication the killer felt remorse for his victims. Each mother lay dead nearby. Sarah was sure she'd missed something in the evidence, but no matter how many times she read her notes and looked at the grisly photos, she couldn't see anything new.

She pushed the files aside and sat back in her chair. What did it matter? Even if she found probative evidence that linked the two cases, how could she tie the cases to Anton Krulak? Most importantly, how could he ever be brought to justice? He couldn't. She knew it, and Patrick had already said as much. It was obvious the same perp had committed the murders, and she knew he wasn't human. But where was this elusive Anton Krulak, and how did she go about finding his lair? She wasn't a detective or even a cop, and Sarah hadn't the slightest idea of even where to begin. Krulak could be anywhere and nowhere.

Perhaps she should talk to Detective Maguire. *Right, Baker. Tell Sean Maguire you know a vampire committed the murders and you want him to find the vampire in question and dispatch him posthaste. You'll be in the loony bin before you know it and out of a job as well.*

But Sarah did want the detective to find Krulak and kill him. Patrick would vehemently disagree with that, saying it was his job to find Krulak and destroy him in the specific, ritualistic Vatican approved manner. It didn't matter what Patrick thought though. All Sarah wanted to do was keep him safe and very far away from the vampire's wrath.

Admitting defeat, at least for the moment, Sarah gathered up the case files and stowed them in her Open Cases file drawer. As she was about to get up and go to the break room for a cup of coffee, her cell phone rang.

It was Sebastian.

"Is this a good time to speak?" asked the deep voice on the other end of the line.

"It's perfect. I was just about to take a break."

"Good. I won't keep you, but I wanted to know if tomorrow evening is still good for us to meet?"

"Yes. Tuesday is one of my regular off-duty nights," Sarah replied, checking the date on her watch to make sure it was actually Monday. Sometimes she lost track of the time, her days and nights blending one into the other.

"Excellent!" Sebastian replied, beaming. "Shall I pick you up?"

"I'll meet you. Even though it's my night off, I'm on call 24/7. If a case comes in, it would be easier for me to get to it if I had my own car."

"I understand. Where do you suggest we meet?"

"There's a pub I like called The Feisty Goat on East Long Street. It's kind of a dive, but it's quiet, and we can hear one another talk. How does that sound?" As Sarah waited for an answer, it dawned on her. The Feisty Goat was around the block from the Dalton crime scene on Rand Avenue.

"Eight o'clock?"

"Perfect. I'll see you then."

"I'm looking forward to it. Until then, adieu," Sebastian said and hung up.

Adieu? *The guy has class,* Sarah thought.

Not even ten seconds had elapsed from the time she'd hung up her cell phone to the time her desk phone rang.

"CSI Baker, how may I help you?"

"Hello, my favorite sheila."

"Patrick! How are you?"

"Can't complain, and even if I did, who'd listen, eh?"

"I would," Sarah protested, a little too much.

"So you would. Ah...I was wondering if I could come to your house tomorrow morning after your shift?"

"Sure. That's fine. About 9:00? I'll text you the directions now."

"That's ace," the priest said and hung up.

"Hey, Baker. You look like the cat that just ate the canary," Grayson said as he shuffled into their mutual office.

"Yeah?"

"What's up?"

"I have a date."

"You go, girl. It's about time," he said with a wink.

"It is, isn't it?"

"I have something else that will make your night."

"What's that?"

"Remember that case where the woman supposedly committed suicide by slitting her throat?"

"How could I forget?" Sarah asked, absentmindedly running her hand across her own throat.

"We have the DNA results on the fluid taken from the woman's clothes. Besides the woman's blood, there was DNA from saliva, and it was from another contributor. A male. I'm going to run it and see if it matches anyone in CODIS."

"If it does, we may have a homicide, not a suicide on our hands."

"Things are looking up, Baker."

"They certainly are."

Chapter 18

Father Martin stood at Sarah's front door, a bag of groceries in one arm and his laptop under the other.

"G'day!"

"Good day, yourself. What's all this?" she asked as she waved him into the living room of her small, but extremely tidy townhouse.

"I thought we could have a working breakfast or in your case dinner."

"Great!"

Patrick followed Sarah to the kitchen where he unpacked enough food for a week.

"Are you expecting more than just the two of us?" Sarah asked as she poured him a cup of coffee.

"You said you were a good eater, so I'm making you a hearty meal."

"There's no Vegemite in there, I hope."

"What? You don't like Vegemite?"

"Honestly? It's disgusting. A college friend of mine brought a jar of it back from her Australian vacation and shared it with me. I could still taste it after two days. Yuck!"

"Ah, sheila, you have no taste."

Sarah knew she wasn't going to win the argument, and she didn't want to either. This gorgeous man was cooking for her, so who was she to argue?

"Where are the frying pans?" Patrick asked and set about his work.

Sarah was happily surprised when Patrick served her a steaming plate of bacon, sausage, fried mushrooms and tomatoes, baked beans, coddled eggs and crisp wheat toast. She couldn't remember when she ate an odder or more delicious meal.

Pushing away her plate, Sarah yawned and stretched. "That was marvelous. Where did you learn to cook?"

"In seminary. I was assigned to the kitchen."

Sarah had briefly allowed herself to forget Patrick was a priest, and her crestfallen face clearly showed it.

"Are you all right?"

"Ah, yeah, I'm fine. I was thinking."

"I imagine you have lots on your mind. Work like yours doesn't end when you come home, does it?" Patrick replied as he gathered up the plates and placed them in the dishwasher.

"No, not really. So tell me. Any developments in our case?"

"There may be. I've been mapping similar murder cases to the Blakely, Dalton and Sandoval-Ross cases over the past eight years, and I think I've found a pattern. I wanted your opinion," Patrick said as he turned on his laptop and opened a file.

A map of the US and Canada appeared on the high definition screen, little red dots scattering across it from one end to the other.

"Each of these dots represents a violent homicide with the same characteristics evident in your cases."

"VICAP has nothing on you, Patrick."

A shy smile tugged at his lips. It may be pride, but he was good at his job.

"What kind of pattern do you see?" Sarah asked, her curiosity definitely piqued.

"It's not a pattern of place but time," he replied, pointing to the screen. The murders are grouped by specific times of the year. The murders in New York City, the Hamptons and Washington, DC all took place during what used to be called the social season. The murders—"

"Social season?"

"The social season was a time when the fashionable and opulent attended balls, symphonies, the opera, yacht races, and lavish dinner parties. It began in Europe and extended to America. Its height was from the 1870s to the First World War."

"Hmm," came Sarah's succinct answer.

"Anton Krulak is still a man of this era."

"So what you're saying is he's making the party circuit."

"Exactly."

"Not to change the subject, Patrick, but I've been meaning to ask you something."

"And what's that?"

"How did you come up with Anton Krulak as the perp in the first place?"

Chapter 19

While doing research in the Vatican archives, Father Martin had come across references to the Krulak family in the town of Sighisoara, Romania. Since the 1870s there had been stories about the family and its break from the Catholic Church. Much of the history regarding this schism revolved around land disputes. Despite the Church seizing large portions of the family's land, the Krulak family continued to prosper and had retained much of its fortune, although how was still unclear.

Folklore contended that the eldest Krulak son, Anton, had made a bargain with the Devil to save his family from financial ruin. These stories had a small, devoted following. However, the Krulaks' fate and history became obscured by the history and folklore of another Sighisoara native, Vlad III, the Prince of Wallachia. The world would come to know Prince Vlad by his patronymic—Vlad Dracula. The Irish born and Protestant raised author Bram Stoker would use Vlad Dracula as his model for the title character of his famous novel, *Dracula*. All modern day ideas and attitudes regarding vampires could be directly traced back to this novel published in 1897.

Father Martin was enthralled by the stories about Anton Krulak and was confident his research would prove Krulak was a true vampire. The first reported murder of a woman found with her throat torn open in the area where Krulak resided was in 1869. Krulak disappeared shortly thereafter, as did the eldest son of the Dragan family. Over the decades, similar murders were reported across the European continent.

Prior to coming to the United States, Father Martin travelled to Sighisoara. Posing as a writer named Patrick Mars, he met with local townsfolk and recorded their vampire stories. Many of the stories were simple folklore revolving around the more famous native son, Dracula, but Anton Krulak figured prominently in several others. The Krulak family still resided in the medieval town, but they were reticent to discuss their famous ancestor or their missing relatives.

When he was about ready to give up searching for Anton Krulak, Father Martin came upon a woman named Anika Radu. Anika was a tiny wisp of a woman, ninety-six but still mentally sharp and quite interested in his endeavors.

On a cold, snowy night in late January, Father Martin met with Anika Radu in her home on the outskirts of town. The night may have been bitter, but Anika's home was warm and inviting. She prepared him a traditional Romanian dinner of caraway seed soup and lamb with okra. After dining the two talked for hours. It was obvious that this lovely, old woman was filled with the Holy Spirit and quite distraught over her family's ties with Krulak, something that had kept her estranged from her relatives for over sixty years.

Anika's first recollections of Krulak were from her father. She often overheard him telling vampire stories, and how the Dragan family had prospered by offering up their firstborn sons to the vampire. As Anika grew older, she dismissed these stories as superstitious nonsense, but when her favorite nephew, the son of her sister Elsa, went into the service of a mysterious benefactor, she began to take credence in these stories.

Young Lucien never returned home. It was said he had died somewhere in France, but there was no record of his death. Anika had demanded answers, and the family's story was eventually revealed. Anika protested and even sought counsel and help from the Church and was immediately exiled from the family and its fortunes.

Before Father Martin departed Anika's home, she slipped a small piece of jewelry into his hand. The oval, hand painted porcelain pendant featured a handsome young man of about thirty years of age. He had coal black hair and piercing blue eyes.

"God forgive me. I stole this from my Uncle Viktor many years ago for this very moment," Anika said softly. "It's the only picture I know that exists of Anton Krulak."

Father Martin gazed down at the pendant in his hand.

"I also know you aren't a writer as you've let everyone believe."

Father Martin's head jerked up in surprise.

"You're a vampire hunter," she said with a wink. "Take this pendant. I pray it will help you in your quest to find this spawn of hell."

The old woman sent Father Martin on his way with a blessing and a kiss. That night she died peacefully in her bed, surrounded by angels.

Chapter 20

"She's not going to like this," Grayson said to the person on the other end of his landline.

"She who?" Sarah asked as she walked into their office.

"She you," he replied, holding up a hand as he finished his conversation. "Okay. We'll be there in a few." After hanging up the phone, Grayson turned to Sarah and said, "We have a 425 that's most likely a 419, and we'll need Animal Control called in."

Please don't let it be what I think, Sarah thought.

The last time they had a call for a possible dead body with animal involvement, an old man had been found dead in the far back part of his rural property. He'd been dead at least a week, and his starving dogs had started to feed on him. Sarah didn't know who she should be sadder for, the old man or the poor animals.

When the CSIs arrived at the scene, it was even worse than Sarah could have ever imagined. It was like something out of an episode of the television show, *Hoarders.* Overflowing garbage cans, trash bags, cardboard boxes, papers, cans, bottles, plastic containers, household items, and clothes covered the gravel yard of the tiny, green clapboard house.

"Be careful," Grayson said as he shined his Maglite along a broken concrete path leading to the front door. "Have you had a Tetanus shot lately?"

"Yeah," Sarah replied as she cautiously followed behind her partner.

The overwhelming stench emanating from the house instantly stopped them at the front door. Decomposition and urine. They could also hear the pitiful yowling of cats.

"Oh, God!" Sarah said with a heavy sigh. "We better wait until Animal Control gets here."

They didn't have long to wait before Animal Control pulled up behind their Crime Scene Unit SUV. A short, wiry man of about fifty jumped from the truck.

"Hey, Baker. Grayson! What do we have tonight?"

"Cats. Sounds like a lot of them," Grayson replied.

"Okie dokie then," Craig Leonard said as he pulled on a pair of thick leather gloves.

Grayson eased the door open. Shadows scattered in every direction as the beam from his flashlight scanned the living room. Glowing yellow-green eyes stared back from the shadows that had hunkered down in the corners of the room, a room engulfed by a sea of trash. A narrow, feces-covered passageway dotted with dead cockroaches trailed through the living room and into the kitchen and bedroom.

The veteran CSI took a deep breath through his mouth to keep from vomiting, but Sarah wasn't as lucky. She bolted from the house, nearly knocking Leonard down as she fled, and ran into the street where she violently emptied the contents of her stomach. She heaved again, wiped her mouth, and then screwed up her pride and returned to the house.

"Sorry about that, guys," Sarah said, embarrassed as she re-entered the living room.

"It happens," Grayson replied sympathetically.

Leonard estimated the number of felines and returned to his truck for pet carriers while Sarah and Grayson struggled through the debris.

"Ah, shit!" Grayson exclaimed as he scuffed his boot across something hard and flat on the floor.

"What is it?" Sarah anxiously asked.

"It's a fucking desiccated cat. It must have been dead for months. Looks like a few more over there," he said, pointing across the room with the beam of his flashlight.

Sarah's stomach did flip-flops again.

When she and Grayson finally made it to the bedroom, they found the rotting corpse of an elderly woman sitting up in her bed as if awaiting her breakfast tray. A rail thin cat sat protectively at her side.

"It's okay, baby," Sarah cooed to the frightened, starving animal. "You're going to get some food and water in just a bit."

"Here, let me have her," Leonard said as he came up from behind and carefully took the cat into his arms and then placed it gently into a pet carrier.

"How in the name of Jesus can people live like this?" Sarah said through clenched teeth, willing herself not to be sick. She never wanted to hear anyone complain about her being an obsessive-compulsive neatnik ever again.

"We'd better treat this DB like a homicide just in case," Grayson said as he tried to figure out where to start documenting the scene.

Eliot Parker could barely manage to get through the house to examine his newest charge.

"It will be tough determining COD and how long she's been dead until a full autopsy," Parker said matter-of-factly as if he saw such a thing every day of the week.

"It's been awhile," Sarah replied. "This woman's cats look to be on the verge of starvation. But they must be getting water from somewhere or more of them would be dead."

"Poor things," Parker replied. "But I'm sure her heart was in the right place."

Parker never had an unkind word to say about anyone.

Five hours later, the CSIs had done all they could. The old woman had been taken to the ME's, and all the cats had been rounded up and taken to the Humane Society. Sarah was more than ready to go back to the station, shower, do her paperwork, and then go home and fall into bed. She was exhausted. For the first time in four weeks, the dashing Father Martin hadn't entered her thoughts.

Chapter 21

As the vampire woke, he felt that all too familiar pain gnaw at his gut, a small, annoying ache at first. Then it rapidly turned into an all-consuming fire, radiating throughout every nerve in his cursed body. He could feel the supple young flesh of his face pull tautly back, slowly stretching over his high cheekbones, fine, straight nose and chiseled chin like aging parchment. The gleaming white incisors, top and bottom, sharpened into cruel, discolored points as the canines morphed into vicious serpent-like fangs. One by one, razor sharp talons akin to that of an eagle replaced his well-manicured fingernails, and his once sparkling blue eyes became black and hollow. The thick, shiny black hair dropped off in dull, matted clumps, revealing a bald, scarred pate that looked even more pitiful as the ears became elongated, pointed appendages.

Krulak's fists tightened into hard, angry balls. Several loud thumps resounded against the coffin lid, alerting Sebastian that the transformation was nearly complete. Then silence. Sebastian leaned closer to the wooden sarcophagus. He could hear a low rasping sound but nothing else. He backed away seconds before the lid exploded off the coffin, landing on the floor several feet from where it once lay.

The vampire flew straight up from where he'd slumbered and came to rest beside one of the little room's dirty windows. The light from a nearby streetlamp streamed softly into the modest accommodation, illuminating the creature in a faint yellow glow. Silently, he stood there, his young, athletic body now stooped and aged, his once well-tailored suit draping his skeletal frame.

Turning his head from side to side, Krulak could feel the crunching of each vertebra as he stretched. Taking a deep breath, he hunched his shoulders several times and then stood ramrod straight. A pair of dragon-like wings tore through his tony coat, emerging from his back like a phoenix. The wings fluttered and then folded across his cadaveric chest as a high, piercing scream tore from his thin, cracked lips.

Sebastian eased closer to his master, his eyes never falling from the satanic face. With one swift and deliberate motion, he flung open the window and then threw himself to the floor. A violent swoosh of air, followed by a thousand demons, grazed his cowering body and then disappeared into the cold night.

* * *

Brittany Anderson had just come home from her shift as a cocktail waitress. Young, pretty, single, and carefree, she worked the 3:00 p.m. to midnight shift at The Max Casino. Falling into her favorite easy chair, she kicked off her high heels and then rubbed her aching feet. As she contemplated whether to watch television or go to bed, Brittany heard a scratching noise coming from her bedroom. Thinking it was her new kitten, she called out to it. "Here, Rascal! Come on, baby. Come to mama."

The kitten didn't meow, but the scratching continued. Concerned, Brittany cautiously tiptoed to her bedroom. She switched on the light and entered the room; a chill instantly swept over her entire body as she stepped across the threshold. She'd left the window open! She ran to it and peered out into the well-lit parking lot beyond. Brittany could see the cars, the bank of mailboxes and a few scattered pieces of trash. If Rascal was out there, she prayed that he was under one of the cars. She had to go look for him.

Brittany turned from the window. This time the scratching noise was right behind her.

The vampire stood next to her dresser, scraping his claws across the highly polished finish, deeply gouging the pristine surface. Fear, stark and vivid, glittered in the young woman's eyes, and her thoughts tumbled anxiously through her brain. Staggering backwards she desperately searched for an escape from this hideous creature.

There was nowhere to run.

The room went dark except for the ceiling that glowed above them, the very maw of hell opening to swallow up all that was unholy. A legion of demons with moldering, naked, corpse-like bodies writhed violently as if they'd come to life from a Hieronymus Bosch painting. Twisting in a macabre dance of death, they beckoned Brittany with harsh whispers and beseeching calls.

Krulak's face was before her, his black eyes cruelly piercing her own. Brittany's mouth opened as she felt a maniacal scream bubble up from the base of her throat, but no sound escaped her quivering lips.

Razor sharp fangs tore at the white flesh until only bloody sinew was visible in the dim light from above. Wave upon wave of ecstasy coursed through Anton Krulak's body and did not cease until the young woman's heart beat no more. As her body went limp in his embrace, the vampire gorged himself with the viscous stream of life.

Sated, Krulak reared back and regurgitated some of the recently consumed blood, spewing it across the walls, marking his territory with a spattering of crimson. Running his blood-covered hand across the length of the bedroom wall, he made his final mark.

His strength regained, Krulak's wings unfurled and he prepared to take flight. But a soft mewling sound halted his retreat. A small black kitten emerged from under the bed and stood crying at his feet. The vampire glared at the tiny, innocent creature then scooped it into his boney, clawed hand and tucked it under his wing.

Chapter 22

Detective Maguire's booming voice could be heard from the bullpen clear into the locker room.

"Who the hell leaked information about today's homicide to the media?"

Uniforms and detectives alike froze in their tracks.

Orlando West had just come on shift. "What are you talking about, Maguire?"

"Today's homicide!" he spat back as if West should know what he was talking about.

"Calm down and come into my office."

Sean Maguire threw himself down in the chair opposite the nightshift CSU supervisor.

"You haven't read the new case file yet, have you?"

"No. I was just getting ready to review the day shift reports."

"Jesus! The homicide Sadler caught today was a carbon copy of our last one and the one in Reno. Worse yet, someone told Kristen Remington of Channel 2 that we have a serial killer running loose in Northern Nevada. It was on the six o'clock evening news. She accused the department and the Reno PD of not protecting the public. She called both me and Jason Gaffney out by name."

"None of my people would leak info on a case," West protested. He could feel his blood pressure rising.

"I know. But I have my suspicions who did. And if I'm right, I'm going to hang that bastard out to dry," Maguire hissed.

The bastard in question was a uniformed officer named Trevor Brown. Maguire had been promoted to detective over him more than three years ago, and Brown was still bitter. He never missed an opportunity to try and make Maguire look bad. Now it seemed Brown had found the perfect way to humiliate him in front of his superiors, the public and Governor Sandoval. Maguire was livid.

"Have you spoken to the Sheriff about Brown?"

"No, but I'm on the verge. This news story could seriously compromise our investigations. Have you found any useful evidence that could ID the perp?"

"Grayson and Baker are still examining the evidence. There's not much, but when they find something, I'll let you know."

"Speaking of Baker, where is she?"

"RDO. Grayson should be in his office if you'd like to speak to him."

West wanted to tell Maguire everything he knew, but he decided to err on the side of caution and remain silent. Maguire had more to lose if this whole vampire thing turned out to be an elaborate hoax and even more if it turned out to be real. With the evidence before him, West was certain the latter would be the case.

* * *

"I hope I'm not too late," Sarah said as she happily greeted Sebastian Dragan.

"Not at all."

"Did you have any trouble finding the pub?"

Sebastian shook his head. "You give excellent directions."

"Carson isn't a big town, so it's easy to get around."

"True, but I have been here before."

"Really? When?"

"About fifteen years ago," Sebastian replied as he eyed the angel sitting before him. He still couldn't believe his good fortune of running into Sarah at the gas station. It was kismet—pure and simple. And if anyone believed in such a thing, it was Sebastian.

"I apologize for not being able to get together with you last week as we planned. Things got crazy at work, and I had to put in more overtime than expected. Having a normal life in my line of work is sometimes difficult."

"Ah, yes. You are the CSI."

A small smile tugged at the corners of Sarah's lips. She found Sebastian's accent and Eastern European syntax charming.

"I make you smile?" Sebastian asked sweetly.

"Yes. You do."

"What shall we have to drink?"

"I always have an Old Rasputin," Sarah replied.

Sebastian burst out laughing. "A what?"

"It's a Russian Imperial stout."

"I see. Then I will have one as well."

"That's ace with me," she replied. She loved using the Aussie slang she'd learned from Patrick.

A quizzical look fell over Sebastian's handsome face. "Ace?"

"It means good. An Australian friend of mine always says that."

"Would this be a gentleman friend?" Sebastian inquired.

"Yes, he is," Sarah said, almost blushing.

"Are you and the gentleman an item?"

Now it was Sarah's turn to laugh. Sebastian sounded like her elderly next-door neighbor Inez, who was always asking Sarah about her love life. For a modern man, Sebastian seemed like someone from another era.

They talked nonstop for the next two hours. She was surprised at how easy he was to talk with and more than impressed that Sebastian was a travel writer. Luckily, he came from a wealthy family, so pursuing his passion for traveling the world wasn't an economic burden.

Sarah wondered how it would feel to be rich. She had grown up in the *system* and learned early on to be self-reliant, never depending on anyone for anything. She never knew her parents. They and her brother Colm were killed in a car accident out on Long Island. Two-year old Sarah survived unscathed. Her foster parents, although loving and kind, were as poor as church mice.

And contrary to what most people believed, CSIs were vastly underpaid, averaging about $30,000 per year or $15.62 per hour for a 40-hour-week. With sixty grand still owed on college loans, Sarah would be poor for many more years to come.

Chapter 23

Maguire interviewed every neighbor in Dalton's building. No one had heard a thing as the young woman was being butchered. Someone on the second floor said they thought they'd heard something that night out by the dumpster but ignored it, thinking it was a stray cat routing through the trash.

That something turned out to be Charlie, an affable street person who regularly made his rounds in the neighborhood, looking for recyclable bottles and cans. Since Carson City didn't require its residents to recycle, most environmentally conscious folks considered the old man to be a godsend. Charlie made a decent haul from his nightly scavenger hunts and was able to rent a cheap motel room during the fall and winter months, while enjoying the outdoor life the rest of the year.

The forensic evidence in Dalton's apartment was useless. None of the fingerprints retrieved were in AFIS, or they belonged to the deceased. The hair samples couldn't be traced to anyone since most didn't contain the root or follicular tissue, and the few that did were Dalton's.

The latest murder of Brittany Anderson was just as baffling as the Evelyn Dalton homicide. However, there was one odd difference. Anderson had recently adopted an eight-week old kitten and that kitten had disappeared. Maguire figured it had simply run away, but considering the food and water bowls, the relatively clean litter box, the scratching post, and the multitude of toys, it didn't seem very likely that Anderson was a neglectful pet parent whose feline had bolted at the first opportunity.

No doubt the kitten would turn up somewhere in the complex in a day or two when its hunger and thirst had finally overcome its fright. Maguire hoped someone would take it in. Although he was a battle-hardened ex-Army Ranger and a ten-year veteran of the Carson City Sheriff's Department, Maguire was an absolute marshmallow when it came to small, helpless things like kittens and children.

Jason Gaffney had been no more successful in his investigation into the Damonte Ranch homicides. Like Dalton's neighbors, none of the Sandoval-Ross's neighbors had heard a thing. What little evidence recovered from the scene was processed, but there were no hits in CODIS, and all the fingerprints in the house belonged to Linda Sandoval-Ross, her children and her husband.

Mr. Ross's fingerprints were on file, but only because he was a lieutenant colonel in the US Marines. Lt. Colonel Ross had been on his third month of a 12-month unaccompanied tour in Iwakuni, Japan during the murders, although he was currently in town on two weeks' leave after having buried his wife and two children.

Detective Maguire was absolutely dumbfounded. He had never worked more frustrating cases, and it was beginning to take its toll. Devouring Tums by the roll full became second nature, and he was convinced he had the beginnings of a stress-induced ulcer.

Weary from his not so restful RDO, Maguire shuffled into the break room and poured himself an extra-large cup of black coffee.

"I have some news that's going to make your night," Grayson said as he came up beside the detective.

"Reno's getting a major league baseball team?"

"Even better. Baker and I've been going over cold cases."

"Okay."

"The DNA came back on a cold case from fifteen years ago. The genetic markers match those of the fluid samples taken from our recent homicides and those in Reno. The perp's the same. Now we just need to ID him."

"That's awesome news!" Maguire replied as he held up his hand for a high five.

Grayson slapped Maguire's hand and was out the door.

The detective's stomach rumbled, this time with optimism. Maybe matching DNA could be found in other cases as well—other cases that identified a suspect by name.

Chapter 24

By mid-December all leads in the homicide cases had been exhausted. There were no more cases on file where the DNA matched the Las Vegas, Reno and Carson City homicides, and despite his best efforts Father Martin could not find Anton Krulak. No person fitting Krulak's description was registered in any hotel or motel in the city or in any of the seasonal rental properties.

The priest's investigation would now have to expand to Reno, and that would take months if not a year or more to conclude. If the Sheriff's Department and the Reno Police were involved, the time could be minimized. But that posed a problem in itself. There was no way for officials to identify Anton Krulak as a person of interest. Father Martin was back to square one.

Sarah continued seeing Sebastian and Patrick, although never at the same time. It wasn't like the two men wouldn't get on well with one another, but three was a crowd, especially when one of the three was a priest. Although her relationship with Patrick was strictly professional and platonic, she still had reservations about introducing the two men.

With Christmas coming on, Sarah was in a bit of a panic. She didn't want either of the men to be alone, nor did she want Grayson to spend his day at some casino. Sebastian's family was still in Hungary, and Patrick's parents resided in Italy. In the end Sarah decided to ask all three to her house for Christmas dinner. Grayson politely declined the invitation. He'd been asked to a friend's house in Lake Tahoe for the day.

Much to Sebastian's disappointment, Anton Krulak decided to spend the holidays in San Francisco, another one of his romantic venues. Sebastian was deeply apologetic, telling Sarah he had to take care of some family business in Budapest but assured her he would return after the New Year.

He wished he could tell Sarah the truth, but he knew she'd be horrified. And what woman wouldn't be? Then there was the unavoidable fact that she worked in law enforcement and would have him arrested if she knew he was complicit in hundreds of gruesome murders. Sebastian had already lost his soul; he couldn't lose the one woman he had ever loved. He had sacrificed enough for Anton Krulak.

Before leaving on his trip, Sebastian told Sarah that he had a Christmas gift for her. She was quite surprised but thrilled even so when that gift turned out to be a kitten. This gift endeared Sebastian to Sarah more than he could realize. Sebastian explained that he had found the tiny creature while out on a walk and was concerned about taking it to the Humane Society, fearing it wouldn't be adopted because it was black. Despite being the 21st century, black cats still suffered from the stigma of being evil, a ridiculous Antediluvian notion that Sebastian couldn't fathom still existed. He knew all about evil, and a black cat wasn't it.

Sarah fell instantly in love with the kitten and named him Bagheera after the black panther from *The Jungle Book*. Bagheera took to Sarah right off too and followed her about the townhouse like a little shadow.

* * *

Christmas Eve couldn't have been more perfect. The snow remained on the ground from two earlier storms, and on this night a light snow was falling. Sarah loved the stillness that came with a snowfall, and she loved cuddling up in her recliner by the fire, drinking hot cocoa and watching old holiday movies.

She was well into *It's a Wonderful Life* when a persistent knock thrummed on her door. Reluctantly, she took Bagheera from her lap and placed him into the charcoal-colored chenille throw she'd been using to keep them warm.

"Who is it?" she called out as she placed her hand on the doorknob.

"It's me, sheila. Patrick."

Who else would call her sheila? She opened the door with a big smile to find Patrick standing before her with an enormous smile of his own and his arms filled with Christmas gifts.

"What's all this?" she asked, a bit embarrassed. She'd gotten him a gift too, but only one.

"It's Christmas Eve!" he replied as if she weren't aware of the day. "Are you ready?"

"Ready for what?"

"Church, my dear. I told you I was going to midnight Mass at St. Teresa's."

It had been years since Sarah had gone to Mass, but how could she tell Patrick *no*?

She ushered him into the townhouse, and he immediately placed the gifts around her little *Charlie Brown* Christmas tree that looked even worse for wear since Bagheera wouldn't leave the branches or ornaments alone.

"There!" Patrick said, pleased with himself. "Now you have some proper gifts for under your tree."

"Thank you," Sarah replied, wanting to kiss his cheek, but resisted the impulse to do so.

Patrick walked to the recliner and took up the black ball of fluff and cuddled it into the crook of his arm. The kitten purred with satisfaction.

"He's even cuter than you described," Patrick said as he scratched under the kitten's chin.

"Yes, he is," Sarah replied, although her thoughts were not on the kitten.

* * *

Minutes later they were packed into a crowded pew with a dozen other Christmas Catholics. Although Sarah was not a fan of crowds or church, she'd never felt happier in her life. As they sang carols more people edged into their pew. Selflessly, Patrick handed an elderly woman his songbook and then placed his hand under Sarah's to share hers. For a moment her hand trembled but stopped when he asked if she were cold.

"Just a chill," she replied with a bashful smile.

A spark of indefinable emotion shined in the priest's eyes as he smiled back.

Chapter 25

Sarah and Patrick hadn't been back to the townhouse for long when she got called into work.

"I'm sorry, but duty calls," Sarah said, feeling a bit ridiculous for her cheesy remark.

"I understand."

"Dinner's still on. Okay? Two o'clock?"

"If you're sure you won't be too tired."

"I'm sure."

"All right then. I'll see you tomorrow. Happy Christmas," Patrick replied, kissing Sarah on the cheek.

Sarah stood in the open door, trembling as she watched Patrick drive away in his snow-covered rental car.

The ringing of her landline instantly interrupted her moment of bliss. "Baker," she snapped.

"It's Grayson. Is everything okay?"

"Yeah, fine."

"I'm on my way now to pick you up."

"I'll be waiting," Sarah said through gritted teeth.

The crime scene tonight was at the William Street off ramp to US 395. A family returning home from Reno had been hit head on by a drunk driver, who in his alcoholic stupor had mistaken the off ramp for the on ramp. Normally, the Crime Scene Unit didn't handle traffic accidents, but since this was a DUI with fatalities, it became the CSIs' job to investigate.

Red and blue lights flashed in disarray in the early morning darkness, lighting the area with a macabre and decidedly unfortunate holiday-like glow. First responders had cordoned off William Street in both directions while the Nevada Highway Patrol had blocked off the ramp from the highway.

What a shitty way to ring in Christmas Day, Sarah thought as she gazed at the mangled chunks of steel. The front ends of both cars were crushed clear into the back seats. The severed head of the drunk driver sat inches above his neck, wedged between the caved in windshield and the headrest, his corpse reeking of alcohol. The parents in the subcompact were barely distinguishable as human beings. Oddly though, the child sitting in the car seat in back of her father looked unscathed except for the jagged piece of metal piercing her small chest above the bands where her protective harness snapped into the lap belt.

"Dare I say, Merry Christmas?" Eliot Parker said as he walked up to where Sarah and Grayson stood, waiting for permission to take over the scene from county deputies.

"It's okay, Parker," Grayson replied. "Somewhere someone is having a Merry Christmas, I suppose, but it aint here."

Eliot Parker did his best at a preliminary exam, notating the condition of each body, as rescue crews anxiously waited to extract the victims from their vehicles. It may seem cruel and pointless, but these people were now evidence and had to be treated as such.

"That should do it for now. Go ahead and take your notes and photos, and then we'll let these guys get to work," Parker said, nodding his head to the men standing in yellow turnouts.

"Thanks, Parker…Eliot," Sarah said softly.

"You're welcome."

"I hope you and Chip have a Merry Christmas despite how it started off for you," she added.

"We will. That man's a rock. I don't think I could do my job half as well if I didn't have him."

"You take care now."

"You do the same, sweetheart," Parker replied.

The crime scene was extensive to document. Sarah and Grayson had to photograph it from the Gold Dust West parking lot—where the drunk driver had first gotten into his vehicle—to the top of the off ramp where the Ericksons' car had departed the highway. Between them over 900 photos were taken of the vehicles' routes, the positions where they came to rest after impact, and every possible angle of each victim before being extracted from the vehicles.

Sarah measured the skid marks made by the Ericksons' car. It was obvious Mr. Erickson hadn't time to avoid the collision and more than apparent that Mr. Young was oblivious he was headed north. Not only had he attempted to get onto the highway the wrong way, he had also been going in the opposite direction of his home in Gardnerville, a town sixteen miles south of Carson City.

Sarah couldn't remember a time when she'd felt more physically and emotionally drained after processing a crime scene. Long after returning to the station, she felt ice cold. Perhaps it had more to do with the call tonight than the weather. No matter. She was determined to shake it off. She'd get a few hours' sleep and then make Patrick Christmas dinner. Fortunately for them both, Sarah had ordered a pre-made Christmas dinner from Smith's, and all she had to do was heat up the turkey, mashed potatoes and gravy, veggies and rolls, and they'd be ready to eat.

A Christmas miracle in itself.

Chapter 26

Anton Krulak loved San Francisco. It had an Old World charm but the energy of modern day. He enjoyed the many gourmet restaurants, the lively pubs, the art galleries and museums, and the theatre. He also loved the Tenderloin District. There he could feed unrestrained among the many derelicts. When one of these people went missing, no one cared, and when one of their shredded, bloated bodies was fished from the bay, the event barely registered in the news—paper or electronic.

Yes, it was the perfect city for him. San Francisco held many memories, and it was there Krulak first fell in love. Her name was Elizabeth Preston. She was the only child and heir to the Preston Railroad fortune, and she was a beauty beyond compare. Eighteen years old with a stunning figure and creamy white skin that accentuated her curly, coal black hair and remarkable violet eyes, Elizabeth was the envy of every debutante and the woman every man sought to call his own.

Krulak first met Elizabeth at the Governor's Ball in 1913, a prominent social event of the time. The ball was the pinnacle of the summer season where the captains of industry, politicians and the nouveau riche came to see and be seen. In his mind's eye, Krulak could see everything like it was yesterday. Elizabeth was a vision in her diamond-accented, black satin dress as she descended the grand staircase of the Spreckles Mansion.

Krulak could barely breathe as her gaze fell upon him out of all the other young men at the party.

He was amazed at his courage and how he had walked up to the young heiress and introduced himself. For the next few weeks they spent hours together, talking of poetry, art and music. They attended soirees at all the finest society salons and dined and drank at the most fashionable restaurants. Not thinking of the consequences or how they would live together, Krulak proposed marriage to Elizabeth within a month of their meeting.

On the night of their engagement party, Anton Krulak felt that all too familiar hunger begin to gnaw at his gut. He prayed it would cease until at least the party was over and his fiancé was safely back home. But God did not hear Krulak's prayers, and if he did the answer was *no* like so many other prayers that had been denied. The legion of demons that were his constant companions heard his pitiful cries to the heavens and became incensed. They whirled about him like a cloud of satanic locust, darkening his vision of all that surrounded him.

Krulak ran from the drawing room of the majestic French Baroque chateau and ascended the grand staircase, the same staircase where he'd first seen Elizabeth. Elizabeth followed. But when she reached the top of the staircase, her beloved Anton was no longer there. In his stead was a vile, loathsome creature. He stood before her, his eyes black and cold and his beautiful black hair all but gone, only a balding, moldy pate remaining. Hideous black-brown wings with membrane-like segments hugged his skeletal frame in an unnatural embrace, holding the tremulous, angry body in place.

As Elizabeth turned to flee, Krulak hissed and then spat out a tirade of ungodly curses. His boney fingers clawed and raked at her slender, pale arm and then found purchase. An ear-piercing shriek tore from her delicate throat, startling Krulak. Instantly, he released his grasp. Elizabeth faltered, took a step and then toppled down the grand staircase, coming to rest at her father's feet, her neck broken.

Krulak reared back his head and screamed a scream that matched Elizabeth's and then some. Flapping his ghastly wings, his body levitated into the air and then crashed through the stained glass window behind him. Jagged, bright colored shards burst in every direction as Krulak vanished into the summer night.

That night the vampire killed not once, but again and again. Nothing seemed to satiate his blood lust. From Pacific Heights to the Tenderloin and down to the Castro and over to Dogpatch and back to the Tenderloin, bodies of both men and women lay where they'd been found, violated and discarded. Only his last victim, a child of three found with his prostitute mother, halted Krulak's ravenous spree.

From that date on, Krulak made a yearly pilgrimage to San Francisco. He'd leave a long-stemmed red rose at the front door of the Spreckles Mansion, now owned by the Romance writer Danielle Steele, and one at the door of the Rescue Mission on Jones Street near the place where young William Smith had met his demise at the vampire's hand.

Chapter 27

Sarah tossed and turned at least a hundred times, repeatedly throwing off her covers and then pulling them back over her shivering body. No matter how hard she tried, she couldn't sleep, nor could she erase the image of the little girl sitting dead in her car seat. If he hadn't already been dead, Sarah thought she could kill Albert Young with her bare hands. She hated the bastard and everyone like him. At least he was dead, and that fact gave her enormous satisfaction.

By one o'clock Sarah gave up and rolled out of bed. Patrick would be over in an hour, and she still needed to take a shower and put dinner in the oven to heat.

As usual Patrick was right on time. The huge smile on his handsome face instantly faded as Sarah answered the door. She looked like she'd been through hell.

"Are you okay?" he asked, barely able to choke out the question.

"Yeah," she replied, waving him into the townhouse.

Not believing her for a second, he put his hand softly on her shoulder and asked again, "Are you sure you're okay?"

Sarah crumpled into the priest's arms, sobbing, the rush of emotion and memories washing over her in a tidal wave of despair. She couldn't be brave any longer. "Oh, God, Patrick! There wasn't anything I could do for her. She was so small, and that drunk bastard killed her and her parents!"

"Who?"

Sarah continued sobbing until she was finally able to speak. "It was the scene I processed early this morning. It was devastating. A drunk driver killed a family of three."

"I'm so sorry," Patrick said aloud, and then began a silent prayer for the souls of the recently departed.

"So am I."

"Listen. We don't need to do dinner today—"

"Yes, we do!" Sarah immediately protested. "It's Christmas Day!"

"All right, but why don't you take a nap first?"

She shook her head as blue eyes beckoned green.

Patrick saw the silent plea and without a word took Sarah's small hand in his and led her to the bedroom. He turned down the covers, and she crawled under them, no longer caring what day it was. Then he slid beside her and enfolded her into his arms. She was warm and soft and smelled like honeysuckle and home.

Sheer exhaustion finally won out, and the urge to rest was overwhelming. Soon Patrick could hear the steady rhythm of Sarah's breath, and he knew sleep had at last claimed her weary body and tortured heart.

It was dark when Sarah woke, and only the nightlight illuminated the bedroom. Patrick was still at her side, his arm tossed gently over her small body. She turned, not wanting to wake him. Sarah had fantasized about such a moment. Now it was happening, and she wanted to commit every last detail to memory—his dark blond curls tousled perfectly, his long, thick eyelashes fluttering slightly, the golden stubble shadowing his cheeks, and his mouth pouty with sleep. She reached out and ran her fingertips across his jawline.

Patrick smiled and opened his eyes. "Happy Christmas," he whispered as he pulled her close.

"Merry Christmas," Sarah whispered back.

Chapter 28

Sebastian was lonely. He was in a city with a population of three quarters of a million people, and he didn't know one god-fearing soul. He tried to occupy his time by visiting some of the sights like the Japanese Tea Garden, the Palace of Fine Art and Fisherman's Wharf, but without Sarah to enjoy such delights with him these places held little interest. Even riding the iconic cable cars was joyless. They were merely another mode of transportation.

Each morning Sebastian found himself at Caffe Trieste, drinking espresso, eating pastry and watching the hustle and bustle of normal life. He had forgotten what *normal* was, and despite the riches his family had secured from his servitude to Anton Krulak, Sebastian now realized as never before the true sacrifice he and his family had made for the vampire. He would gladly give up his fortune and live his life as a penniless ditch digger if it meant having Sarah at his side. He even dreamt of having children with her.

When his daydreams became overwhelming, Sebastian would take out his pen and write about his travels with Krulak. He noted the places they went, where they stayed, and detailed the weather, the restaurants, and the attractions just like any good travel writer would do. For a while this would keep his mind off Sarah, but not completely. When he began missing her desperately, he'd write long love letters to her. He'd never be brave enough to send them, but he wrote them nevertheless. When he'd finish pouring out his heart to her in letters she'd never read, Sebastian wrote poetry. The Muse favored his subject, and Sebastian's mind took flight as he thought of his beautiful angel.

One night when the melancholy became too much to bear, Sebastian found himself in a dive bar down in the Tenderloin, close to where Krulak had made a kill when they'd first arrived in the city. The old man's body, or what was left of it, had been discarded in a dumpster and wasn't found until Waste Management had put it through one of its industrial trash compactors. No telltale signs of the vampire's mark could be seen on Krulak's latest victim. Authorities chalked up the old man's death as an accident, assuming he was a street person who had sought shelter from the frigid San Francisco nights in one of the many dumpsters behind the rows of bars and adult bookstores.

After his seventh vodka, Sebastian decided to head back to the hotel. He needed to be at the Mark Hopkins before Krulak came in from his night on the town. Fumbling with his keycard, Sebastian dropped it several times before opening the door to his master's suite.

Shuffling and bumping into furniture, he made his way to the first bedroom and then collapsed in a drunken heap upon the soft, cream-colored satin comforter of his king-sized bed. With one last thought of Sarah, he drifted to sleep with a smile on his face.

The shaking of his bed awakened Sebastian an hour before dawn. His mind was still cloudy from the amount of alcohol he'd consumed, and he never gave it a second thought that an earthquake might be what was rattling him from his slumber.

With a groan Sebastian opened one eye and then the other. Stretching, he rolled over to discover Krulak standing at his bedside, his silhouette clearly visible in the dim light that gently streamed through the nearby picture window.

"Who is this Sarah you moan about in your sleep, Sebastian?" Krulak asked. "Some vixen you met while on our holiday?"

Ice cold fear gripped Sebastian's heart. Krulak could never know about Sarah.

"Sarah?" he replied, as if the name didn't mean a thing to him.

"Come now, my dear companion. I know when a man is dreaming about a woman."

"I don't remember what I was dreaming about, sir. It must have been a name I heard somewhere."

"Ah, I see," Krulak said. "Perhaps it was a dream of precognition, and you will meet this mysterious Sarah one day. Fate is odd that way, you know."

"Fate is an odd thing indeed. After all, fate has brought us both here, has it not?"

"Yes, Sebastian, it has." Krulak's voice broke slightly as he spoke. The memories of Elizabeth flooded his mind, and the place where once there'd been a heart now ached deeply as if rent in two. "The hour is late, and I must prepare for sleep," he said as he turned and left for the master bedroom.

"Do you wish me to secure the drapes?" Sebastian asked. While on a brief holiday like this, Krulak's coffin was left at their home base, in this case the St. Charles Hotel. Sebastian made sure their rooms remained undisturbed while they were gone by paying the hoteliers and the housekeeping staff quite handsomely for the privilege of security as well as anonymity.

"No need. The management has installed room-darkening drapery as requested, and I will make sure everything is quite tight. No light will disturb me."

"Then rest well, sir," Sebastian said.

"Enjoy your day."

With that the vampire left before the sun could rise, and Sebastian went back to sleep and dreamt of Sarah once more.

Chapter 29

Except for the Ericksons' crime scene, this Christmas had been the best ever for Sarah. Her store bought meal tasted like a gourmet banquet, and the entire evening had been pure bliss. After dinner she and Patrick spent the night on the couch with Bagheera cuddled between them, watching old movies and drinking hot cocoa.

It was crazy to have such deep feelings for a man she'd only known a couple of months, but Sarah was sure she was in love. Then again she did have a penchant for falling in love too quickly. Maybe it was desperation. Men could smell desperation, and her love affairs always seemed to be over as quickly as they began. Was Patrick just another love affair, a one-sided love affair? Sarah quickly dismissed the thought. Patrick did have feelings for her; she could see it in his eyes. But whether he'd act on them was something else entirely.

The period between Christmas and New Year's Day was always slow for everyone at the Sheriff's Department except for the patrol officers who were gearing up for the rash of DUIs that would certainly happen in Carson and other cities throughout the state and the country. Sarah thought if everyone who wanted to drink and drive on New Year's Eve, or any other holiday, could see the crime scene photos she took on Christmas, they'd never so much as look at a drink before getting into a car.

As she rummaged through her desk, Sarah found her vampire novel. Smirking, she looked at the beautiful young people adorning the cover and then tossed the book into the trashcan without a second thought. Her days of romanticizing vampires were definitely over.

"What's cookin', good lookin'?" Grayson said as he sat down at his desk and shoved a tin of homemade fudge toward Sarah.

"Ooh, thanks," she replied, grabbing a large chunk of the chocolate and walnut confection. "Did Kelly make this?"

"Yep. That girl can do anything—cook, bake, make candy, and she's pretty and super smart too."

"I think you've found a keeper," Sarah replied as she bit into the decadent candy.

"What about you? Have you met anyone interesting lately?"

"Actually, I have."

"Tell me about him."

"He's kind, funny, intelligent, handsome, and..."

"And?"

"He's perfect. Absolutely perfect."

"I'm glad you met someone nice, Baker. You deserve a good man in your life. I hope it works out."

"Me too," she replied and grabbed another chunk of fudge and went back to her paperwork.

An hour later Sarah signed off on the last crime scene reconstruction report and placed it atop a pile of completed case files. Whoever thought being a CSI was glamorous was sadly mistaken. The paperwork alone was enough to break the strongest spirit, let alone cases like the Blakelys, Evelyn Dalton, Brittany Anderson, and Linda Sandoval-Ross and her children. These cases were far outside the normal purview of forensics, but Sarah figured her skill set, as well as Patrick's, would certainly aid in the discovery and demise of their killer Anton Krulak.

As Sarah gathered up the reports to file them away, Patrick swooped breathlessly into the office. He was as white as the sand on an Australian beach, and she thought he might pass out.

"What's wrong?"

"My rental car's been stolen!"

"Calm down. It will be all right. I'll call Detective Maguire. Not to worry. The rental contract should cover accident, vandalism, theft—"

"You don't understand."

"Understand what?"

"The vam—" The priest's words were instantly cut short when he realized Thomas Grayson was also in the office.

"Did you have valuables in your car, Father?" Grayson politely asked.

"Yes. Property from the Vatican archives," Patrick replied surreptitiously. "Can you help me?"

"I hope so," was all Sarah could say in response.

Chapter 30

Sarah knew her supervisor needed to be informed of the current 411, and she also knew she had to let Detective Maguire investigate the case without knowing anything more than the fact it was a car theft with the additional theft of personal property. The thieves had gotten more than they'd bargained for and were looking at charges for not only grand theft auto but felony larceny as well. She picked up her desk phone and dialed West's extension. He answered on the second ring.

"I have a situation, boss."

"What kind of situation?"

"Father Martin is here, and we need to talk."

"Enough said. Come to my office," West replied with a shiver. *Please, God, not another vampire killing,* he thought.

Sarah and Patrick were ushered into West's office. The nightshift supervisor stared at the priest and then at his CSI.

Patrick nervously raked his fingers through the thick jumble of blond curls. This situation had complicated matters immensely, and more lies would need to be told to maintain his cover.

"My rental car was stolen this evening. The case containing the vampire dagger was in the trunk."

West's mocha-colored skin turned ashen. "Good Lord!"

"Obviously, we need to find the car before the perp finds the dagger," Sarah said as she gazed at Patrick. A combination of love and fear shined from the depths of her beautiful blue eyes. The look was not lost on either man.

"I'll have Maguire put out an APB right away."

"How should we explain the...the contents of the case to Detective Maguire?" Patrick asked haltingly.

"We can simply say it's a priceless church artifact," Sarah interjected before West could speak.

"Yes, that's good," West agreed. "You could say you were here on tour, showing the artifact to churches and museums in the area."

Patrick nodded slightly. For a man of the cloth, his life was filled with endless transgressions and deceptions. He wondered if these sins were forgivable, despite being done in the name of God and the Church. He had never revealed these sins in the sanctity of the confessional, and that was a sin in itself. Perhaps he was just as damned as Anton Krulak.

Detective Maguire joined the CSIs and began jotting down the case particulars in his notepad.

Patrick shifted uncomfortably in his chair.

"Don't worry, Father. I'm sure our deputies or the Nevada Highway Patrol will find the car in no time at all. Hopefully, your church antique will still be locked safely away in the trunk. It was probably just some kids out for a joy ride. After all, a Kia Rio isn't exactly on the top ten list of the cars most stolen by professional car thieves," Maguire said with a little chuckle.

"I suppose not," Patrick replied.

Sarah desperately tried to maintain her professional distance, fighting the urge to lean over and hold the priest's hand. She nearly cracked when Patrick turned and gave her a relieved smile and a slight wink.

"I think I have all the information we need for now," Maguire said, closing his notepad. "I'll be in touch as soon as the vehicle is located and your property is recovered."

"Thank you," Patrick replied as he extended his hand to the detective.

Maguire shook the priest's hand and then headed out to speak with his deputies.

"When the car is found, rest assured my team will process it with the utmost professionalism," West offered confidently.

"I have no doubt of that, Dr. West, and I do hope CSI Baker will act as lead on the case."

"If that's what you wish, I'll make it so. You couldn't have a better forensic tech processing the evidence. She's absolutely amazing when it comes to dusting and lifting prints."

Sarah blushed even though she knew West wasn't simply stroking her ego. She was damn good at her job, and she was proud of that fact. Pride may be a sin, but this sin just might save the day and Patrick too.

Chapter 31

Late the next day, Patrick's rental car was found abandoned in Zephyr Cove on the Nevada side of Lake Tahoe. The car was towed to Carson City and arrived at the station just about the same time Sarah was beginning a new shift. Patrick had already been notified and was eager to know the disposition of the dagger. Unfortunately, that couldn't be determined until the car was completely processed like any other crime scene.

Sarah began her case notes detailing the time Douglas County sheriff deputies found the vehicle near the Zephyr Cove marina to the time it arrived in the motor pool at the Carson City Sheriff's Department. She notated its model year, color, license plate number, its general condition, mileage, and gas level. Then she took complete overall photographs of the vehicle, as well as close-up shots of the front and back license plates. When that series of photos was finished, she began the interior shots: front and back, floorboards all around, under the seats, the dashboard, speedometer, and the exterior and interior of the glove compartment.

"Need help?" Grayson asked as he came up behind her.

"You could scoot under the car and notate any undercarriage damage and take photos for me."

"What are you dusting with?" he asked as he slid under the car.

"I thought I'd use silver for the interior because of the black vinyl seats and magnetic black for the exterior."

"Good choices," came the muffled reply from below.

Sarah pulled on a pair of latex gloves and then grabbed a jar of fingerprint powder and a squirrel-hair brush designed for small area coverage. Twirling the brush between her thumb and index finger, she applied a thin layer of powder to the places most commonly touched inside a car like the steering wheel, dashboard, rearview mirror, windows, door handles, visors, seats, glove compartment, and the tops of the door panels where they met the windows.

One by one full and partial prints appeared like magic on the vehicle's interior surfaces, revealing an array of silver loops, whorls, arches, and deltas. Many of the fingerprints were Patrick's, but he had already given elimination prints, so hopefully the remaining prints could be traced back to a suspect.

After all the interior areas were dusted and photographed, Sarah dusted the exterior windows with black powder and then photographed each print or cluster of prints. Then she carefully lifted all the processed prints using transparent sticky lift tape, a kind of clear, cellophane tape resembling heavy-duty packing tape. Each lifted print was placed on a white, cardboard backing sheet. Finally, the location of where the print was retrieved, along with other information, including the name of the CSI who processed the print, was notated on the card.

Afterward, Sarah tagged and bagged all the items in the vehicle. She smiled as she placed the movie ticket stubs she'd found tucked behind the driver's side visor into an evidence bag. *Patrick must be a romantic*, she thought. He'd saved both their ticket stubs from the movie they'd seen together last month.

Sarah repeated the dusting process on the exterior of the car but used a black metallic powder designed exclusively for use on metal. A special applicator had to be used for the powder. This powder very much resembled the fine, black metallic substance found in the old fashioned children's toy *Wooly Willie*, which was used to draw a beard, hair and eyebrows on a red, bulbous-nosed cartoon face situated behind a plastic window on a cardboard base.

Painstakingly, she depressed the applicator's plunger, revealing an interior rod. Then she released the pressure on the plunger ever so slightly. As the rod retracted, particles of the metallic powder were caught up on the magnetic tip. As expected the dusting process revealed a multitude of latent prints on the trunk lid and around the lock.

The processed prints came out quite nicely and were easily photographed and lifted. Sarah mentally congratulated herself on a job well done. As she stepped back from the vehicle, she gave a heavy sigh, hoping Patrick's dagger would be in the trunk.

"Nice job, Baker," Detective Maguire said as he ambled up to the vehicle.

Sarah nodded slightly at the detective.

"Who's going to do the honor of popping open this puppy?" Maguire asked as he looked back and forth between Sarah and Grayson.

"I'll do it," Grayson volunteered. "Baker's the lead on this case, and she should be the first to see what's in there."

"All righty then. Pop it!"

Grayson leaned into the car and released the trunk lever.

Maguire donned a pair of latex gloves and then slowly opened the trunk lid. Light from the overhead fluorescent lights quickly illuminated the darkened compartment, revealing its contents.

Sarah let out the breath she'd been holding and sighed in defeat. Except for the spare tire, the trunk was empty. How was she going to tell Patrick? More importantly, how was he going to tell his superiors in Rome that he'd lost the only weapon that could kill the vampire Anton Krulak and send his soul to hell?

The ringing of her cell phone instantly snapped Sarah from her panicked thoughts. "CSI Baker," she said without looking at the caller ID.

"It's me, sheila. I couldn't wait any longer. Did you recover the dagger?"

Chapter 32

"Ah...ah," Sarah stammered, trying to find the words to tell Patrick the bad news. "I'm afraid your dagger wasn't in the car. The vehicle was processed thoroughly. I'm sorry."

There was only a deafening silence in response.

"Are you there, Patrick?"

A few seconds passed before an agonizing voice replied, "I'm here." Another silence followed before he added, "I'll have to go back to Rome and explain to my superiors what's happened."

"Don't leave yet," she replied in a panic. "I got some good prints from both the interior and exterior of the vehicle. I'll run them through AFIS as soon as I'm done talking with you. Okay?"

"How long will that take?"

"It depends. If there's a print match in the system, it shouldn't take long. But—"

"But what?" the frazzled priest asked.

"If the prints aren't on file, there's no way to trace them back to a suspect."

"I see."

Sarah could hear the defeat, painful and rough, in Patrick's voice.

"Please be patient. If we get a hit on the prints, Detective Maguire can begin investigating the suspect or suspects right away."

"There's something else you need to know," Patrick said. "In fact, it's imperative, and it's the reason we need to find the dagger and the suspect sooner than later."

"And what's that?"

"The dagger can only be possessed by someone with pure intentions. When it falls into unholy hands, that is, when someone with nefarious motives gets hold of it, he'll die. I'm afraid our suspect is most likely dead even as we speak."

"This changes everything," Sarah rasped. "I think it's time we come clean and tell Detective Maguire everything."

"I agree.

"I'll go run the prints now, and I'll call Parker to see if he's had a new DB come in lately."

"DB?" Patrick asked.

"Dead body."

"All right. I'll wait and see what happens," Patrick replied in a voice more optimistic than expected.

"Just sit tight. I'll call you back as soon as I can."

"Sarah..."

"Yes?"

"Thank you. I know you're doing all you can."

"You're welcome. Talk to you later," she said and hung up. "I love you," she whispered to the silence on the other end.

Sarah returned to the CSU office and scanned the lifted prints into the Automated Fingerprint Identification System all the while praying these prints would have a match. If not, that was it. Patrick would return to Rome and never come back to Carson City. She wondered if he'd be fired. Could a priest even be fired, and if so where would he go and what would he do? Would someone else replace him?

Sarah didn't even want to think about it. She wasn't ready to say good-bye to Patrick, not yet. Who was she kidding? She would never be ready to say good-bye to the man. Yet Sarah knew deep in her heart that she would have to do just that one day, but not today or even tomorrow.

* * *

"And where did you say you got this?" the pawnbroker asked as he examined the exquisite silver dagger.

The gangly, dark-haired teenager replied, "My dad."

"And where did your dad come across this dagger? It's quite unusual."

The boy's eyes darted around the cluttered pawnshop as he searched for a plausible answer.

"Ah...he got it from my granddad. It's a family heirloom. My dad died last year, and now my mom is really sick. I need the money for her operation," the boy said with a smile, pleased with his lie.

Stanwood Johnson brought a loupe to his eye and examined the dagger once more. The workmanship was flawless, and he recognized the Vatican seal on the pommel. He knew the inscription on the blade was Latin, but he didn't understand its meaning. He did know, however, that a piece like this was priceless, and he was sure his friend Abel Montoya in the antiquities department of the Nevada Museum of Art would be very interested in it. Montoya was a connoisseur and had an extensive private collection of religious artifacts. The pawnbroker was sure he'd pay well for such a piece as this.

"I'll give you $500.00 for the dagger."

The teenager nearly jumped out of his well-worn Nikes when he heard the figure. "You got a deal, mister," he said, holding out his hand.

The pawnbroker shook the sweaty, proffered hand and then filled it with five, crisp one hundred dollar bills. The boy stared briefly at his bounty and then hastily stuffed the money into his pocket and ran out the door.

Carefully, Johnson wrapped the artifact in a chamois and placed it in his safe. Then he grabbed the old, black dial up phone that sat on the dusty counter next to the dusty cash register.

"Abel Montoya."

"Abel. It's Stanwood Johnson. I have something you might be interested in."

"Excellent. When can you meet me?"

"How about tonight? Seven o'clock."

"That would be fine. Our regular place?"

"Sounds good. I'll see you then," the pawnbroker replied with a smile as big as the Sierra Nevadas.

Chapter 33

"Hello, my friend," Abel Montoya said to the pawnbroker.

"Good to see you again. It's been too long, but I think you'll find the wait has been well worth it," Stanwood Johnson said as he handed Montoya the cream-colored chamois containing the dagger.

Montoya took the package and gently opened it. His eyes sparkled as brightly as the silver dagger inside.

"This is magnificent! However did you come across it?"

"It came to me," Johnson replied with a snort. "A kid about seventeen years old came into my shop claiming it was a family heirloom. He said he needed to sell it so his mother could have an operation."

"Strange how many treasures land up in your pawn shop because the owner's mother needs an operation."

Both men laughed.

"What will you offer me?" Johnson asked.

Montoya ran his fingers gently across the engraved inscription on the blade. Then he grasped the dagger by its hilt and held it up to the light and inspected every detail of the incredible artifact.

"Judging by the small nicks on the blade, I assume this dagger has been used at one time or another. However, there's no hallmark or date on it, and the detailing and inscription aren't worn. So I must assume it was crafted in the latter part of the 20th century or perhaps even sometime in this one."

"Will that make a difference in the price?"

"Not in the least," Montoya replied with a greedy smile.

"Then we have a price?"

"Shall we say $35,000.00," Montoya offered.

"$35,000.00 has a nice ring."

The art dealer opened his fine leather briefcase and grabbed several stacks of one hundred dollar bills and then placed them into the pawnbroker's ratty, green duffel bag.

"As always, it's been a pleasure doing business with you," Johnson said.

"The pleasure has been all mine," Montoya replied.

The two men shook hands and went their separate ways.

Chapter 34

"Woo hoo!" Sarah squealed as the prints she'd taken from Patrick's rental car matched a person on record.

The suspect in question was a juvenile offender named Bradley Jenae, seventeen and a ward of the court. He had an extensive criminal record for breaking and entering, truancy and drugs.

Sarah grabbed the desk phone and anxiously dialed Patrick's cell. "Patrick!" she breathlessly said as he answered.

"Yes?"

"I have good news."

"Tell me you found a suspect."

"I have! I'm going to give Maguire the info as soon as I hang up. We'll have the dagger soon. I'm sure of it."

Sarah could almost feel Patrick's relief radiating through her phone.

* * *

Bradley Jenae had felt nauseated ever since he consumed those two steak dinners at the Gold Dust West, celebrating his good fortune. But a little stomachache was well worth eating like a king. Bradley couldn't remember the last time he'd eaten meat, let alone a steak. Boxed mac and cheese was the nightly staple in his foster home, but it was better than going hungry as he had when he was on the streets.

When he was only thirteen, his alcoholic mom tossed him out of the house to make room for her new boyfriend who didn't like kids. Bradley had lived on the streets until Father Chuck Daniels, the parish priest of St. Teresa's, found him and placed him into the foster care system. But that was last year and by then Bradley had a juvenile record and a taste for the things only money could buy like good food, nice jeans and new sneakers.

Even though he still felt queasy, Bradley decided to hitchhike up to Famous Footwear on the south end of town to buy a new pair of Nikes. When he reached US 395, he felt like vomiting. A cold sweat trickled down his back and his gait became more halting with each successive step. As Bradley watched the steady stream of cars pass him by, he stuck out his thumb, hoping someone would stop and give him a lift.

No one paid any attention.

By the time he made it to the Highway 50 on ramp, a right hand turnoff from US 395 South, Bradley was nearly delirious. Not paying much attention to where he was going, he stumbled across the road against the light. Seconds later a blue Ford F-10 pickup truck hit him at full speed. His gangly body hurtled into the air like a ragdoll, flew over the pickup's hood, and finally landed on the other side of the Highway 50 intersection like so much road kill.

Chapter 35

"Congrats, Baker," Detective Maguire said as he reviewed Bradley Jenae's rap sheet. "We'll have this kid cuffed and back in juvie in no time at all."

Sarah should have been happy, but she found herself almost as worried about Bradley Jenae as she was about Patrick. The kid had no idea what he was getting himself into when he'd broken into Patrick's car and stolen the dagger. She truly felt Bradley's punishment wasn't going to fit his crime.

"I'd better call my wife. It looks like I'll be working overtime," Maguire said.

Sarah hesitated, unsure if she should tell the detective the truth about Patrick and the dagger at this point in time. Perhaps it would be prudent to wait and see if he could find and arrest the kid before she said anything. She'd call Patrick and see what he thought. She looked at her watch. It was almost the end of shift. Was he asleep now? She knew he'd been up the better part of the night worrying and must be as exhausted as she. Before calling him though, Sarah decided she'd better tell West what was going on. He needed to be updated on the case.

"Yes?" came a voice from the other side of the door.

"It's me. Baker. Can we talk?"

"Come in," Orlando West replied.

Sarah felt like a rookie as she entered her boss's office. This whole situation with Patrick was getting more complicated and more bizarre by the day, and she wondered if West might think it was affecting her judgment as well as her ability to perform her job.

"I'm glad I caught you," Sarah said.

"I was just about to call it a night."

"I have some good news. The prints I lifted from Father Martin's car had a hit, and Maguire is looking for the suspect now."

"I'm sure Father Martin will be relieved, and hopefully he'll have his property back soon."

"I hope so too."

"Is there anything else?" West asked.

"There's something we need to talk about," Sarah said as she pulled up a chair and sat down.

"I thought as much."

She explained to West what would happen if the dagger fell into the wrong hands. Although it was difficult to believe, Sarah had to come to terms with this eventuality as she had the many other elements of Patrick's life and profession that were not of this world or in the realm of her own scientific worldview. Although she was still incredulous in many respects, the evidence didn't lie, and if Sarah believed in anything at all, it was the unfailing truth of cold, hard evidence.

Chapter 36

Detective Maguire could hear the wailing of several children before he even knocked on the door. As he waited patiently for Mrs. Hoyt to answer, he looked about the dirt-covered yard strewn with broken toys, derelict tricycles and mounds of dog crap.

The door opened slowly, and a thin, middle-aged woman with stringy, prematurely gray hair stood before him, a crying child in each arm.

"Good morning, Mrs. Hoyt. My name is Detective Sean Maguire. May I have a word with you?" Maguire asked politely.

"I suppose so," she replied, hunching her shoulders.

Mrs. Hoyt waived him into a cluttered living room where two more toddlers sat on the floor playing blocks. As she sat down in an overstuffed couch, one child slid from her arms while the other child squirmed and fussed as she wiped his nose and then ran her snot-covered hand across her jeans.

Maguire tossed the clothes from a chair opposite the couch and sat down.

"What's this about?" Angela Hoyt asked as she looked the detective over with a wary eye. "Are you from CPS? I passed my inspection last month."

"No, ma'am," the detective replied. "I'm looking for your foster son Bradley Jenae."

"He's in school."

"No, he isn't. Do you know where he goes when he's truant?"

"I didn't know he was," the woman replied defiantly.

"Well, he is. As a matter of fact, Bradley hasn't been in school for a week."

"I'm sure there's some kind of mistake."

"I was at his school this morning."

"I do the best I can with the money the state gives me—"

"Yes, ma'am, but this isn't about your performance as a foster mother. I see you have your hands full, and I apologize for bothering you today," Maguire said. He knew he wouldn't get anywhere with Mrs. Hoyt, and it was obvious she had no idea where the kid was.

A crashing noise, accompanied by a feverish wailing, ended the conversation for good.

"I'd better go now, so you can take care of things."

"Thank you," Mrs. Hoyt replied as she began picking up the pieces of the broken lamp one of the toddlers had just knocked to the worn, hardwood floor.

For the first time in many months, Sean Maguire thanked God for his well-behaved brood and his lovely wife. He saw himself out the door and then gratefully slid into the driver's side of his black, unmarked Crown Vic and drove back to the station.

Chapter 37

Sarah met Patrick for dinner at a local chain restaurant a couple of hours before her shift began. Although she was disappointed Maguire hadn't yet found Bradley Jenae, she was still optimistic, and that made Patrick optimistic too.

"I've never seen someone so small eat so much," Patrick said with a wink, glad that the heaviness of their meeting had been lightened by Sarah's good mood and hearty appetite.

"You don't do so badly yourself," she replied, taking another bite of her double bacon cheeseburger followed by a sip of chocolate shake.

"You've got me there, sheila. Eating is the next best thing to surfing."

"When was the last time you went?"

"Crikey!" Patrick exclaimed. "It's been yonks. I don't get a lot of time off with this job. I haven't even seen my folks in three years."

"I'm sure they understand," Sarah said with a hint of envy, knowing Patrick had parents to go home to see.

"They're more than understanding despite..." Patrick replied and then paused.

Sarah waited and when he didn't continue, she continued for him. "Despite what?"

Patrick took a deep gulp of his Foster Lager and then said, "Despite the fact neither my mum nor my dad has ever been very keen on me being a priest."

Sarah was more than a little surprised. Most Catholic parents would have been delighted to see their son enter the priesthood. "Why's that?" she finally had the nerve to ask after a few beats had passed.

"I'm an only child of two only children. I suspect they were hoping I'd give them half a dozen grandchildren."

Sarah caught herself just before she could say, *It's not too late.* Instead, she asked Patrick to tell her more about surfing.

"If I say so myself, I'm not too bad. I can ride the waves with the best of blokes. Ah, Sarah! There's nothing like it. Have you ever surfed?"

"There aren't any waves on the East River," Sarah replied, laughing.

"Then we'll have to take a trip to the West Coast this summer and go surfing. That's all there is to it!" Patrick said emphatically. "We're only ten hours or so away from a brilliant California beach called La Jolla Shores. And I'd say we're both due for a holiday. What do you say, sheila?"

"I say, yes!" I'm game if you are."

A vacation getaway with Patrick! *I wonder what his superiors in Rome would say about that?* Sarah thought. Well, it wasn't like she was taking him south of the border for a quickie wedding. The man needed a break, and so did she. Hopefully, by summer Anton Krulak would have been found and dispatched back to hell, and their lives would return to normal. The happy thought soon faded when Sarah realized Patrick's life would never be normal.

Patrick could tell Sarah's mood had changed. "Is there anything wrong?"

"No. Just thinking."

"About what?"

"I…I just hope there aren't any sharks when we go surfing."

Patrick tossed back his head, and the happy sound of his laughter surrounded them. "No worries, sheila. But just to make you feel safe, we'll double check with the lifeguards before going into the water," he said, grabbing her hand and shaking it reassuringly.

Sarah could feel her heart begin to pound wildly as the priest's hand held hers. She was sure she was blushing, but knowing Patrick he'd just chalk it up to her being embarrassed by her childish fears.

"That's what mates are for," he replied with a devastating smile, totally unaware of how handsome he was or how he made her feel.

"So we're mates then?" Sarah asked teasingly.

"Of course!" Patrick replied, raising his glass of Fosters to toast their friendship.

Sarah raised her milkshake and clinked it against Patrick's beer glass. "To good mates."

"To good mates."

Chapter 38

When Sarah came into her office, she instantly noticed the plastic evidence bag sealed with red tape sitting on her desk. A note from Eliot Parker accompanied the item.

> *Sarah:*
> *I had a John Doe come in; Caucasian;*
> *Approximately 17- 19 years of age; no ID.*
> *The only thing in his jean pockets was this*
> *pawnshop claim ticket.*
> *Could you please see if you can pull some prints for me?*
> *Thanks!*
> *Parker*

Oh, God! Was Parker's latest guest Bradley Jenae? And if the kid pawned the dagger, then who had it now? An additional life could now be at risk.

Hurriedly, she took the evidence to the department's small lab for processing. In a glass beaker, Sarah combined two grams of ninhydrin; ten milliliters of methanol; thirty-five milliliters of ethyl acetate; five milliliters of acetic acid, and five hundred milliliters of petroleum ether along with a small magnet to facilitate the mixing process. Then she placed the beaker on a mixing platform.

When the chemicals were thoroughly combined, the resultant solution was poured into a glass pan. The claim ticket was dipped into the solution for five seconds and afterwards rinsed in distilled water. Next, the claim ticket was laid onto a flat surface, dried with a hair dryer and then subjected to heat and steam from a common household steam iron until the amino acids in the latent prints were visualized by turning a bright purple color.

Sarah grinned with satisfaction as she stared at two full prints and two partial prints, which contrasted nicely with the pale yellow paper of the claim ticket. She photographed the prints, and downloaded them into her laptop computer. The prints were then run through AFIS.

Two IDs were confirmed. The full prints belonged to a petty criminal named Stanwood Johnson, who had several misdemeanor convictions but no felonies, and the two partial prints were from Bradley Jenae.

Sarah was about to call Patrick with the news when her phone rang.

"Hello, Sarah," came Patrick's happy but anxious voice.

"I have good news and bad news. Which do you want first?"

"Give me the bad news."

"I just processed a piece of evidence taken from a John Doe at the ME's. The prints matched Bradley Jenae.

Sarah could hear Patrick reciting some kind of prayer in Latin before he replied.

"I'm sorry, Sarah. And the good news?"

"The prints were retrieved from a pawnshop claim ticket. I think Jenae pawned the dagger. Fortunately, the claim ticket has the name of the pawnshop, and it's local. It's down the street from where you're staying. Maguire will follow up."

"That's good news...and bad."

"I know. We need to find out if the pawnshop owner still has the dagger. If he does, then our troubles are at an end," Sarah stated optimistically.

"And his are just beginning."

Chapter 39

Stanwood Johnson was almost ready to close his shop. It was Saturday night, and he was looking forward to a few drinks, a prime rib dinner and several hands of poker at Bodine's.

He hastily counted the few bills and coins in the cash drawer, filed away his paperwork, turned off most of the lights, and grabbed his keys. But before leaving, he decided to relieve himself and headed to the lavatory in the back of the shop.

"Are you sure this is a slam-dunk, Shemar?" a small, teenaged boy asked his companion.

"I'm sure, my little peep. We'll be sitting pretty in just a few."

The night was moonless, and the dark faces of the boys were hardly noticeable in the faint light from a streetlamp a few yards away from the pawnshop.

"You go first," Shemar said to his friend.

"Okay," Andre replied as he pulled his bandana over his nose and his hoodie up over his short, curly, black hair. Slowly, he opened the glass door and looked about.

The shop was empty.

"This is gonna be easy peezy," Shemar said as he followed Andre inside. The older boy eyed the cash register and swooped around the dusty counter. After pushing several buttons, the cash register drawer popped open. "Cha-ching!"

Andre came up from behind and grabbed the few bills and stuffed them into the pocket of his jeans.

They gave one another a high five and headed to the door.

"What the fuck do you think you're doing?" came a booming voice from behind them. The old man moved like a flash and grabbed the shotgun hidden under the counter. "Stop right there!"

The boys froze.

Johnson held his shotgun in one hand and grabbed the receiver of the old rotary dial phone that sat next to the cash register and began to call 911.

"He's calling the cops," Andre cried.

"No, he aint," Shemar spat as he spun around, ducked and then charged Johnson.

A loud kaboom, instantly followed by a white flash, erupted from the weapon's muzzle. Buckshot peppered the shelf containing DVD players, boom boxes and small appliances as well as the chest of Andre Wilson.

Shemar gazed in horror at his friend lying on the dirty shop floor. In a blinding rage, he grabbed the shotgun from Johnson's hand and slammed the butt of it into the old man's face.

Stanwood Johnson fell unconscious to the floor, but Shemar continued to pound his face until it was nothing but a caved in mess of red goo and white bone fragments. When his anger had finally been quelled, Shemar dropped the shotgun on the floor and then ran out of the pawnshop as fast as Usain Bolt.

Chapter 40

Sebastian finished the last line of another love letter to Sarah, a letter he would never send. He carefully folded it and then neatly tucked it into the inner breast pocket of his tony, navy blue wool blazer. It seemed like half an eternity had passed since he'd last seen Sarah, and his heart raced at the very thought of her. He entertained several scenarios of what they'd do when he returned to Carson City. First, he wanted to take her out for a nice meal and then maybe go to Reno for a concert or a show.

Suddenly, Sebastian's thoughts grew dark and sullen. Perhaps she'd forgotten all about him. Even worse, she could have met someone else and even fallen in love. That thought was unbearable, and he could feel his chest tighten with each passing second as he envisioned her in the arms of another man. And the man he saw was the handsome, blond-haired priest.

"Sebastian!" Krulak said, interrupting his manservant's dark thoughts.

Sebastian jumped at his master's voice.

"Did I startle you?" the vampire asked.

"No, sir. What is it you wish?"

"I want you to make a reservation for the Black and White Winter Ball this Saturday evening at the Hyatt Regency. Even at this late date, I am confident a single ticket can be secured for a generous donation."

"I have no doubt, sir," Sebastian replied with a nod of his head and a slight bow.

Nowadays, the Black and White Winter Ball was the highlight of the winter social season in San Francisco. Long gone was the Governor's Ball of years past. Pity. That had always been a grand affair, but Krulak was eager to see what the new gala had in store.

* * *

Arriving at a fashionable hour, Anton Krulak surveyed the grand ballroom, filled with all the finest citizens of the city on the bay. The mayor and his wife were there along with most of the city council and many members of the city's pro sports teams.

The vampire was indistinguishable from both those with old money and the nouveau riche. Effortlessly, he mingled among the beautiful people, introducing himself and dropping his title where it would be most appreciated. As he talked with one native son, an actor of national prominence, Krulak couldn't help but be distracted by the lilting laugh of a woman a few feet from where he stood.

"Excuse me," Krulak said as he retreated from the actor and curiously walked toward the source of the laughter.

The young woman was surrounded by a host of handsome men: stockbrokers, doctors, lawyers, and the like. As Krulak made his way through the throng, the laughter continued but then stopped abruptly when she saw him. He was the most beautiful man she had ever seen.

Krulak's world stopped revolving and time stood still. He was in another place and another time as his cool blue eyes beheld the reincarnation of his beloved Elizabeth Preston.

The circle of gentlemen parted, and the petite woman with stunning violet eyes and long, black curls that sparkled like diamonds came near. With a dazzling smile, she held out her hand, and Krulak accepted it. Gallantly, he kissed the top of the creamy white hand in true continental fashion. The young woman blushed fiercely.

"My name is Count Anton Krulak of Sighisoara, Romania," Krulak said as he gazed into the violet depths staring back.

"I'm Katrina Bello...of Daly City," she replied giggling. "It's a pleasure to meet you."

"The pleasure is all mine."

Katrina blushed once more. She had never dreamt she'd meet a member of a noble family at the Black and White Winter Ball. She was only in attendance because her law firm was one of the sponsors of the annual event. Katrina had recently landed a job as a junior clerk and was surprised as everyone else that her boss Terrance Gage had invited her to the gala. Gage had a reputation as a womanizer and most likely thought he'd score with the young beauty if he invited her to the event.

"Do you believe in déjà vu, Miss Bello?" Krulak asked sweetly.

"I'm not sure," Katrina replied with another nervous giggle.

"What about destiny?"

"Oh, yes. I believe in destiny."

"Then if I may be so bold, let me say but this. You are my destiny, and I am yours."

* * *

"I had to tell Cardinal Fontani about the dagger. It's my obligation to keep him informed about my mission," Patrick stated firmly.

"But why couldn't you have waited a bit longer?" Sarah's small body shook with every word.

"I'm sorry."

"So am I!"

"I won't be gone long. I promise."

"Right."

"Please be reasonable, Sarah. I need—"

"I have to go. I've got another call coming in. It's work. I'll call you later," Sarah said and hung up.

"Baker," Detective Maguire said. "We have another 420. It seems our sleepy little Carson is rapidly becoming murder central."

"Another murder? This is unreal."

"I've never seen so many murders in such a short time span," he replied and then added, "Funny how they all began just about the time your friend Father Martin arrived in town."

"You can't seriously believe a Catholic priest had anything to do with these murders. Come on, Sean," Sarah snapped.

"I suppose not, but you're going to be damned surprised when I tell you the name of our latest vic."

"So tell me."

"Stanwood Johnson. His body was discovered about twenty minutes ago. He was killed in his own pawnshop. Looks like he was beaten to death with the butt of a shotgun."

Sarah was speechless as she processed the information.

"Are you still there, Baker?"

"I'm here. I'll meet you at the scene in ten minutes."

"See you then," Maguire said and hung up without further formality.

Sarah called Patrick, and he answered on the first ring. "Is everything all right?"

"I'm fine, but the same can't be said for Stanwood Johnson."

Chapter 41

Sarah met Patrick at the airport to say good-bye. She was physically exhausted from processing the Johnson crime scene and emotionally exhausted from wrestling with her anger over Patrick's departure. Instead of sleeping after her shift was over, Sarah tossed and turned, debating what to say to Patrick and whether or not she should tell him she loved him. What did it matter? He was bound for Rome and a visit with the Pope. Why would he care what she thought or felt?

"I'm glad you came," Patrick said as Sarah met him at the American Airlines ticket counter.

"I couldn't let you leave without saying good-bye."

"My flight doesn't board for another half hour. Let's talk. Can you tell me about the Johnson homicide?"

They walked to a row of chairs and sat down a few feet away from several other waiting passengers.

"You can tell your supervisors that as of today two people involved with the dagger have met violent, untimely deaths. As far as we can ascertain, Johnson was the last person in possession of the dagger, but it wasn't in his shop or in his home. At this point we can only assume a third party now has it, and finding that person is going to be next to impossible."

Patrick sighed heavily.

"Detective Maguire will continue to investigate, but I think it's time you started praying for a miracle," Sarah said, trying desperately to contain her raging emotions.

"I do appreciate your and Detective Maguire's dedication to this case, Sarah. I truly do."

"It's my job," she responded harshly.

"Don't be angry, sheila. Please," Patrick begged as he reached for her hand.

She wanted to pull away, but her will to keep physically connected with this man, even on the smallest level, was just too great.

Patrick could see the tears beginning to pool in Sarah's beautiful blue eyes. A sharp pain caught in his chest because he knew he was the cause of those tears.

A feminine voice came over the loudspeaker, announcing the rows to be boarded first. Passengers stirred, grabbed their carry-ons and headed to the boarding gate.

"I've got to go, but I'll be back," Patrick said as he rose to his feet.

Sarah grabbed the sleeve of his black dress jacket. "I...I," she stammered as she gazed at the Roman collar Patrick now wore and then into the green sea of pain looking back.

"I know," he replied and pulled Sarah to her feet. His strong arms enfolded her into a loving embrace, and his cheek rested on the top of her head.

Tears unabashedly streamed down both their faces. Patrick forced a slight smile and then slowly withdrew, grabbed his briefcase and walked away without looking back.

"Good-bye, my love," Sarah whispered.

* * *

"I have decided we should stay here permanently," Krulak announced to Sebastian and then continued dressing for the evening.

"But, sir! Do you think that's prudent?" the handsome manservant asked in a calm voice even though his guts were roiling with anger and frustration.

"Why not? I am weary of travel, Sebastian, and I have all I need here. The hunting is good, and—"

"Does this decision have to do with Miss Bello?" Sebastian asked before he could stop himself.

Deathly anger consumed the vampire, and his strong, pale hand was instantly around Sebastian's throat. "Who are you to question my motives for this decision or any other?" Krulak hissed.

"No one," Sebastian replied as he stood perfectly still.

"As I thought. You are my servant, and you do as you are told."

"Yes, sir."

The vampire's hand slid from Sebastian's throat. The manservant retreated, glad that the confrontation with his master had not escalated.

"Did you make dinner reservations?" Krulak asked matter-of-factly as if nothing untoward had just happened between them.

"As directed."

"Excellent! Now bring the Escalade around," the vampire commanded as he looked at himself in the mirror and straightened his tie once more.

"Very well," Sebastian replied and was out the door and headed to the garage before Krulak could turn around.

As the elevator descended, Sebastian's thoughts raced and his heart pounded harder with each passing floor. By the time he reached the garage, he had made up his mind. Krulak had to die.

Chapter 42

Winter in Rome was colder than Patrick had remembered, and the chilly air in the stonewall library of the International Association of Exorcists seemed to confirm this suspicion with each passing hour. He shivered and then pulled his black wool sweater over his long-sleeved black shirt. It did little good. Perhaps the cold he felt was in his heart and not in his body.

"Good day, Father," the old, heavyset monk said as his sandaled feet shuffled across the worn marble floor. "How's it coming along?"

Patrick glanced up at Brother Ciaran and then down at the man's feet. How he could wear sandals and a Franciscan robe rain or shine was beyond Patrick's ken, but the monk had done so for some sixty years. Patrick thought the man's feet must be as thick as a rhinoceros's hide.

"As well as can be expected," Patrick replied, looking over the pile of manuscripts and journals on the table.

"Good, good. I'm glad to hear that. Soon your penance will be over, and you'll be back in the field. I'm sure you're excited about that."

Patrick nodded.

The council had been more lenient with him than he'd deserved. For his penance Patrick was given a month of solitary contemplation, and when that was finished he was assigned the task of translating several volumes of vampire hunters' notes, memoirs, and diaries, which was rather easy considering he was a linguist. The amount of work, however, was the real penance, and his task had already consumed a full month of sixteen-hour days, seven days a week.

Although the dagger may never be recovered, Patrick knew it was unlikely that its real purpose would actually be discovered. No doubt whoever had it now saw it only as a beautiful artifact and not as a weapon against unnatural creatures of hell.

"This too shall pass, Father," Brother Ciaran said in his lilting Irish accent as he patted Patrick's shoulder.

"I realize that."

"Then why do you look so sad? What troubles you?"

"It's nothing," Patrick replied stoically.

"As you know, I'm not an ordained priest and can't hear confessions, but if you'd like to talk, I'd be more than happy to listen. Whatever you tell me will be kept between the two of us and the angels."

Patrick considered the monk's offer. His secret had gnawed at his heart for far too long, and it needed to be shared, or exorcized if that were the case, before it consumed him completely.

"Come to my cell after vespers, and we'll talk."

"I will. Thank you, Brother," Patrick replied, feeling better already.

* * *

Patrick knocked on the large, rough-hewn wooden door of Brother Ciaran's cell directly after vespers had ended. The monk opened it with a smile, his chubby cheeks pink from the cold.

"Come in," he commanded sweetly.

Patrick stepped inside Brother Ciaran's modest room. A bed, a nightstand, a wooden chair and a small wardrobe were the only furnishings. A crucifix decorated the wall above the headboard of the twin-sized bed.

"Please. Have a seat," the old monk said, pointing to the chair.

Patrick sat down while Brother Ciaran went to his wardrobe and removed a tall, clear glass bottle and two earthenware mugs.

"Do you like mead?"

"I've never had it."

"Then you must try it. It was invented by our people, you know."

"That I did," Patrick replied with a grin.

Brother Ciaran was one of the Association's best cooks and its beekeeper. The Association maintained a large apiary atop its main building within Vatican City, and the honey was sold to help finance the Association's enterprises. Brother Ciaran could make anything from honey: sauces, cookies, cakes, and candy, but he was famous for his mead.

He poured Patrick a generous glass and then one for himself. "Slainte!"

"Slainte!" Patrick echoed. He sipped the sweet honey wine with appreciation. "This is quite good."

The cherubic-faced monk beamed with happiness.

When they had finished their drinks, Brother Ciaran sat down on the edge of his bed and waited for Patrick to begin the conversation. When several minutes had passed without any dialogue, he spoke up. "Tell me about her."

"Her?" Patrick asked, sheepishly.

Chapter 43

Sarah checked her e-mail for the second time in an hour, and still there was no word from Patrick. Her heart sank. It had been two months since he'd left Carson City, although to Sarah it seemed like a lifetime had passed. She couldn't understand why he hadn't sent at least a short note to let her know he was all right. Various scenarios of what had happened to him rampaged through her mind from him sitting in a dank, Vatican dungeon to him being exiled to some remote corner of the world to do missionary work.

Since Patrick's departure there'd been no more homicides or other felonies and only a handful of calls that required the CSI team such as the suspicious arson at Carson High. The case was processed and solved quickly when Grayson determined a heat source had been left on in the chemistry lab, resulting in an easily contained fire.

Sarah was back to reviewing cold cases. The Dalton and Anderson cases were both now considered cold and would likely remain so until the end of time. Still, Sarah found herself reviewing her crime scene notes and photos, probably more as a way to keep some kind of connection with Patrick than to discover probative evidence that could link the cases to Anton Krulak. The evidence they did have tied the cases together and to the Sandoval-Ross case, but there was no way to link the evidence to Krulak and never would be.

Just when her spirits had hit rock bottom for the night, Jamie Taylor, a newly graduated deputy sheriff, came in with the mail.

"Hi, Sarah," he said shyly. "How are you tonight?"

"Hey, Jamie! I'm fine. What about you?"

The probie flashed a big toothy grin at Sarah. "Fine," he replied as he dropped an envelope on her desk and scurried out the door.

Sarah grabbed the envelope and examined the writing on it. It was definitely written by a European. Not bothering to look at the postmark, she carefully opened it. Her brow scrunched with curiosity and a hint of apprehension. *Please, God, let it be from Patrick.* The fleeting disappointment that initially swept over her face was quickly replaced by surprise and satisfaction. The letter was from Sebastian. He'd be returning to Carson in two days and was eager to see her.

"Good news?" Grayson asked.

"As a matter of fact, it is."

* * *

Sebastian placed his last article of clothing in his Louis Vuitton suitcase and firmly snapped the locks shut as Krulak watched on. The vampire had agreed that his manservant was in need of a holiday. Sebastian had been uncharacteristically dour for the last several weeks, and Krulak contributed the malaise to the man's need of female companionship. Why should he deny Sebastian such a small pleasure as a holiday away at some tropical resort filled with native beauties? After all, he had

Katrina to keep his nights occupied, and he could manage quite well on his own for such a short period of time.

"Do you have everything you need?" Krulak asked as if he were a doting father sending his son away for a fortnight at summer camp.

Sebastian nodded dutifully.

"Excellent! Then I will see you in two weeks' time."

Sebastian nodded again as a glimmer of hope sparkled deep in his dark brown eyes. If all went as planned, he would find a way to kill Krulak. Then when the vampire least expected, he'd return and carry out the deed and that would be the last time he'd see Anton Krulak in this world or in the next.

Chapter 44

Detective Maguire knocked on the faded apartment door; flakes of peeling paint dropped off with each successive thump. "Shemar Lewis! Carson City Sheriff's Department. Open the door!" he demanded.

A rotund black woman with a sweet face and a head full of cornrows answered seconds later. "Shemar don't stay here no more."

The detective held up his shield and then handed the woman his card. "Could you please tell me where he is, ma'am?"

"That boy? Since he's been running with that no good for nothing Andre Wilson, I haven't seen hide nor hair of him," Shemar's aunt replied.

"Then you don't know about Andre."

"What about Andre? Is he all right?" Concern hardened the soft edges of her voice.

"I'm afraid not. Andre's dead."

"Lordy, lordy! Aint no surprise though. That boy has been messed up with gangs since he could walk. Been selling drugs and no telling what else."

"Gangs?" Detective Maguire asked.

"The Eastside Kings was the last one I heard he'd hooked up with."

"Thank you for the information."

"You're welcome," the woman replied and then closed the door without further comment.

Lewis's pal was a banger. Most likely Shemar Lewis was too. Maguire decided to check in with one of his confidential informants and see what the word on the street was about the Eastside Kings. For fifty bucks and a carton of Kools, Cleavon Tuttle would rat out his own grandmother.

The detective checked his watch. Tuttle should be at Duke's Bar by now. Maguire would drop by Wal-Mart for the smokes and then swing by the bar before he headed home for lunch. He knew his wife was already mad at him for pulling another double shift, but the money was good and they needed it for their kids' college tuition. Maybe he should go by The Flower Bucket for a dozen roses on his way home from work. That always soothed Kathleen's hot Irish temper.

When Maguire arrived at the dingy bar, the regulars were all lined up on their favorite stools. Floyd, the bartender, knew everyone by name from the old man who used to work in the silver mines before his back gave out to the young tattoo artist who sold weed on the side to supplement his income.

Until Maguire joined the force, he hadn't realized there were so many bars and sketchy areas in Carson City. At one time the city had been the jewel of Nevada. Anything seemed possible. Now it seemed as if the city was divided into the "haves" and "have nots." Even the middle class seemed to belong more to the "have not" camp than to the "have."

"Why, Sean Maguire! My man!" Cleavon Tuttle said as Maguire sat down at the bar.

Heads rose from assorted alcoholic drinks and bleary eyes looked on with mild curiosity then returned their attention to the business at hand.

"Cleavon," Maguire said. "Can I buy you a drink, my friend?"

"You certainly may," came a quick reply. A dazzling smile of pearly white in a field of ebony gleamed back at the detective. "Floyd! Another whiskey, if you please," Tuttle ordered.

The man behind the bar nodded, grabbed a bottle of Jim Beam and refilled the shot glass sitting in front of Cleavon Tuttle.

"What you want, Sean?" Tuttle asked. He was a man who didn't like drinking alone.

"Club soda," Maguire said to the bartender and then leaned close to his CI and whispered, "I'm still on duty."

Floyd served Maguire his drink, and the detective clinked his glass against Tuttle's, saying, "Here's to beautiful women."

"Here. Here!" Tuttle agreed as he emptied the glass and then smacked his full lips with satisfaction. "Much obliged, Sean."

Maguire grabbed his drink and nodded toward a table on the far side of the bar near the pool table and a couple of slot machines. Tuttle grabbed his own empty shot glass and followed behind.

"It's been a while," the CI said as he sat down. "What brings you to this fine establishment in the middle of the day?"

"Have you heard any chatter about a kid named Shemar Lewis? He runs with the Eastside Kings."

"Shemar, Shemar," Tuttle chanted and then his face lit up like a Christmas tree. "Yeah, Shemar! He's Delorian Lewis's little bro."

"And?" the detective pressed.

"The last time I heard, Delorian and the family was staying in those apartments that sound like a politician. You know. The ones on Roop."

"The Senator?"

"That's the one. Delorian's mom got Section 8, so they moved to The Senator last summer."

"Thanks," Maguire said and then added, "How about one for the road?"

"Don't mind if I do," Tuttle replied as he raised his glass in Floyd's direction.

Chapter 45

Instead of going home for lunch, Maguire grabbed a sandwich at Subway and wolfed it down as he headed straight for The Senator Apartments on South Roop. He arrived at the apartment complex just as he finished his last bite of ham and cheese. He parked his black, unmarked Crown Vic in front of the rental office and called for backup in case Shemar Lewis wasn't home alone.

"Good afternoon," Maguire said as he entered the rental office.

The young woman behind the desk eyed the handsome detective, and his wedding ring, and then asked if he'd come about the two-bedroom unit that was currently available.

Maguire shook his head, produced his shield, and politely asked the unit number of the Lewis family.

The office clerk began to shake as if she were the focus of the investigation.

"Apartment 114, first floor," she finally said after several beats had passed.

"Thank you," Maguire replied with a wink.

She blushed, offered a shy smile and then calmed.

The detective found the apartment with relative ease and cautiously knocked on the door. After several knocks with no answer, he announced himself in a thunderous voice. Immediately, a crashing sound came from within followed by the slamming of a door.

Maguire instantly recognized the sound and hurriedly headed for the opposite side of the building.

"Going somewhere, Shemar?" Maguire asked the young man who was halfway out the bedroom window.

"Don't shoot!" he begged, even though Maguire had not unholstered his service weapon.

"Shemar Lewis, you're under arrest. You have the right to remain silent," Maguire said as he grabbed Lewis's arm with one hand and his handcuffs with the other.

The teenager twisted like a ferret on crack, and a sudden popping noise punctuated the quiet day. Without a sound Maguire fell backward and collapsed to the ground. A trickle of crimson slowly seeped from the small hole over his right eyebrow as his lifeless blue eyes stared up at the gray, cloudless sky.

Shemar Lewis jumped from the window and ran toward the parking lot, but a burly sheriff's deputy thwarted his retreat a few feet from where Detective Maguire lay dead. "Stop or I'll shoot!"

The youth momentarily froze, desperately debating his options. Then he spun around and leveled his .22 caliber revolver at the deputy's head. But before he could shoot, Deputy Trevor Brown fired his Sig Sauer P226 with lightning speed and impeccable precision.

Lewis grabbed his shoulder as his weapon flew from his hand. He dropped to the ground, whimpering like a child, and called out for his mother. His bravado and bravery gone.

Deputy Brown roughly cuffed the young killer and propped him against the side of the apartment building. Then he stifled the rage that had welled up in his chest and called in the 10-00: *Officer down. All units respond.*

"Why didn't you kill me?" Lewis asked in amazement.

"Because that's too good for you, you little bastard. I'm going to take great pleasure watching you squirm when you get the needle."

* * *

"Baker, ah, Sarah," Orlando West rasped into the phone.

"What time is it?" she replied, stretching.

Bagheera rose and stretched as well.

"Just after two o'clock."

"What?"

"In the afternoon. It's two in the afternoon."

"For a minute there I thought I'd really overslept," Sarah said, her voice still tinged with sleep and her mind foggy with dreams of Patrick.

West was not a man who let his emotions rule him, but he was finding it difficult to speak as the anger engulfed his entire being. "You need to come to work. Dayshift needs all hands. There's been a—"

Sarah was instantly pulled from her sleepy stupor when she heard the desperation in West's voice.

"What's happened?" she demanded in a clear, even tone.

"It's Sean. He's been shot."

"Shot?" The words barely escaped her lips. "Where is he? Is he all right?"

"I'm afraid he's...he's gone, Sarah."

"Gone? No! That's impossible," Sarah cried, refusing to believe the tragic news.

"Sean would have wanted us to stay focused and professional. We have the shooter, but the scene still needs to be processed and the evidence collected. I'll do that along with the dayshift techs, but I want you to process the suspect. Can you do that for me? For Sean?"

"Yes," Sarah replied softly. "I can do that."

"All right then. I'll see you later."

Sarah tossed her cell phone onto the nightstand then grabbed Bagheera and cuddled him close to her chest and cried, first for her friend and then for herself.

Chapter 46

Deputy Sheriff Trevor Brown brought Shemar Lewis into the small exam room. Shackles bound the teenager's hands and feet. His shoulder throbbed from the gunshot wound, and he swore under his breath that he'd make Brown pay for what he did.

"Stand here!" Brown demanded, ignoring the comment as he shoved Lewis in front of the white painted wall and directed him to put his toes on the red line taped onto the linoleum floor.

Sarah gazed indifferently at Lewis, trying desperately to hide the contempt she was feeling. Shemar was just another piece of evidence in the case and had to be treated as such. She grabbed her camera and methodically began taking pictures. First she took overall shots from head to toe with the suspect looking straight ahead and his arms at his side. Then she repeated the process with each side view and the back. Next she took close-ups of Lewis's face, side and the back of his head. Then she took close-ups of his hands: palms up and palms down.

Too much time had elapsed from the time Lewis had been arrested and treated for his injury to do a gunshot residue test, but Sarah did do a fingernail scraping and combed his hair for any trace evidence.

"You can take him back to his cell," Sarah said to Brown, her voice wavering slightly. She sighed with relief as the deputy and suspect disappeared through the door.

If Shemar Lewis had been in her presence one minute more, Sarah thought she could have beaten him to death with her camera. How she hated him. Maybe one of his cellmates would do her the favor and save the taxpayers a boatload of money on a trial.

Grayson hesitantly opened the door and looked into the room. His heart went out to Sarah when he saw her sitting alone, her head bowed, a single tear running down her cheek. "You doing okay?"

Sarah looked up and brushed the tear away with her fingertips. After sniffling a couple of times, she forced a smile and replied, "Yeah."

"Parker's on the phone. Now that you're done with Lewis, he needs you for the autopsy photos."

"Autopsy?" she rasped.

Grayson grimaced and nodded his head.

"Tell Parker I'll be there in half an hour. I need to make some notes before I leave."

"Will do," Grayson replied. He began to close the door and then stopped and asked, "Do you want me to go instead?"

"No. I have more experience than you. Maguire...Sean would have wanted me to do it. I'll be okay. This will be my last favor for him."

* * *

"Thank you for coming," Eliot Parker said as Sarah came into autopsy. The white tile walls gleamed, reflecting the light from the lamps overhead, and the smell of chemicals permeated the immaculate room.

Sean Maguire lay on the stainless steel table, still sealed in a black body bag. Parker stood at the head of the table. Like most medical examiners, Parker was in the habit of talking to his charges. But he made a mental note not to speak to the deceased while Sarah was in the room.

"May I begin?" Sarah asked politely.

To Parker's surprise, the question hadn't been directed to him.

"Okay, my friend. If you're ready, then so am I," Sarah said and began her photo documentation.

First she took an overall photo of the bag and then one of its plastic seal and nametag. The bag was opened and overall photos of the body were taken. When that was done, Parker waved to his assistant to remove Maguire's body from the bag and then replace it on the autopsy table.

Maguire looked like he was merely sleeping, his eyes closed and his russet-colored hair gently tousled. The small caliber entry wound above his right eyebrow caused by an intermediate gunshot had darkened, and the stippling, or powder tattooing, was now clearly visible. Contrary to what most people thought, stippling was not blood spatter or even burns, but rather unburned powder grains that exit a weapon during firing, causing pinpoint abrasions on the skin.

While the body was still clothed, overall photos, head, side and back, were taken. Segmented photos; left, right, overhead and back, and head to chest, chest to waist and waist to feet followed.

Sarah pursed her lips as she took a close-up of Maguire's face and then his hands and feet. Afterward, she took medium and close-up shots with and without a scale of the gunshot wound and the damage to the skull.

After the clothed photos were taken, Parker meticulously washed Maguire's body, and another series of photos were taken in the same manner.

"That was the easy part. Are you ready to continue?" Parker asked, his voice soft and encouraging.

Sarah simply nodded.

The ME drew his scalpel down each side of Maguire's chest and then down along his midsection to the pelvis, making a perfect Y-incision. He pulled back the skin, the newly formed flaps draping the window of the open cavern, and removed all the major organs and weighed each of them. Afterward, he took a trajectory rod and carefully inserted it into the skull at the wound site. Sarah documented each stage. Parker then removed the rod and looked up at Sarah, indicating the most difficult part of the autopsy process was about to begin.

After a moment's hesitation, he made a cut from behind Maguire's left ear, across the forehead, and then to the right ear and around. The cut was then divided, and the scalp was carefully pulled away from the skull in two flaps. The front flap was placed over the detective's face and the rear flap over the back of the neck, exposing the top of the skull.

Sarah could feel her hands begin to shake, but she summoned all her experience and strength to do her job and continue on as if the man before her had not been her friend. She cringed slightly at the high-pitched whining noise the electric saw made as it cut into the skull but kept steady.

Then the moment Sarah dreaded most happened. A sickening, sucking noise resonated throughout the quiet room followed by a popping sound as the top of the skull was detached. The brain was removed, weighed and placed on the autopsy table where Sarah took her obligatory photos displaying the brain's overall condition and damage.

She couldn't help but wonder at how such a small organ was the sole repository of a person's entire life: his personality, memories, experiences, and education—everything that made him human and unique.

"I think you have all the photos you need," Parker said gently, interrupting Sarah's philosophical reverie.

"Okay," she replied to the medical examiner. Then she leaned close to Sean Maguire and said, "I'll see you on the other side, my friend. Put in a good word for me when you meet the boss."

Chapter 47

Sarah debated whether or not to text Patrick and tell him about Detective Maguire. In the end she decided he should know. Patrick had liked Sean and a few prayers from a priest on his behalf couldn't hurt.

She scrolled through her contact list and stopped when she came to Patrick's name. The image of his smiling face peered back from the cell phone's plastic screen, and a tsunami of emotions swept over Sarah as she remembered their time together. She forced the memories from her thoughts, pursed her lips and began her message.

> *Patrick:*
> *Sean Maguire was killed Tuesday in the line of duty.*
> *Please keep him and his family in your prayers.*
> *Sarah*

Sarah hit the send button, tossed the phone onto her desk and returned to her paperwork. Not a minute later, her phone dinged, alerting her of a new text message. She sucked in a couple of choppy breaths when she saw the message was from Patrick.

> *Sarah:*
> *My deepest condolences on your loss.*
> *I will say a Mass for Sean.*
> *Be well,*
> *Patrick*

No *I miss you*. No *I love you*. No *I'm coming back soon*. Nothing!

With all her might, Sarah heaved her phone against the door. The phone crashed against the thick wood and then plummeted to the floor, its screen a spider web of cracks.

"Holy freaking moly!" Grayson shouted as he entered the office. "What happened?"

"Nothing! Nothing at all!" Sarah shouted back and then ran from the room in tears.

"Geez! I'd hate to see how she'd act if something happened," Grayson said to the empty office.

"I'm sorry," Sarah said, returning a few minutes later.

"No apologies necessary," Grayson replied. "I loved the guy too. He was like a brother, and I'm pissed that he's dead while some worthless banger is having three hots and a cot courtesy of the Great State of Nevada. I wish to God Brown had killed the little bastard."

So do I, Sarah thought.

"Excuse me," Jamie Taylor said as he entered the office. He handed Sarah a pink message slip. "This call came in for you. The man said he couldn't reach you on your cell phone."

She offered the probie a slight smile. "Thanks."

"You're welcome," the young man replied, beaming.

Sarah's slight smile broadened when she saw the call had come from Sebastian. He was back in town. She grabbed the office phone that sat on the corner of her desk and punched in his number.

A deep voice answered.

"Sebastian. It's Sarah."

"I'm quite happy you got my message and called back so quickly," Sebastian said, the excitement welling up in his chest.

"So am I. I can't really talk now, but call me tomorrow after I get off work. Okay?"

"I'll count the hours until then. Good-bye Sarah Baker, CSI."

"Bye."

"Is that Mr. Perfect?" Grayson asked.

"Maybe."

Chapter 48

Katrina ran her warm hand across Krulak's smooth chest. Even in the moonlight, she could see how ghost-pale he was, and she wondered why he was always so cool to the touch. Even in the throes of passion, Krulak never broke a sweat.

Concerned, Katrina asked him if he suffered from a medical condition. Krulak laughed and explained he was from a cold climate and had always lived in other cold or cool climes, so he tended to be naturally colder. "Cold hands, warm heart," he teased.

That answer had never truly satisfied Katrina's curiosity about her lover's body temperature, and he could never give her a satisfactory answer as to why they couldn't see one another during the day. Krulak would merely shrug off her inquiries by saying he was too busy with work, although he was never very specific about what he did.

Nevertheless, Krulak had proven to be a generous and attentive lover and never failed to surprise Katrina with beautiful gifts. He took her to the finest restaurants, attended the plays or movies she wanted to see, and he always listened to her when she needed to vent about work, her friends or any issue that came up in her life.

Katrina knew Krulak would make an excellent husband and father despite his workaholic tendencies. Perhaps when he was settled down, he'd realize there was more to life than work. Katrina hoped that would be someday soon. Now that she was settled into her position at Gage, Carmichael and Waters, it was time she too thought of a future outside of work.

Katrina snuggled close to Krulak and kissed his chest. He stirred from his sleep and enfolded her into his arms.

"I had the most wonderful dream," he whispered.

"Tell me about it," she replied with a sigh.

"I dreamt I was..." Krulak caught himself before he could say the word—*human*.

"Was it about me?" Katrina asked sweetly as her hand made lazy circles on his chest and then ran down the length of his torso.

"How did you know?" the vampire replied as he rolled on top of Katrina and kissed her passionately.

* * *

"I'm so happy to see you," Sarah said as she rose from her chair and reached out to embrace Sebastian.

He smiled at her words, enfolding her into his strong arms. She was so small and fragile in his powerful embrace, and that made him feel even more protective of her.

"Where do we begin? How was your trip home?" Sarah asked cheerfully.

Sebastian's chest tightened. He hated having to lie to her, but it was even more important now that he had abandoned Krulak. His master must never know his whereabouts or anything about the people in his life, especially Sarah. Someday soon he would find a way to kill the vampire, but until that day came Sebastian needed to be a ghost.

"My trip was fine. Thank you for asking."

"What will it be, folks?" the waitress asked as she sauntered up to the table.

"An Old Rasputin," they said in unison. They looked at one another and then burst out laughing.

"Good choice," she replied and headed for the bar.

"How have you been, my dear Sarah?"

"I'm fine, but it's been an incredibly tough week."

"May I inquire why?"

"One of our detectives was killed in the line of duty. He was a friend, and I'll miss him more than words can say. His memorial service is Friday."

"I'm so very sorry, Sarah. So very sorry."

"Detective Maguire, Sean, was a good man. He left behind a wife and five young children."

"How sad," Sebastian replied with true sympathy.

"Let's talk about something else," Sarah said as she swiped at the tear that threatened to roll down her pale white cheek.

"Yes. No more talk of sadness. We should celebrate my return to America. Let me take you to dinner. We'll go somewhere very elegant. Anywhere you'd like."

"Why don't you come to my house for dinner?" Sarah asked as she put her hand atop Sebastian's.

"I'd like that very much," Sebastian replied. "Will your friend the priest be joining us?"

"No. Patrick won't be joining us. He's gone back to Rome."

"For how long?"

"Forever, I suppose."

Chapter 49

Sarah regarded herself in the full-length mirror. Black was definitely not her color and dresses did nothing for her figure except make her look like a dumpy singleton. She wasn't actually dumpy, but she was definitely single with a capital S. Sara smoothed her skirt, took another look in the mirror, grabbed her purse, and headed out the door.

St. Teresa's parking lot was packed, so Sarah had to park on the street. Hundreds of police officers from all over Nevada and Northern California had come to pay their respects to a fallen brother in the thin blue line. Kathleen Maguire had already returned to Boston with her children where her husband would be buried, so only a memorial service would be held today in Carson City.

When Sarah reached the church entrance, she found Sebastian waiting for her.

"I hope you don't mind, but I thought I could pay my respects to your friend."

Sebastian put his hand gently on the small of Sarah's back and guided her into the church. The last time she'd been here was on Christmas Eve when she attended Midnight Mass with Patrick. Now this sad occasion would replace that happy memory.

Sarah looked about the crowded church. A sea of dress green and dress blue was all she could see until she finally spotted West and Grayson dressed in black civilian suits. They had saved a seat for her. Surprised that Sarah wasn't alone, they nodded a hello to the stranger as she and Sebastian slid into the pew.

The low murmuring of voices stilled as a young man in dress greens approached the pulpit.

"Atten hut!" he commanded.

The police officers stood in unison, coming to attention.

"Detective Sean Maguire, front and center."

No one came forth.

"Detective Sean Maguire, front and center."

Again no one came forth.

The command was repeated once more.

A moment of silence followed and then the young officer spoke again. "Detective Sean Declan Maguire is off duty. End of watch March 20th."

The deputy backed away from the pulpit and returned to his seat in the front pew. When he was seated, a bagpiper entered from the rear of the church, and the familiar, bittersweet tune of *Amazing Grace* filled the large sanctuary. Tears welled up in the eyes of every person present, including Sebastian.

Sarah choked down the lump in her throat as her own tears flowed freely down her cheeks. Sebastian's heart went out to her, and he gently laid his hand on hers and gave it a light squeeze. She gasped softly at his kind gesture and offered him a smile in return. Sebastian was a good man and a true gentleman. Sarah was grateful to have him in her life.

Chapter 50

"Thank you so much for being there for me today," Sarah said as Sebastian saw her to the front door of the townhouse.

"You needed a friend at your side on such a day."

"I appreciate it more than you know."

"You're very welcome, Sarah Baker."

Sebastian kissed Sarah's cheek and turned to leave, but she grabbed his arm and stopped his retreat. "Don't go. Not yet. Come in and have a cup of tea and some cake."

"Are you sure? Wouldn't you like to rest a bit?"

"I'll rest later. Right now, I'd like your company."

Sebastian didn't argue and followed Sarah into her home.

They had barely gotten through the door when Sarah threw her arms around Sebastian's waist and hugged him fiercely. He hugged her back and then kissed the top of her head. She looked up at him in surprise and found dark brown eyes filled with love and desire gazing back. She pursed her lips slightly, beckoning him. Sebastian's lips came down softly upon hers in reply.

"Stay with me. I don't want to be alone."

"I'll stay with you as long as you wish."

"No. You don't understand," she replied, her voice cracking. "I want you."

Sebastian's whole being had been filled with such

longing for this woman. He couldn't remember a moment when he hadn't loved her. Since he had first seen Sarah, he had thought of no one but her. Sebastian had fantasized about hearing these words; wished for them and even prayed for them, and now she was in his embrace, offering herself to him. He could not refuse her loving plea.

"I want you too." His large hand cupped the side of Sarah's face, holding it gently before reclaiming her lips.

Returning his kiss passionately, Sarah savored the taste of Sebastian's mouth and the heady sensation coursing through her body. It had been so long since she'd been wanted, and she trembled with excitement and anticipation.

As she began to speak again, Sebastian put his fingertips to her lips. Then to Sarah's surprise, he lifted her into the warm circle of his arms and carried her to the bedroom where he gently let her slip from his embrace.

They stood face to face in momentary indecision until Sarah made the first move. She took the jacket from his broad shoulders and tossed it onto the upholstered chair that sat next to the nightstand. Then she tugged at his tie until the knot was loosened and the choking material was freed from his neck. Slowly and seductively, Sarah unbuttoned Sebastian's dress shirt and pulled it open, exposing a muscular chest covered in thick brown hair. She grazed his warm skin with kisses, whispering her desire as she trailed her lips across his chest and down his abdomen.

Sarah turned around so Sebastian could unzip her dress. Without a word, he obeyed her silent command, and the dress dropped silently to the floor, a wave of black lapping about her feet. Sarah stepped out of the material, her blue eyes never wavering from the dark brown eyes gazing back.

Sebastian gently slipped his fingers beneath Sarah's bra strap and caressed her shoulder before removing the lacy garment. His large, warm hands held each perfect breast with awful reverence, and Sarah gasped as an all-encompassing sensation of love and acceptance came over her.

"Tell me what you want, my love," he rasped as his passion swelled.

Sarah's breath caught in her throat, and the words evaporated from her lips as she pulled away. A cold knot formed in Sebastian's chest. She had changed her mind. But the fear disappeared in a heartbeat when Sarah unbuckled his belt. Now there was only surrender, surrender to Sarah and surrender to their mutual desire.

Chapter 51

Life was good. Abel Montoya had everything he'd ever wanted. He was independently wealthy, had a job he loved with the Nevada Museum of Art, and his nights were spent with riches even a sultan would envy. Each night after dinner, Montoya retreated to his finely appointed den where he'd drink rare brandy, smoke his exquisite Cubans and admire his treasures.

Tonight was no different as he pulled the picture window drapes closed, blocking out the lights of the city so that only the gentle glow of his antique Tiffany lamps illuminated his beloved sanctuary and the artifacts, paintings and sculptures he loved more than life itself.

Montoya took a long, fat Havana from his humidor and rolled the illicit tobacco between his short, thick fingers. He deemed it satisfactory and carefully clipped the end. A blue flame with a white-yellow tip danced from a sterling silver lighter, and he puffed and puffed until the end of his cigar glowed red like the eye of an angry dragon. Then he bent back his head, inhaled deeply and after a few moments blew the smoke from his lungs.

With the cigar still in his fingers, Montoya took the stopper off a vintage Waterford crystal decanter and poured himself a generous snifter of 1904 Marquis de Montesquiou Armagnac. This bottle had set him back almost $7,000, but it had been worth every cent.

With his cigar and drink in hand, Montoya settled down into his original Eames chair and propped his feet on the matching ottoman. He loved the soft crunching of the expensive leather, and he smiled with satisfaction as he made himself comfortable. He took another puff of his cigar and then a long, slow swallow of the Armagnac.

As he went to set the snifter on the end table, he accidentally sloshed the brandy on his trousers. He cursed the loss of even a drop of the rare vintage as he ran his fingers over his leg and then tried to lap up at least a few drops of the expensive liquid from his stubby fingertips. He took another puff of his cigar and then grabbed his prized dagger with his free hand from the same end table where his crystal snifter sat.

As he raised the dagger to the light, Montoya could see the finely inscribed blade and marveled at its words. Although he collected religious artifacts, Montoya was not a man of faith, an irony at which he often chuckled. He actually despised the pious and the faithful, deriding their childlike devotion to ancient superstitions and long dead gods. If there was anything that Abel Montoya revered, it was money. Money alone could buy treasures beyond imagining, and it was money that made his world revolve.

Montoya puffed at his cigar once more and then exhaled a thick, blue cloud of smoke. It floated mere inches from his face, refusing to dissipate in the warm environs of the burnished paneled room. Closing his eyes with contentment, he savored the moment. As he opened his eyes, Montoya could have sworn he saw what looked like an angel's wing through the smoky cloud that still lingered before him. He snorted at such a silly notion. Then a piercing white light stung his eyes, and the same vision of an angel's wing enveloped his vision.

His mind refused to believe what his eyes so clearly saw—the image of Michael the Archangel standing a few feet from where he sat. The angel reached out his hand and demanded the dagger, but Montoya laughed cynically and refused the heavenly being's request.

What kind of hallucination had this Armagnac produced? He was incensed and vowed to return the tainted vintage to his wine broker for a full refund. When he had finally finished cursing the man, Montoya looked up just in time to see Michael release his golden sword from its scabbard. Overhead the heavens opened up, and a multitude of angels watched from their celestial dwelling place as Michael's righteous blade came down swiftly and cut the art collector's throat from ear to ear.

Montoya's hand dropped to his leg, and the cigar instantly set the Armagnac-soaked material ablaze. As the blood gushed from his throat and the searing flames consumed his body, the final frantic pleas to heaven and the god he did not believe in echoed throughout the elegant room.

Sonia Garcia surveyed the charred remains of Abel Montoya's home, clearly visible in the bright lights that had been installed around the perimeter of the property. Nothing but ash, twisted metal beams, melted glass, and blackened brick remained.

Montoya himself had been reduced to mere ash and bone fragments as if he'd been through a crematorium, which basically he had. But unlike a crematorium that burns at 1800 degrees Fahrenheit, a normal house fire burns between 1200 and 1700 degrees. However, judging by the destruction of both the body and the house, the temperature had exceeded that, yet no accelerant presented which would account for the extreme heat or the amount of time the fire had burned.

As Garcia and the Fire Marshal sifted through the ash, she was stunned when she came across an odd silver dagger that appeared to be completely unscathed. It was totally illogical the silver had not been seared off the steel, but she couldn't dispute the evidence.

The nightshift supervisor motioned her forensic tech to place a number placard at the evidence and then take photos before Garcia removed the dagger from its resting place. When that had been accomplished, she slipped on her latex gloves and carefully removed the dagger from the ash and placed it into an evidence bag. Garcia notated the item with the time, day, date, and location of where it had been discovered along with her name and ID number.

"How do you think this dagger survived?" she asked the Fire Marshall, Ted Stevens.

"You got me on that one. I've been on the job twenty-three years, and I've never seen anything like it."

"I suppose I'll just have to file this one under *truth is stranger than fiction.*"

"I think you're right," Stevens replied, scratching his head.

A newbie CSI, trying to look like she knew what she was doing, passed her superior and nodded.

"How's it going, Harper?" Garcia asked.

"Okay," came the insecure response.

"If you find any evidence like a wick or any other flammable item, make sure you put it in an airtight metal can."

The newbie acknowledged the directive and went out to the Crime Scene Unit SUV to gather some cans.

"Isn't that like sending the kid on a snipe hunt?" Stevens asked as he surveyed the ruins.

"Not like...is. It will keep her out of trouble."

"You're a sly one. I'll give you that. It looks like I've done all I can do here. I'll head back to the station now, make my report and fax you a copy when I'm done."

"That would be great. Thanks."

Sonia Garcia looked at the evidence bag containing the pristine dagger and shook her head. This crime scene reconstruction report was definitely going to be an interesting one.

Chapter 53

The sweat poured down Patrick's face, stinging his eyes, but he continued punching the sand-filled bag before him. With every thump, thump, thump, he saw Krulak's face taunting him for his multitude of failures. A final punch and he was done, exhausted beyond measure. Yet he felt better than he had in days.

"Will you be in shape in time for the new cadre of students?" came a voice from behind.

Patrick turned around to see Brother Ciaran standing with a water bottle in one hand and a white terry cloth towel in the other.

"Thanks," Patrick said as he grabbed the towel and wiped his glistening face. He took the water bottle and drained the contents in two gulps. "As for your question, let's hope so, but I'm not as young as I used to be. Getting into shape has been harder than I expected."

"None of us are as young as we once were except maybe the Pope," Brother Ciaran replied with a laugh.

Patrick chuckled. The Pope was amazing. One would never know he was a man in his late seventies. It seemed the pontiff could work rings around everyone in Vatican City and still be ready for a pickup game of football if the opportunity presented.

"If you're not too busy this afternoon, would you mind helping me in the apiary?" Brother Ciaran asked.

"I'll be glad to help. What time?"

"Say about three?"

"I'll see you then."

The monk gathered the water bottle and towel from Patrick and happily sauntered away.

It was just past noon, and Patrick had enough time for a long shower and a late lunch. He gave the punching bag another few jabs and then walked about the gym and then into the adjoining armory. Whereas the gym held an array of modern exercise equipment, the armory looked like something from the Middle Ages. Racks of sabers, halberds, lances, axes, daggers, and knives lined the ancient stone walls.

He selected a dagger and grasped its hilt firmly before swiping it through the air several times. This dagger wasn't too heavy, nor was it too light; it was well balanced and fit his hand perfectly like his own lost dagger. When Patrick thought of all he had lost, his heart sank. He never dreamt he could lose such a priceless artifact or lose his heart to a woman. He loved Sarah almost as much as he loved God, and this fact made his heart ache more than the loss of his weapon or his failure to find and destroy the vampire Anton Krulak.

Patrick returned the dagger to its shelf and then surveyed the rows of armaments, selecting various weapons to try out. His students would never use any of these weapons in the field except for the daggers, but it was useful to learn how to defend one's self as vampire hunters had in days of old.

Before the International Association of Exorcists had commissioned the school for vampire hunters, students were selected and trained by their parish priests. However, training was usually substandard and much of the cause for the demise of many vampire hunters. Now with training regimented and uniformed, all students were versed in the art of ancient warfare such as archery, fencing with foil, épée and saber and also in the modern Israeli self-defense technique Krav Maga, which encompassed boxing, combat sambo, judo, wrestling, aikido, and grappling.

Patrick was quite adept at Krav Maga and pitied any street thug who may think taking on a priest would be an easy task. Luckily, he never had to use this particular skill set on anyone except a vampire, and he found it more than useful when in hand-to-hand combat with his satanic foe. Vampires as a whole seemed quite surprised when attacked in such a manner, thus effectively putting them off balance and making the final death blow with the holy dagger that much easier.

Chapter 54

Sarah woke with Sebastian cuddled against her on one side and Bagheera on the other. She could hear the steady, even breathing of her lover, and when she touched the kitten he began purring. Soon Bagheera was awake and making his hunger known, pawing the faces of both Sarah and Sebastian.

"You're a little panther," Sebastian said as he sat up and cuddled the kitten. "I can't believe how big he's getting."

"He's like Clifford."

"Clifford?" Sebastian asked, somewhat puzzled.

"It's a big, red dog from a children's book. He grows bigger and bigger, and soon he's as big as a house because he's loved so much."

"Then Bagheera will be enormous. But I'm already a big man. Whatever will become of me when you love me so much? I'll be a giant!" Sebastian proclaimed with a laugh as he put the kitten on the bed and then pulled Sarah into his arms and kissed her.

When the kiss ended, Sarah could barely catch her breath. Sebastian's ardor was intoxicating. He was an amazing lover, and she wondered how it would feel to actually be in love with him. Perhaps one day she'd feel the same way about him as he felt about her. Right now, Sarah just wanted to relish being loved and all the possibilities it offered.

"What time is it?" Sarah asked as she looked over Sebastian's broad shoulder at the clock on the nightstand. "Damn! It's almost seven. I need to get into the shower."

"Couldn't you take the night off?"

"I'll be off tomorrow."

"Then we should do something. Tell me what you want to do, and we'll do it."

"Let me think about it." She kissed Sebastian's cheek and was out of the bed before he could take her into his arms once more.

"Very well then," he replied and settled back down into the satin sheets.

Bagheera was having none of that and jumped onto Sebastian's chest. Bright yellow eyes stared with determination, demanding to be fed.

"Okay. Okay, my little panther. I'll feed you."

Sebastian carried the kitten into the kitchen and fed him a can of tuna. Then he put on a pot of coffee for Sarah and began her breakfast. Like Patrick, Sebastian was a marvelous cook, and he enjoyed caring for her.

"I could get use to this," Sarah said as she came into the kitchen and put her arms around the big man.

"I already am," he replied with a smile. He turned and kissed the top of her head and then sweetly ordered her to the kitchen table where her juice was already waiting.

"Sebastian?"

"Yes, my love?"

"I was wondering..."

"Wondering what?"

"Since you haven't found a house yet, I was wondering if you'd like to stay here with me? I'm sure you're tired of living in hotel rooms."

Sebastian could barely speak and was unsure of how to respond. "I'm not sure."

That wasn't the response Sarah expected to hear, and her temper flared. "So! I'm good enough to have sex with but not to live with?" she spat as she stormed from the kitchen and into the bedroom, slamming the door with a curse.

Sebastian quickly followed. "You misunderstood me," he said at the bedroom door.

"Oh, I think I understood you just fine," she snapped back.

"No, you didn't. I don't want us to be housemates."

"Then what do you want us to be?"

"Husband and wife."`

Sarah couldn't have been more stunned than if Sebastian had told her he was a priest. She did have deep feelings for him and would enjoy living with him to see if they were actually a good, long-term match. But marriage? Even though Sarah desperately wanted to get married and have children, she hadn't known Sebastian long enough to say yes to his proposal.

Then there was the question of Patrick. It would be grossly unfair to make vows to Sebastian when she was still in love with the priest. Although that ship was never going to come in, Sarah couldn't stop loving Patrick no matter how hard she tried. The more she tried to forget him, the more she thought of him and remembered everything he'd ever said to her; the warmth of his arms; the color of his eyes, and the way he made her feel when he smiled and gave her a little wink.

Sebastian had his qualities too. He was kind, patient and intelligent. He was also handsome, sophisticated and financially comfortable. He was the perfect package and hers for the asking. Then why hadn't she fallen in love with him as quickly as she had Patrick? The answer eluded her.

Sarah told Sebastian she wanted to wait to accept his proposal until they knew one another better and she was sure of her heart. Marriage was forever, and she didn't want to end up being another statistic in that *fifty percent of all marriages in the US fail* category.

Although Sebastian was disappointed, he understood Sarah's reluctance to rush into marriage. She had been on her own for a long time, and he knew she valued her independence. Becoming someone's wife must be an overwhelming prospect no matter how much she liked the romance of it. Sebastian also knew Sarah loved Patrick, and it would take time for her to forget him. That was all right with Sebastian. Now that he'd left his life with Krulak, he had all the time in the world and anything was possible.

* * *

Krulak paced nervously around his hotel suite. Sebastian was a week overdue returning from his holiday, and there'd been no word from him. The manservant hadn't answered his phone or responded to the texts Krulak had sent. Even worse when the vampire had contacted the hotel in Fiji where Sebastian's holiday had been booked, the concierge told him that Mr. Dragan had never arrived.

Krulak was incensed and frightened. Sebastian had been a good and loyal servant. It would be a pity if he had befallen an untimely death. But what if he hadn't died? What if he had run away? Disappeared? No! That was impossible. Sebastian would never do such a thing. There had to be a logical explanation as to why he hadn't arrived for his holiday and for why he hadn't returned to San Francisco.

If Sebastian didn't arrive in the next day or two, Krulak knew he would be obligated to tell the Dragan family that one of their favorite sons was missing. He would also have to send for young Marius. Krulak may be able to manage for a few weeks without a servant, but he definitely needed one for an eternity.

Chapter 56

"The air is still rather chilly," Patrick said as he buttoned his black cardigan.

"Yes, it is, but don't forget it was a long, cold winter this year. A cold spring should be expected," Brother Ciaran replied as he donned his white beekeeper suit, a not so easy task for the robe-wearing monk.

"What would you like me to help you with this afternoon?"

"I have a confession to make, Father. I actually don't need any help. My little beauties here do most of the work. I just wanted your company. Besides, I think you could use a wee bit of a rest. You've been training ever so hard these past few weeks."

Patrick raised his brows, nodded and smiled in agreement. His days and nights had been consumed with preparing to teach vampire hunting to a new class of men and women who had no idea what they were actually getting themselves into. Even when he told them of the dangers of their prospective profession, they wouldn't believe him, not until they faced their first vampire out in the world and alone. Until then his training would be merely academic.

Brother Ciaran checked each hive and made notes of their condition and that of his charges. Since Colony Collapse Disorder had become a pressing issue for beekeepers throughout the world, the monk had become even more vigilant with his bees. The slightest variation in their numbers was reason for instant concern. And Brother Ciaran was a concerned father. The bees were his family.

"Have you been praying on the matter?" the old monk asked casually.

"I pray constantly about everything. Which matter are you asking about in particular?"

"The beautiful one," Brother Ciaran replied without missing a beat.

"I've been praying about that too."

"Has the Lord given you an answer?"

"He has. It's the same answer with each prayer: *1 Corinthians 13.*"

"Ah, yes! 'Faith, hope and love. But the greatest of these is love.'"

"How can I not love her when the Lord has put this burden on my heart?"

"That's a good question, Patrick. God has given you a great capacity to love. It's up to you to figure out how he wants you to share that love. There's no sin in loving a woman. Woman was made for man, and to be married and have children is one of life's dearest blessings."

"I agree, Brother. I just wish I had met Sarah twenty years ago."

The monk chuckled. "If that were so, I'm afraid I'd be visiting you in prison."

Patrick gave Brother Ciaran a horrified look. "Why?"

"Because twenty years ago, lad, Sarah was ten years old."

Patrick blushed and then burst out laughing. "I see your point!"

Chapter 57

Another day had passed, and there was still no word from Sebastian. Krulak had resigned himself to the fact he would have to inform the Dragans that Sebastian was missing and call on young Marius to take his place. Krulak had never had such a young manservant and wondered if the boy would be up to the rigors of the job. At least he was old enough to drive, so that was something positive in this unfortunate and baffling situation.

Krulak sat down at the desk and grabbed a couple of sheets of stationery and a pen and began to write. He got as far as *Dear Madame Dragan* and stopped. For the longest time, he stared at the cream colored paper with the gold Mark Hopkins logo. Then he smiled. The last time he'd taken pen to paper was to write a love letter to Elizabeth. Krulak had written her volumes of love letters, pouring out his heart with each word. She in turn replied with love letters of her own, revealing her deepest secrets and most ardent desires.

If ever there had been a perfect match, it had been he and Elizabeth. She was his soulmate. Katrina was exceptional too, but although Krulak knew he had been destined to meet her, only Elizabeth would be his one true love.

He began his letter again, first with condolences to the family and then with a directive to send Marius to America posthaste. When he finished detailing all that had happened, as well as his urgent plea to have Marius replace Sebastian as soon as possible, Krulak wrote a generous check for Sebastian's parents and one for Marius's travel expenses.

"What are you doing, Anton?" Katrina asked as she awakened from her nap. She and Krulak had spent the evening making love, and she had fallen asleep soon afterward.

"I am writing a letter," he replied.

"Do people really still write letters?"

"People? No," he said, "But *I* do."

Katrina gathered her robe and slipped out of bed, pulling on the red silk wrapper as she walked to the desk where Krulak sat. She put her arms around his shoulders and hugged him tightly. "That's what I like about you. You're such an old fashioned gentleman."

"Yes, I am old-fashioned, but is that not part of my charm?"

It was nearly midnight and time for Katrina to go home. Krulak turned around and gazed at her beautiful face and then her gorgeous body that he had so recently ravished.

"It's time, I know."

"You are a working woman. If you stayed with me, you would never get any sleep."

"I think you're right."

Katrina dressed and then kissed Krulak once more before leaving. She was halfway out the door, when she suddenly stopped.

"What is it?" Krulak asked.

Katrina spun on her heels and began to speak, but then the words left her lips and her courage dissolved. "Nothing really."

"You can tell me anything."

"It can wait for another night. As you said, it's late and I need to go to work in the morning."

"Very well."

Katrina left without another word, but she vowed to speak with Krulak the very next time they got together.

Krulak stared at the door long after it closed and wondered what that had been all about.

Chapter 58

Sarah shuffled into her office. She wasn't in the mood to work tonight. The city had been working on her street all week, and she hadn't slept but more than a few hours each day the entire time. Consequently, she was Little Miss Cranky Pants, and folks had better stay out of her way if they didn't want to bear the brunt of her bad mood.

She hadn't said yes to Sebastian's proposal, and he hadn't pressed her further for an answer. He understood it would take time. Sarah did repeat the offer to have him move in with her, and he accepted. Fortunately, both he and Bagheera were able to sleep through anything and remained in remarkable good spirits despite her less than happy demeanor.

Grayson eyed his co-worker. "You look like hell."

"I feel like it too."

"The city's still working on your street?"

"You got it."

"How about a cup of coffee?"

"That would be awesome," Sarah replied as she fell down heavily into her chair and put her head on the desk.

Her eyes closed, and she could feel herself drifting away. *Oh, great! Now I can sleep!* Yawning, Sarah surveyed the piles of brown case files stacked in every direction. At least most of them were completed and just needed filing. As she grabbed a stack of files, her arm brushed against the pile of mail that sat precariously on the edge of her desk. The magazines, envelopes and flyers tumbled to the floor, and Sarah was instantly on her knees scooping them up.

She glanced at the new forensics magazines and a couple of the postcards advertising a recently opened pizza parlor and a Chinese restaurant's take out menu. She was just about to toss the postcards into the circular file when she spotted another postcard in the mix. Instantly, she began to tremble when she saw it was a photo of St. Peter's in Rome. Slowly, Sarah turned the postcard over, willing it to be from Patrick. She felt her heart skip when she saw the signature, but she hadn't a clue what the message meant.

1 Corinthians 13
Patrick

"Here's your coffee," Grayson said, handing Sarah a mug of her favorite French Roast. "Who's the postcard from?"

"Father Martin."

"How is he?"

"Beats me. He just wrote a reference to a bible passage."

"Don't look at me. You know I'm a heathen."

"Don't I know it!"

Sarah tossed the postcard onto her desk and Googled *bible quotes*. Thousands of results appeared. She clicked on the BibleHub.com link and quickly looked up

1 Corinthians 13. And now these three remain: faith, hope and love. But the greatest of these is love. A large, salty tear rolled down her cheek, but she quickly brushed it away.

"You okay?"

"Never better."

Chapter 59

Sarah was coming down from the clouds when West called.

"You have a new scene," the nightshift supervisor said in a pleasant voice. "Major case."

"Okay. I'll tell Grayson."

Eliot Parker had arrived at the Courtyard Carson City minutes before Sarah and Grayson. He and his assistant were already headed to the second floor room.

When the CSIs entered the hotel room, they found Detective Brown standing next to the king-sized bed, taking notes. A Caucasian male, who looked to be in his mid-fifties, lay dead in the bed, a single gunshot wound to the neck.

"My, my. What do we have here tonight?" Parker said as he walked up to the deceased.

"The guy in the next room discharged his handgun during an altercation with his girlfriend. The bullet went straight through the wall and into Mr. Winters. He never knew what hit him."

"I should say not," Parker replied as he slipped on his latex gloves.

"What about the shooter?" Grayson asked the detective.

"He's been taken into custody. I took the girlfriend's statement and released her. Go ahead and start processing the scene. We'll need a trajectory reading on the ballistics."

Sarah and Grayson nodded. This wasn't Brown's first homicide, but it was the first major case since being promoted to detective. Whatever bad blood there'd been between him and Maguire, it seemed that Brown was trying his best to prove himself and honor the memory of his fallen comrade by doing an exemplary job.

Sarah removed the laser light from her field kit and aligned it from the hole to the gunshot wound in the victim's neck. She made her notes and then repeated the process, but this time she directed the laser beam from the victim through the bullet hole in the wall and into the room next door to gauge the height at which the fatal shot had been made. This would have been a fun exercise had it not been for the resultant lethal consequence.

When the trajectory measurements were completed, Sarah took her own notes, sketched the room and took the mandatory photos. Three hours later, she was more than ready to wrap it up.

On the short drive back to the station, Sarah fell asleep. Grayson didn't bother waking her. He knew she was exhausted, and besides, she'd do the same for him had the situation been reversed.

Sarah mumbled something as Grayson pulled into their parking spot.

"What was that, Baker?"

"Love you, Patrick," came the dreamy reply.

Patrick? Father Patrick Martin?

Sarah stirred again "We're here already?" she asked.

"Yep."

West met Sarah and Grayson on their way into the office. "How'd it go?"

"It was an interesting scene," Sarah replied. "Like something straight out of a TV show."

"Hmm," West offered. "When you get a minute, I need to talk with you."

"Sure. I'll be right there."

Grayson looked at Sarah, and she looked at him and shrugged her shoulders.

"Please. Have a seat."

"It's one of those kinds of talks, huh?"

West chuckled. "No. It's not."

Thank God! "What's up?"

"You're being transferred."

"What? Where? Why? What have I done?"

"Settle down. You haven't done anything wrong. In fact, you're always so top notch that the Washoe County Sheriff's Department has asked for you to fill in for one of their techs who will be out for the next two weeks."

"Can you spare me?"

"Not really, but they need you."

"When do I start?"

"Tomorrow night."

"Yes, sir," Sarah replied dejectedly.

"Not to worry. You'll be working with Sonia Garcia. I've known her for years, and she's a great lady and one hell of a CSI."

"All right then," Sarah said and left the office.

Chapter 60

Another month of nights was almost over, and soon Krulak would feed once more. With each passing hour, the incessant gnawing in his gut festered, devouring his body and whatever humanity within him that remained. He told Katrina he was going out of town for a few days, so there'd be no possibility she would come by the hotel room. Her safety was paramount.

Krulak's hunt would take him back down to the Tenderloin District where he would be free to roam through the refuse of society. Old men and women whose names and lives had been forgotten were the easiest prey, but he preferred the younger ones who had lost their way. The homeless veteran with PTSD scarred by the horrors of war or the teenage prostitute eager to sell herself to any stranger who came by fed his dark soul as well as his ravenous body.

It was time to leave the safety of his sanctuary. Krulak checked the drapes of the picture window that looked out over the city and then glanced around the suite before heading off to the service elevator that would take him to the delivery dock behind the Mark Hopkins. There he could come and go undetected by the other guests and residents of the luxury hotel. He opened the door and froze, his body in shock as much as his brain. Katrina!

"I'm glad you're still here," she said sweetly. "I need to talk with you."

"Yes, yes," Krulak replied, stuttering as he willed the demons inside him to calm. "Come in. I only have a moment."

"That's all I need."

Katrina walked haltingly into the well-appointed, European influenced suite and stopped near the French provincial desk. She turned and gave Krulak a nervous smile. "I wanted you to know the good news before you left."

"Good news?" Krulak asked, intrigued.

"I think so, and I hope you will too."

"Do go on."

"You're going to be a father, my darling," Katrina said bravely.

White-hot anger welled up from the darkest depths of the vampire's being. "No! Impossible! Whose child is it?" he demanded as he grabbed her slender throat in his strong, pale hand.

"It's yours! I swear!"

"I will ask you one more time. Whose child is it?"

Katrina tried vainly to escape her lover's grasp, but the more she struggled the harder he held on.

"The baby is yours. I love you!" came the rasping words.

As Krulak tried to comprehend Katrina's words, the cloud of demons appeared above him, swirling maniacally. His mortal façade was rent apart, and the eternal vampire rose like a satanic phoenix.

Naked fear filled Katrina's violet eyes. As she let loose a wild, consuming scream that even those in the deepest parts of hell could hear, Krulak's razor sharp fangs tore into her neck. Her delicate body went limp as the life force violently escaped, but Krulak continued tearing away at her throat until the white vertebrae gleamed through the sea of red.

Krulak drank his fill of his lover's blood and then discarded Katrina as he would any other prey. He could hear the joyful cries of the demons as they swirled around him, urging him to flee into the night. But before he did, Krulak regurgitated a mouthful of blood and spewed it across the suite's walnut-paneled walls. Then he plunged his clawed fist into Katrina's abdomen, aborting the living fetus that still dwelt inside its dead mother, crushing it into oblivion.

Chapter 61

"God almighty!" Detective Paul Devereux said as he looked about the elegant suite. "What the fuck happened here?"

His newly promoted partner Chris Alcott stood motionless, unable to say a word. Neither man had ever seen anything like it, not even in a war zone.

Katrina lay in a pool of blood on the gold and brown floral carpeting, her wide, violet eyes staring at the nothingness above.

"The ME should be here shortly," the younger man was finally able to choke out.

Devereux nodded and walked around the corpse, trying not to step in the blood and contaminate the evidence, which was not an easy task. "The concierge said the suite was leased to a foreign national named Sebastian Dragan, but there's no female guest on record."

"What's a guy need a suite for?"

"Who the hell knows, but we need to find this Sebastian Dragan. Maybe he's some kind of diplomat, and this was a terrorist attack. He could be a hostage right now or be dead for all we know."

"He could also be the perp," Alcott replied.

"True."

"At any rate this place needs sealed off, and CSU needs to get in here ASAP."

Alcott nodded his head and went to secure the room while Devereux took his preliminary notes. He knew the hotel would want this incident taken care of swiftly and most importantly quietly. It wasn't every day a homicide like this happened in one of the city's finest and oldest hotels.

Devereux, a compact man of forty, had seen his share of brutal crime scenes in sixteen years on the force. He thought he'd be used to them now, but he wasn't. In fact, they seemed to bother him more as he aged. His wife said it was about time for him to retire, and after tonight he was beginning to think she was right.

"Okay for the techs to come in?" Alcott asked as he shuffled back into the suite.

"Yeah. That's fine. I'm heading off now to interview the neighbors and the housekeeping staff. I want you to stay here and keep any reporters at bay who may have picked up the story through one of the hotel employees."

"You got it."

Devereux walked the halls up and down, checking the exits. Elevators in the middle of the floor and stairs on each end allowed easy entry and egress. He knew those elevators would have cameras, so maybe he'd get a good shot of the perp on the surveillance footage. There was also a service elevator on the floor, and Devereux knew most likely there'd be no camera in it. That made him deduce it was the likely mode of escape the killer had taken. He also knew the killer could now be anywhere in the city or in the world.

Chapter 62

Through the darkness Krulak soared over the garbage-covered streets, eying the refuse, both human and nonhuman, below. Katrina's death had not satiated his bloodlust. If anything it had increased his desire to kill. He was a killer. He was death incarnate. That was his true destiny. He'd been a fool to think he could live as a man and enjoy a life as such. Krulak would delude himself no longer. He would seek out the innocent and those who deserved to die. All were equal. All were prey. He was a vampire and nothing more.

In the distance Krulak saw the faint movement of something in the shadows. He swooped down and came to rest near a dumpster outside the Rescue Mission. His thin lips turned up into a feral smile. He knew this place.

A figure appeared before him, a garbage bag in each hand.

"Good evening, Father," the vampire hissed at the old priest standing before him.

A scream lodged in the cleric's throat as the garbage bags slipped from his hands and crashed to the ground. He tried to make the sign of the cross, but his arm refused to move.

Krulak circled his victim in an agonizing pas de deux, his hot breath scorching the priest's skin as he spat out a tirade of hate toward the old man and all those of his kind.

"Dear God!" Father Hooper pleaded. "I beseech you to take me to heaven!"

"God? There is no God. There is only Satan, the Lord of all things living and dead!"

A segmented wing slashed through the dank air, enveloping the priest in one swift motion, crushing him to the vampire's chest. Then the other wing closed about from the opposite side, securing the old man in a suffocating cocoon.

As Father Hooper struggled to breathe, Krulak's fangs sunk into his throat, instantly severing the carotid artery. A warm sea of blood gushed into the creature's mouth, making his body shudder in orgasmic ecstasy. He drank with satisfaction until the priest was drained. Then with a thunderous scream, Krulak opened his wings and hurled Father Hooper into a mound of trash that had spilled from the overfilled dumpster. Staring at his victim with naked contempt, Krulak vomited a mouthful of blood across him before flying away.

Victim after victim, Krulak tore through the rundown neighborhood without mercy. As the thin line of dawn appeared on the horizon, Krulak felt his skin begin to tingle, and he frantically searched for shelter. The transformation was upon him, and he could feel the hideous dragon-like wings and the serpentine fangs begin to retract. The long, vicious claws disappeared, and were replaced by the polished fingernails of a gentleman. Glistening black hair slowly covered the bald, scarred pate, and his glowing red eyes cooled to the color of a cloudless azure sky.

Completely exhausted, Krulak stood naked and shaking at the back door of an abandoned bakery. He tried the doorknob, but it wouldn't budge. So he threw his shoulder against the door. A cracking noise resounded in the air followed by a loud squeaking of rusty hinges as the door gave way.

Inching through the darkness, Krulak navigated the kitchen, opening cupboards and doors in search of someplace to rest. At the far end of the room, he opened another door and stumbled into a utility closet where he tripped over a mop.

Expecting to hit the hard linoleum, Krulak was surprised to find only softness beneath him as he landed. His slender fingers rummaged through a pile of what felt like towels, flour bags and clothing. Within that cotton pile, Krulak found a tee shirt and a pair of pants. The clothing smelled of dust and sweat, but he didn't care. He hurriedly dressed and then fell fast asleep in the welcoming shelter.

Chapter 63

Krulak slept the day away then stirred as a new hunger gnawed at his gut. His human body needed food. Cautiously, he left the safety of his newfound sanctuary and ventured out to the alley and then into the street beyond. Eyeing the open businesses, he spotted a bodega's neon sign flickering on and off. He entered the small store and scanned the sparsely stocked shelves. A dark-haired Latino man about twenty years of age sat behind the counter, reading a comic book. He gave Krulak an indifferent glance and returned to his reading.

The vampire casually walked up to a crate of fruit, grabbed a couple of apples and an orange and then ran from the bodega as fast as his legs could carry him. The clerk never bothered looking up.

Once outside Krulak hurriedly consumed his forbidden fruit, enjoying it more than he had any food in a very long time. When he was refreshed, Krulak made his way back to the Mark Hopkins Hotel where he hoped somehow to gain access to his suite and his belongings.

As he had done many times before, the vampire entered the posh hotel through the delivery area and took the service elevator to his suite on the sixteenth floor. The crime scene tape had already been removed at the request of the hotel manager, but Krulak knew what had happened inside not so long ago.

Looking up and down the hallway, he wiggled the doorknob. To his surprise the door was unlocked, and Krulak hurriedly slipped inside unnoticed. He turned on the overhead lights and surveyed the once pristine suite. Splashes of brownish red marred the burnished paneling, and a pool of coagulated blood, which had also turned deathly dark, stained the carpeting where Katrina's body once lay.

Momentary remorse filled his being, but the vampire willed it away as he did the memory of Katrina and what he had done. He showered and dressed and then grabbed a valise from the closet and stuffed it full with as many clothes as it could fit. When he had gathered all the belongings he needed, Krulak removed the vent cover on the air duct of the master bedroom wall and collected the fake passport and the money hidden within. He placed a stack of hundred dollar bills into the breast pocket of his tony Valentino suit and the rest of the money into the Louis Vuitton valise.

With one last look around the elegant suite, Krulak opened the door and slipped back into the hallway. But this time he took the main elevator down to the lobby and walked out of the hotel and into the dark night as if he were just another guest.

Chapter 64

Her shift was only halfway over, but Sarah was already exhausted. Reno's crime rate was double that of Carson City, and the members of the Crime Scene Unit definitely earned their pay. The night had been nonstop since she'd punched in, and so far Sarah had gone to four scenes: two burglaries, an assault and a robbery.

She had finished logging in the evidence from the assault and was now wandering through the property room looking for a place to store it. The shelves were packed with cardboard evidence boxes two and three high. As Sarah approached the end of one storage rack, a chill shot up her back, and she could feel the hair on her arms stand up. The property room was well lit and looked much like any other, but something about this one made her feel like someone had just walked over her grave. Perhaps it had to do with all the weapons stored in there, weapons that had been used in homicides.

Sarah chided herself for being superstitious and then continued. From the corner of her eye, she thought she saw a light. Sarah turned around and gazed back down the row of shelves. One evidence box sat precariously on the edge of a shelf, looking like it could fall off any second. She wondered how she'd missed that on her initial walk through. She pushed the box back and returned to her desk where she found two more evidence boxes waiting. With a sigh Sarah gathered the boxes and returned to the property room. *I see. I'm the loaner who's getting all the scud work.* She chalked it up to another glamorous aspect of forensics.

Casually, Sarah walked down the same row where she'd stored the first box but was stopped halfway there. The box she had pushed back onto the shelf was again perched on the edge. Puzzled, she looked around, ducking her head up and down so she could see between the shelves. She was alone now, but someone had to have been in the property room within the last ten minutes. She took the box and put it on the bottom shelf of the storage rack and left.

An hour later Sarah had more evidence boxes to store. After stacking the new boxes in a different area of the property room, she walked to the row of shelves where she had stored the first box. She froze in midstride. The box was back on the original shelf and once again sitting precariously on the edge of it, ready to fall off.

That was it! She angrily grabbed the box, slammed it on the floor and then yanked off its lid. Instantly, a bolt of searing, white light shot out of it. Sarah stumbled backward and fell on her behind with a jarring thump. Shaking and barely able to process what had just happened, she crawled on her hands and knees to the box and then peaked inside.

She blinked several times, trying desperately to clear her eyes and her thoughts. This was too incredible to be true, but there it was—Patrick's vampire dagger!

Chapter 65

Sarah's eyes glistened as brightly as the silver vampire dagger encased within the evidence bag. She was astonished and couldn't wait to tell Patrick the unbelievable news. But first she had to take the evidence to Sonia Garcia.

Sarah took a deep breath and then knocked on her temporary supervisor's office door.

"Come in." Garcia glanced up from her paperwork with an inquisitive look and a smile on her full lips. "Yes, Baker. What can I do for you?"

Sarah walked haltingly into the office and set the evidence box on Garcia's desk. "While I was storing evidence from tonight's scenes, I happened to see this box sitting askew on one of the racks. To make a long story short, it fell off the shelf."

Garcia's smile turned into a horrified grimace. "Was anything broken or compromised?"

"No, ma'am. Nothing like that."

"Good. Then go ahead and return the box to the property room."

"Before I do there's something you need to know."

"What's that?"

"This evidence is from a crime scene I worked in Carson City. It's the dagger that was stolen from Father Patrick Martin, and it's part of a Vatican collection of religious artifacts that was on tour here in America,"

Sarah lied. "I'm not sure how it ended up in the Abel Montoya evidence, but it did."

"Are you sure it's the same dagger?" Garcia asked incredulously.

"I'd bet my soul on it."

"That's quite a bet."

"Yes, it is. I can tell you what's engraved on the blade," Sarah offered.

Garcia opened the evidence box and retrieved the plastic bag from within. She held it up to the light so she could read the dagger's inscription. "Uero Stipen—"

"Uero stipendium mors est Satanae. Vita aeterna est donum Christi. Death is the reward of Satan. Eternal life is the gift of Christ."

"That's right," Garcia said, more than a bit surprised.

"Father Martin needs the Church's property back. He was recalled to Rome when this dagger was stolen and no doubt reprimanded harshly for its loss."

"The Montoya case is still open. It hasn't been determined whether it was arson and homicide or an unfortunate accident. Detective Gaffney and the Fire Marshall are still investigating."

"So how can Father Martin get the dagger back?"

"Seeing that it wasn't the cause of Montoya's death, I don't believe there's any reason why the dagger can't be returned to its rightful owner. Let me clear it with Legal first, and I'll get back to you."

"I know Father Martin will be quite happy about having the Church's property returned."

"I'll make it my priority."

"Thank you so much," Sarah said, relieved.

Chapter 66

Sarah's thumbs flew over the cell phone's keypad, furiously texting her message to Patrick. It was 2:00 a.m. Reno time, which made it 10:00 a.m. Rome time. By now Patrick would have been up for hours and already showered, dressed, eaten a Spartan breakfast, and gone to Mass. No doubt he was presently working away at whatever vampire hunters did when they weren't out in the field. She reviewed the message, hit the send button and then said a prayer that he'd be in contact soon.

The rest of the night was blessedly uneventful, and Sarah had plenty of time to catch up on paperwork. Garcia came by around 0400 hours to see how Sarah was doing but otherwise nothing else occurred to keep her rational mind off the irrational event, which had led to the discovery of the vampire dagger. Since meeting Patrick, Sarah thought she'd be use to the improbable and the bizarre, but she was still a CSI and logic and reason were foremost in her worldview. *No wonder people go crazy*, she thought.

Sarah was bone tired when she got home, but thankfully Sebastian had her dinner waiting. He'd already fed Bagheera, cleaned the litter box and vacuumed and dusted the townhouse. The man was amazing, and she was so lucky to have him in her life. So why wasn't she madly in love with him? She did love Sebastian, at least as much as her heart would allow her to love anyone other than Patrick. But was that enough for her? For him?

Sarah sat wearily down at the kitchen table, and Sebastian filled an oversized mug with coffee and then kissed her cheek.

"Busy night?" he asked.

"Nonstop," came the weary reply.

"You'll feel better when you eat and get some sleep."

She nodded in agreement. They ate in comfortable silence and then Sarah showered and fell into bed. Sebastian and Bagheera were now both in the habit of cuddling with her until she fell asleep, although Bagheera stayed in bed long after Sebastian had gotten up and began his day.

Sebastian wrote daily in his journal, detailing his life and travels with Krulak. He thought his stories would make a good book. Paranormal stories were always popular, and the public never seemed to tire of vampires. No one would ever know his stories were based on fact. Truth was definitely stranger than fiction.

Thanks to the money he'd saved over the years, Sebastian was able to contribute to Sarah's mortgage and to the household budget. Yet the thought he could do more always plagued him. He entertained the idea of getting a job, but what kind of job? What could he do? There wasn't much need for manservants in the area, and he had no references except for Sarah. Sebastian was suddenly feeling quite useless.

Sarah stretched and yawned. She felt wonderful and had managed to sleep an entire seven hours without waking up or even dreaming. Rolling over, she grabbed her cell phone from the nightstand and checked her messages. Not one was from Patrick. As she began to text him, Sebastian came into the bedroom, and Sarah instantly stopped and tossed her phone down on the bed.

"Texting your boyfriend?" Sebastian asked with a laugh.

"No!" Sarah shot back, a bit too emphatically.

"Good!" Sebastian replied with a wink and then brought his lips to hers in a sensuous kiss.

She returned his kiss with an urgent passion, willing the handsome priest from her mind. Sarah's life was here and now and so was Sebastian.

Chapter 67

Patrick was beside himself. How could he have dropped his cell phone in the middle of La Montecarlo? He could still hear the terrible crunching of plastic as the passing Fiat crushed the device into pieces. Now he had to requisition a new phone and that could take weeks, knowing how slowly paperwork travelled through the organization's supply department. At least he wasn't out in the field, so being without a phone wasn't a major issue.

His new class of recruits was shaping up nicely. A feisty, young Argentinean named Sofia Pereyra was proving to be his number one student. She was small, incredibly strong and athletic, and her entire life since childhood had been devoted to becoming a vampire hunter. In many ways Sofia reminded Patrick of Sarah. Such determination and drive in one so young and beautiful always gave him pause. Like Sarah, this young woman could have chosen an easier life, but instead chose a life few people could endure. He prayed her career would be a long one.

"Buenos días, Padre," Sofia said as she and a few of her classmates came into the gym.

"G'day!" Patrick replied happily.

"What are we doing today, Father?" asked a young Russian with a thick accent.

"You'll all be pleased with today's assignment."

"We're fencing?" came the eager reply from a French student.

"Something even better."

"Wrestling?" came another query.

"No, but close. Today you're going to have the chance to give me a good thrashing."

The bright faces of the students dulled with shock.

"We're boxing," Patrick said as he opened up the storage locker filled with well-worn training gloves, new mouthpieces, and various sized headgear.

"Cool!" the Russian replied, beaming.

"But when will we ever box with a vampire?" Sofia asked in a huff.

"Never, but boxing is good for physical conditioning. You'll need fast reflexes when you're out in the field. The vampire is faster than anything you can imagine, and it will take everything you have, mentally and physically, to defeat him."

Sofia grabbed a pair of gloves and slipped them on. "Ready, Padre?"

Patrick donned his own gloves, headgear and mouthpiece and within minutes he was sparring with the young woman. It was all he could do to keep up with her as she easily danced around him, landing punches here and there when he least expected. Patrick knew he couldn't go easy on Sofia even if she was at least sixty-five pounds lighter than he and a woman. A vampire would have no mercy, so the priest gave as good as he got.

With the final punch, he sent the young woman crashing to the floor. Stunned, Sofia slowly pulled herself up. Patrick removed his headgear and was about to shake her hand when she delivered a devastating right cross to his chin. He stumbled backward and then fell onto the floor. Several students rushed to help him up, but he waived them away.

"You fight dirty," Patrick said, shaking his head.

"So do vampires!"

"That they do."

He smiled. This young woman would do well in the field.

Chapter 68

Young Marius arrived in Carson City two days after Krulak's return to the Capitol. He hadn't been pleased about being yanked out of school to begin his service with the vampire two years sooner than expected. But Krulak had paid the Dragans handsomely for their son's inconvenience, and they sent the boy off to America with happy hearts and few reservations.

Although Marius was only sixteen, he stood over six feet tall and had broad shoulders and large, strong, hands. His hair was a dark chestnut color, and he had the same soft, unguarded brown eyes as his uncle. Krulak felt as if he'd stepped back in time. He could have sworn he was looking at a young Sebastian.

The vampire felt an unfamiliar pang in his chest and realized he missed his faithful manservant. Sebastian had disappeared completely, and Krulak had to accept the fact his companion had died in some kind of accident and would never return. Still, he wondered about Sebastian's fate and hoped that his death had not been too dreadful. A quick and painless death was something all mortals hoped for in the end.

"Have you settled in now?" Krulak asked Marius as he came into the young man's room, a room adjoining his own on the top floor of the St. Charles Hotel.

Krulak had been undemanding those first few days Marius had been in Carson City. The young man needed to rest from his journey and mentally prepare for the life he had ahead.

"Yes, sir," came the dutiful reply.

"Good," the vampire said as he patted Marius on the cheek. "There is much you need to know, but I trust you will be a quick learner."

Marius nodded. Despite his outward confidence, he knew very little of what to expect. Since he was a child, Marius had listened to the stories his grandfather told about his days in service to Krulak, but those stories had always been told after the consumption of copious amounts of vodka. Marius put little stock in his grandfather's words, believing them to be an old man's fanciful imagination inspired by worldly spirits and not by those from beyond the grave.

Krulak explained in detail the time frame in which he needed to feed. He wanted to make sure the young man would be prepared for what he would see and not flee in response. Krulak also assured Marius he'd never have any reason to fear him as long as he did as he was told.

A week later Marius experienced something he would remember to his dying day. Nothing could have prepared him for the hellish transformation he witnessed as his handsome, young benefactor morphed into a vile, hideous monster. As the demons swirled above them, beckoning Krulak into the night, the young man cowered on the floor and frantically prayed. Weeping and clutching the silver crucifix he wore around his neck, Marius begged God for forgiveness in doubting his grandfather's stories.

The vampire threw open the window and took flight, the army of demons following close behind.

Marius had no idea how much time had passed since he'd thrown himself to the floor, but when he finally had the courage to rise, he slowly picked up his quivering body and warily gazed about the hotel room. He took a deep breath and crossed himself, fearing God was nowhere to be found here.

Chapter 69

"We may have a break in the Bello homicide," Paul Devereux said as he tossed a stack of paperwork onto his partner's desk.

Chris Alcott flipped through the lab report on the trace evidence recovered at the Bello crime scene. Although the DNA was unidentified, it did match DNA found at recent crime scenes in Carson City and Reno and from a cold case more than fifteen years old.

"You've got to be kidding!" Alcott said, looking up from the lab report.

"Looks like our Sebastian Dragan has been a busy boy," Devereux said. "Now we just need to find him and match his DNA to the DNA in these scenes and our case will be closed along with all the others."

Alcott offered his partner a high five. Devereux slapped his hand against Alcott's, grinning like a rookie on his first assignment.

"I think it's time we took a road trip," the veteran detective said.

"I hear Northern Nevada is nice this time of year," Alcott replied.

"I've called the Carson City and Washoe County Sheriff's Departments and the Reno PD. We'll stop in Carson City first and talk with Detective Trevor Brown and then go onto Reno and see Detective Jason Gaffney. Both these guys have seen Dragan's handiwork up close and personal. Hopefully, by now they have a few leads on where he might be," Devereux said.

* * *

"It's nice to meet you," Detective Brown said as he shook hands with Detective Devereux and then Detective Alcott. "Please have a seat. Dr. West and CSI Baker will be here shortly."

The two San Francisco police officers sat down opposite Brown's desk and patiently waited for the nightshift supervisor and his lead CSI.

"My predecessor, Sean Maguire, was the detective on the Dalton and Anderson cases. Unfortunately, he was killed in the line of duty a few months ago."

"I'm sorry for your loss," came the automatic response from Devereux. How many times over the past sixteen years had he said that to someone? He'd lost count.

"Thank you. Anyway, I only know the cases through Maguire's reports. Dr. West and CSI Baker processed the scenes, and I'm sure they can answer any questions you—"

"May we come in?" West asked politely at Brown's door.

Brown waived his CSIs into the cramped office. "Detectives Devereux and Alcott, Dr. West and CSI Baker."

Everyone politely nodded and then West and Sarah slid up a couple of side chairs behind the visiting detectives.

Devereux was the first to speak. "It seems our cases have become one, and after looking at your crime scene photos, I can definitely say the murders were committed by the same perp. The crime scenes are identical."

"And so is the DNA," Alcott offered.

"The person of interest in the murder of Katrina Bello is a Romanian named Sebastian Dragan. He's been here in the US on a work visa for the better part of eight years," Detective Devereux stated.

Sarah gasped and turned the color of chalk. *Romanian?*

Chapter 70

It took every ounce of professionalism Sarah had to remain calm. She was incensed Sebastian had lied to her and more than a little afraid he was involved with Anton Krulak.

"What's wrong, Baker?" West asked as he noticed Sarah becoming paler by the minute.

"I'm afraid I don't feel very well. I haven't eaten this evening," she replied, hoping her supervisor would believe her lie.

"Why don't we all take a break?" Brown suggested. "Baker, go get something to eat and meet us back here in fifteen minutes."

Sarah gratefully accepted the detective's offer and was out the door before she could collapse. Frantically, she routed through her desk drawers until she found a small package of crackers. She poured a handful of the tiny, crispy goldfish and then gobbled them down, desperately trying to quell the nausea that had erupted in the pit of her stomach. After Sarah had swallowed the last mouthful of crackers, she took a deep breath and then a shallow sip of water from the bottle that always sat on her desk.

What was she going to do? Should she tell West that she was living with a murder suspect? How was she going to face Sebastian and ask him about Krulak and more importantly ask if he had anything to do with

Katrina Bello's death or the deaths of all the other people Krulak had killed?

After her brief respite, Sarah returned to Brown's office. For the next hour, she and West went over crime scene photos and notes with Devereux and Alcott. Throughout their meeting she was perspiring so profusely that she could feel her shirt clinging to her back, and she was sure the men sitting around her could see her shaking. Never was she so glad to have a meeting end.

"We're going over to Reno now to speak with Detective Gaffney, but you can reach me on my cell. While we're here, we'll be staying at the Motel 6," Devereux said as he prepared to depart.

"Good to know. Don't hesitate to call us if you need anything," West replied.

"Will do," the senior detective said and left with Alcott at his heels.

"I really need to go now, boss. My shift starts in less than an hour, and I don't want to be late."

"That's fine. Go ahead and take off."

Sarah started for the door.

"Oh, Baker," West called out.

Sarah froze.

"We'll all be glad when you're back."

She turned and gazed fondly at him and said, "Me too."

Sarah could barely keep her mind on the road as she drove the thirty-two miles to Reno. There wasn't much traffic this time of night, and the long stretch of darkness before her only intensified her despair.

Approaching the Eastlake exit, Sarah saw something large and black swooped across the windshield. She automatically jerked the steering wheel in response, and the little roadster swerved erratically from one side of the highway to the other until she could correct her action and bring the sports car back into its proper lane.

"What the hell?" Sarah slowed and looked out the windshield and both side windows but saw nothing. She shook her head, thinking she was seeing things, and then accelerated until she resumed cruising speed once more. But then the same dark object swooped across the windshield again. Sarah slammed on the brakes and came to a squealing stop on the side of the road.

She switched on the emergency flashers, grabbed the Maglite from the glove compartment and then jumped from the car. The strong beam searched the night sky. Few stars could be seen in the overcast firmament, but the beam clearly caught something on the second pass.

The flashlight crashed to the ground.

The vampire and its demonic minions circled overhead, laughing and cursing as they flew around the frightened young woman. Then as quickly as they had appeared, they disappeared into the night.

Chapter 71

Krulak's harsh laugh echoed in the empty sky. He was enjoying his little prank and his new found freedom. Since returning to Carson City, Krulak discovered he could change his form from human to vampire anytime he wished. Perhaps he could have done it all along, but it wasn't until after Katrina's death and the acknowledgment of his true nature did Krulak realize he could transform at will. Now he took to the skies in search of a victim to kill for the sheer pleasure of it, and he enjoyed terrorizing the unsuspecting traveler as a way to pass an eternity of time.

A speck of light shone far in the distance, piquing the vampire's interest. The demons urged him on until they hovered en masse above a desolate, rustic cabin. Krulak made a passing sweep across a small, dirty window. Inside, an old man sat in an equally old wooden rocker, reading by the light of an antique oil lamp. He hardly seemed worth the effort, but then again he was old and useless. Krulak would be doing the man a favor by killing him. No longer would he sit alone. Instead, he'd be a part of the multitudes in heaven…or hell.

The vampire lit down near the same window he'd just flown by. A sound much like that of a small animal screeching in pain resounded through the still night as he slowly dragged his claws across the glass pane.

The old man continued reading.

Krulak repeatedly scratched at the window but to no avail. Angered by the man's seeming indifference, the vampire smashed his boney fist through the glass and then soared through the gaping hole and into the dimly lit cabin. Before the old man could move, Krulak's serpentine fangs dug mercilessly into his neck. The vampire twisted his head maniacally back and forth until he could hear each cervical vertebrae crack.

He reared back his head and laughed. That had been far too easy. Unsatisfied and wanting more, Krulak decided to find the little sports car he had encountered a short time earlier. He was sure the young woman inside it would put up more of a fight than this old man.

Chapter 72

Sarah was still shaking when she got to work. She checked in and then went straight to the locker room and texted Patrick. Tears rolled freely down her pale cheeks as she hit the send button. Surely, he'd answer this message. Sarah didn't know what to do; she was so frightened.

A hand gently touched her shoulder, and Sarah nearly jumped off the wooden bench she was sitting on.

"Anything wrong?" came a pleasant voice from behind.

Sarah sniffled, wiped the tears away and looked up to see her temporary supervisor standing over her. "If I tell you, you'll think I'm a lunatic," Sarah replied, echoing Patrick's own words from a past not so long ago.

"Try me. I've seen and heard a lot of strange things in my lifetime."

"You've never heard anything like this."

Sonia Garcia sat down on the bench, smiled and waited.

Sarah proceeded to tell Garcia everything from the time she met Patrick and processed her first vampire crime scene to the incident that happened on her way to work. She did, however, leave out any mention of Sebastian.

"Oh, chica! What you've been through! But I appreciate you sharing this information with me."

A puzzled look fleeted across Sarah's beautiful face. "I really thought you'd relieve me of duty when you heard my story."

"Not at all."

"So you believe me."

"Yes, I do. Since I was a child in Mexico, my parents and older siblings called me *loco*."

"Why?"

"Because I've seen what you've seen."

Sarah gasped.

"I was almost ten years old. It was late August and very hot and very humid. I couldn't sleep, so I decided to sit in my open window and gaze at the stars. I remember the Northern Star seemed brighter than usual, and I thought that was a good omen for making a wish. Just as I finished my wish for a gatito, a kitten, this horrible black creature flew past my window. It passed by several times before it came to rest in front of me."

"Oh, my God!"

"I will never forget what it looked like. It was like a rotted corpse with wings and gruesome fangs and claws. Its eyes burned like hot coals, and I was paralyzed with fright. I tried to call for my parents, but no sound came out of me. The creature just stood there laughing, and then it lunged at me. As his claw grazed my arm, I finally cried out, and my papa came running into my bedroom."

"Your father must have believed you when he saw your injury."

"No. Papa thought I had scratched my arm on a nail in the window frame. He told me I had a bad dream and put me back to bed."

"Did the creature return?" Sarah asked in a small voice.

"Luckily no, but I feared it would. And now it looks like it has."

"It may be Krulak or even another hellish creature. There are probably more of them than even Father Martin is aware."

"I imagine so."

"What do we do now?"

"I suppose we need to wait until Father Martin contacts you. This is more than the two of us can handle."

"I agree."

"Now that we've told one another our stories, I have a question for you," Garcia said sweetly.

"Okay."

"The dagger that was stolen from Father Martin, I've never seen anything like it. Is it for killing vampires?"

"Yes. That's why he was so distraught when it was stolen and the reason why he had to return to Rome. The dagger was specially crafted of tempered steel and the highest grade of silver. The main blade and the two smaller daggers represent the Trinity. Only a holy dagger like this one can kill a vampire."

"Let's hope it will soon be put to use."

"God willing," Sarah replied.

Chapter 73

The key rattled softly in the lock, and Sarah wearily opened the door, uneasy about finding Sebastian home. She called out his name, but only Bagheera answered. He scampered up to her feet and pawed at her leg, demanding to be held.

Sarah grabbed the sleek black cat and cuddled him close. He purred with contentment.

"Have you been fed this morning?" Sarah asked as she carried him into the kitchen.

A full bowl of food and water sat on the floor near the refrigerator. A vase of red roses that hadn't been there the night before sat on the kitchen table. Beside the vase was a note.

My Love:
I've gone to the Farmer's Market.
Your dinner is in the oven.
I will see you later when you wake.
Sweet dreams.
Your Sebastian

Detective Devereux was wrong. Sebastian was a good man. There was no way he could have been involved in Katrina Bello's death or with Anton Krulak. At best it was all a horrible mistake and worst an unfortunate coincidence. He'd explain everything when he got home, and then they'd go see Detective Brown and explain everything to him.

After eating Sarah tried desperately to sleep but found it impossible. No matter how she tried to explain things to herself and deny the truth, the facts were there: the horrific crime scenes; Patrick and Sebastian's arrival in town the same time the vampire killings began; Sebastian lying about being Hungarian; and then there was Bagheera. Brittany Anderson's black kitten had disappeared at the time of her murder, and Sebastian suddenly appeared with a black kitten as a Christmas gift.

Sarah finally gave up on sleep and decided to watch TV for a while. Listlessly, she shuffled into the living room and threw herself down in the recliner. As she channel surfed, her mind wandered and her gaze followed. On the desk next to a pile of mail, Sarah noticed Sebastian's journal. Normally, she wasn't one to spy on anyone, but the circumstances were quite different now.

As expected the journal entries covered Sebastian's travels in America. He detailed the cities he'd visited with their restaurants and tourist sights, but more than that the journal was filled with comments about Anton Krulak.

Sarah felt like vomiting, but she willed away the nausea and continued to flip through the pages, stopping to read random entries.

June 15th, New Orleans: The master was in excellent spirits tonight. He won big at the roulette table. The Maison Blanc Gaming Club has always been extraordinarily lucky for him.

July 30th, Las Vegas: This is a lonely city. Although the master has found several lovely companions on our many trips here, I can find no one other than gold diggers and whores.

August 23rd, New York: The social season will begin soon. This is the master's favorite time of the year. The city is beautiful, especially at night. Krulak will make the most of our time here.

September 19th, San Francisco: The master has been in a foul mood for several days now. I questioned him on some trifle and was punished with the full fury of his anger. I can still feel his pale hand around my throat. I thought tonight would be my last.

October 12th, Carson City: We arrived in Carson City today. The master loves this town, although I cannot understand why. While here, he insists on staying at the St. Charles, a dilapidated relic from another time. I find it quite depressing.

October 15th, Carson City: Words cannot express my feelings about today. I saw the blond priest and was seized with incredible fear both for my master and myself. However, that fear suddenly disappeared when I saw his companion. At first I thought she was an angel, but then I realized she was only a woman, the most beautiful woman I have ever seen. She had short, auburn hair and eyes the color of cornflowers, and her laugh was as sweet as honey. When I was granted a glimpse of her smile, I knew my heart was lost forever.

"What are you doing?" came the harsh demand.

Sarah began to tremble, the fearful images of Krulak's deeds violently forming in her mind. The vampire had killed countless men, women and children, and the man standing before her was his faithful servant.

Chapter 74

"Everything you've told me from the moment we met has been a lie!"

"Please, Sarah! That isn't true!"

"Isn't it?"

"No!" Sebastian pleaded.

"Then how do you explain this?" Sarah spat, throwing the journal in his face.

Sebastian flinched as the journal sailed past his cheek, grazing it ever so slightly.

"Please listen to me. I love you!"

"How can a man who serves a monster love anyone?"

"I never had a choice. Believe me. My family has been indentured to Krulak for almost one hundred and fifty years."

"Your family in Hungary?" Sarah snapped, her voice heavy with sarcasm.

"No. I'm Romanian," Sebastian confessed. "I come from Sighisoara at the foot of the Carpathian Mountains. It's the home of many vampires, Anton Krulak being one of them."

"Yet you have no reservation about serving a vampire, a creature of hell?"

"I'm tortured daily by what I've done. My soul is damned, have no doubt about that!"

"As it should be."

The big man's shoulders drooped in despair, and he bowed his head in shame. Sarah would never forgive him, nor would God.

"I—"

"What? Are you trying to spit out another lie?"

"I left Krulak in San Francisco. I couldn't go on with my life. I came here until I could find a way to kill him."

"Only a vampire hunter with a sacred dagger can kill a vampire! You know that!"

"Is your friend the priest a vampire hunter?"

"Yes! And one day he'll kill Anton Krulak and you!"

Sebastian stumbled backward, stunned by the fierceness of his lover's words.

Sarah relented when she saw the devastation on Sebastian's handsome face, but her anger remained. "If you want to live, get out of my house and out of this town! Now!"

Sebastian's soft brown eyes pleaded once more for forgiveness, but Sarah turned her head, refusing to accept the unspoken plea. Crushed, he said nothing as he turned and stormed from the townhouse, slamming the door in his wake.

Sarah crumpled to the floor with remorse and wept.

Chapter 75

Brother Ciaran ambled into the gymnasium and looked around. He spotted his friend on the far side of the enormous room, surrounded by students.

"Excuse me," Patrick said as he moved from the throng and walked toward the monk.

Sofia's gaze followed. She adored him.

"G'day!" Patrick said happily.

"And a good day to you! Graduation is here at last, and I'm sure your students are excited."

"They can't wait to get out into the field. After Mass this evening, they'll pack their bags, and tomorrow bright and early they'll receive their first assignments and be off."

To the far ends of the earth they shall scatter. Brother Ciaran mused. "When's your next class?"

"Another cadre of students won't arrive for at least a month. But until then, I'm sure I'll find something to keep me busy."

"You can always help me in the apiary. You're getting very good at beekeeping, Patrick."

"I'll have to add that to my resume," the priest replied with a wink. "Did you come by to chat or was there anything you needed?"

"My needs are few, my dear lad, but I did want to tell you that the cell phone you requisitioned is no longer manufactured, so I had to begin your paperwork all over again. You'll have a new phone in two to three weeks."

"It's not that important. It's not like I'm waiting for a call from the Pope."

"You never know. I'm sure the Holy Father would enjoy hearing about your many adventures."

"No doubt he would."

"Excuse me, Padre," Sofia said, interrupting the conversation. "I need to ask you something."

"What is it?"

"After Mass tonight, we're all going out to celebrate graduation, and we wanted to invite you to come along."

"I appreciate the invitation, but you and your friends should go by yourselves. You don't need an old bloke like me hanging around."

Sofia wouldn't take no for an answer and insisted that the handsome priest join her and her fellow graduates for a night on the town. After all, when would they ever be together again? She didn't say anything about some of them not surviving long in their new careers and tried to put that thought in the back of her mind.

"Okay! Okay! I'll meet you at Boomerang Jack's at nine o'clock."

"Great!" Sofia gushed. "You're going to have a terrific time."

* * *

Boomerang Jack's was an Aussie pub that Patrick enjoyed going to on occasion. It wasn't like being back home in Ballina, but it was the next best thing, especially in Italy. *Sarah would like it there*, Patrick thought.

A sharp pain lanced at his heart, and he rebuked himself for not calling her since he returned to Rome. But what would he say to her? She knew he loved her, but what could he offer her? If he left the priesthood, how could he make a living? He'd never been anything but a priest.

It was better for them to go on with their separate lives. Speaking and writing to one another would only bring them pain and unfulfilled promises. Sarah was young and beautiful; she'd meet someone and get married and have a family. She deserved that. She deserved to be happy, and more than anything else in this world, Patrick wanted Sarah to be happy.

Chapter 76

It was Friday night, and Boomerang Jack's was roaring as Patrick made his way through a crowd of young people.

"Evening, mate!" came the greeting from several of the regulars, a greeting he returned in kind.

Patrick was dressed in civilian clothes, a black Oxford shirt and black jeans. The appreciative glances he received from the women he passed by did not go unnoticed, not by him nor the other men in the pub. It still amused him that women found him attractive. *Must be the accent.*

"Padre!" Sofia called out over the crowd, waving him to where she and a dozen other students sat at a long, wooden table. "I'm so glad you could come."

"Me too," he replied shyly as a passing patron jostled him.

"What are you drinking, Father?" the young Russian named Arkady Petrov asked.

"What else? A Fosters."

Arkady grabbed a barmaid as she passed by their table. "A Foster Lager for Father Patrick," he ordered.

The pretty brunette eyed Patrick up and down. "Father?"

"The finest priest in all of Rome!" Arkady declared with pride.

What a waste, the barmaid thought as she took the order. "Anything else?"

"Another round, my good woman," John Hampton, a student from Coffs Harbour, Australia ordered.

"Sit, Father," Arkady directed, patting the seat of the chair he'd been saving for his teacher.

"Thanks!" Patrick replied and sat down. But before he could get comfortable, the students began bombarding him with questions about his time out in the field. Each of them was eager to hear more details about the stories he had used as classroom lessons. After sixteen years of hunting vampires, Patrick had enough stories to fill half a dozen books.

Several rounds of drinks were ordered during the course of the night. Patrick was beginning to feel their effect, or maybe he was just feeling his age.

"I'd better call it a night," he said, after draining his last pint of the golden brew.

Despite the overwhelming protest, Patrick insisted.

"Before you go, Padre, we need to take pictures," Sofia said as she grabbed her cell phone from her purse.

Her fellow students gathered behind the priest. Their youthful smiles were filled with happiness and unabashed confidence. She clicked a few photos before turning the camera on herself and Patrick.

"This one is for me," Sofia said. But just before she took the shot, she turned and kissed Patrick on the cheek.

He could feel his face flush.

"Don't worry. No one will ever see our selfie," she whispered. "I just want to remember tonight; the way we are now. Who knows what heaven has in store for us."

Sofia's words hit him hard. She wasn't much more than a child, and neither were her classmates. And Patrick knew he was likely sending many of them to their deaths.

Chapter 77

"Hey there, Baker. Grayson," Detective Devereux said as he and Detective Alcott came into the office.

"Detectives," Sarah replied politely.

Grayson looked up from his paperwork and nodded a hello.

"I wanted you to know that we'll be heading back to Frisco first thing in the morning. There's nothing more we can do here. Looks like this Dragan guy is in the wind, and we have other cases that need our attention at home."

"I'm sure you do. Have a good trip, and please know Detective Brown will keep you apprised of any developments here on this end," Sarah said.

"Sounds good. Thanks again for all your help," Devereux replied as he extended his hand.

Sarah shook hands with the detective and wondered if he could feel her anxiety. She hadn't seen or heard from Sebastian in over two weeks, and she hadn't told anyone about her involvement with him. If Detective Brown, or even West, had the slightest idea she had withheld this information, she could be arrested for obstruction of justice. Her career and life would be over.

She was still trying to come to terms with Sebastian's lies and life. The Sebastian Sarah knew was kind and gentle, and she finally realized he had lied to protect her. Yet that didn't change the fact he was indirectly responsible for the deaths of countless people by abetting the vampire in his evil existence. How could she forgive and forget that?

"Don't be so down," Grayson said as he gazed at his forlorn partner.

"Huh?" she replied, emerging from her dismal thoughts.

"The Dalton and Anderson homicides will go into the cold case files for now, but that doesn't mean they won't be solved eventually."

"I suppose you're right. We need to remain positive."

"Yes, we do, and we need to concentrate on the evidence in the cases that can be solved."

"I'll try."

"Good! Want to help me finish up these case files?"

"Sure." Sarah grabbed a stack of file folders and went to work. She had just signed off on the first case file when her desk phone rang. "CSI Baker."

"Hello! It's Sonia Garcia."

"Hi! How are you?"

"I'm fine," Garcia replied. "More importantly, how are you? Have you had any more incidents?"

"I'm well, and nothing else has happened."

"That's good to hear. I know you're busy, so I won't keep you, but I wanted you to know that Legal has finally given the go ahead to release Father Martin's property."

"That's excellent news. I'll let him know."

"When will Father Martin be returning to Nevada?"

"I don't think he's ever coming back."

"Then who will take custody of the property?"

"Could I?" Sarah asked, the optimism evident in her voice.

"I don't see why not. I'll let Sergeant DeAngeles in property know you'll be retrieving the dagger."

"Great! I can pick it up after shift."

"That would be fine. Take care, Sarah. Keep me informed if anything else happens."

"I will."

Sarah was beaming. Patrick would be so relieved, that is if he got her message. She was beginning to suspect he hadn't received her last few texts. So instead of texting him this time, Sarah called his cell, but the phone rang and rang without answer or even going into voicemail. She called Patrick's number several more times with the same result. Undaunted, Sarah went online and tried to find a phone number for the International Association of Exorcists. There was no listing for any such organization in Vatican City or Rome or anywhere in the world.

Chapter 78

Sarah and Grayson caught only one case that night, a robbery at a local convenience store. The perp had worn gloves, a Halloween mask and a hoodie and was in and out of the store in less than two minutes. None of the surveillance cameras had been operational, so there was no video footage to review and no physical evidence left by the robber to process. It had been an utter waste of time, and something the rookie deputy, who had initially responded to the scene, could have handled alone.

Sarah was completely disgusted. Her dissatisfaction in her night's work only acerbated her overall bad mood and desire to be off shift as soon as possible. She was anxious to get to Reno and retrieve the vampire dagger, but she was still unsure what she'd do with it after she had.

Sarah thought about putting the weapon in her safe deposit box but then wondered if she should keep the dagger near should she have any further encounters with a vampire or even Anton Krulak himself. She also wondered if it would be effective in her own hands, beyond making superficial wounds.

It's not that Sarah was afraid to use the dagger, but she wasn't trained in the ritualistic methods of killing vampires, nor was she a member of the clergy. Perhaps she'd only enrage the creature in her feeble attempt to physically kill it and thus extinguish its immortal life force. She could very well be a casualty of such foolishness.

"Ready to go home?" Grayson asked. He gathered up his case files and neatly stacked them on the corner of his desk.

"More than you can ever know."

"All righty then. I'll see you tonight. Safe home."

"You too," Sarah replied as she watched her partner leave the office.

Her trip to Reno this morning was blessedly uneventful. Although Sarah had always loved the night, she was more than happy this trip was being made in the daylight. It seemed as if the heavens agreed. A bright ray of sunshine pierced a fluffy, white cloud in a sky of deepest azure, giving Sarah a profound sense of peace.

Having spent two weeks working at the Washoe County Sheriff's Department, Sarah was comfortable as she walked down the halls of the station. Several people still on shift from that night warmly greeted her.

"Are you Sergeant DeAngeles?" Sarah asked the uniformed officer behind the property room counter.

Next to Patrick this officer was the most beautiful man she had ever seen. His hair was the color of winter wheat, and his eyes were cobalt blue. His skin was fair and flawless and as smooth as alabaster.

He nodded and offered a gentle smile.

"I'm here to collect a piece of evidence from the Abel Montoya case. Sonia Garcia should have informed you the article was being released into my custody."

The officer nodded again and left the reception area, disappearing into the rows of shelving behind him. He returned a few minutes later and handed Sarah the evidence.

She thanked him and then put the plastic encased dagger into her messenger bag. As Sarah was leaving the property room, she nearly ran into a portly, dark-haired police officer coming in. "Excuse me!" she exclaimed.

"Are you Baker?"

"Yes."

"I have your evidence ready. Just give me a minute," the man said as he opened the locked inner door and walked up to the counter. He grabbed a clipboard and handed it to Sarah.

"I don't understand."

"You need to sign for the evidence."

"But I already have it. The other officer gave it to me."

"What other officer?"

"The young man with the amazing blue eyes. I didn't get his name."

"You must be mistaken. I'm the only one on duty."

Chapter 79

Marius had adjusted nicely to his new life as Krulak's manservant. His homesickness was starting to wane, and he was becoming comfortable in Northern Nevada. He enjoyed spending his days hiking in the Sierras, going to museums, and exploring the many ghost towns that dotted the countryside. His nights were devoted to building model cars, a hobby he'd had since childhood. Although he would never become accustomed to watching Krulak transform or seeing the legion of demons that were the vampire's constant companions, Marius accepted his fate. He understood that through his sacrifice his family would continue to prosper.

The day was clear and warm, so Marius decided to walk to the Farmer's Market a couple of blocks from the hotel. He tired of eating in restaurants and enjoyed the fresh fruit and vegetables offered in the summer. He was amazed by the variety and abundance of food in America and wished he could send some of it back home to Romania.

As he wandered through the stalls of produce, Marius felt as if he were being watched. He brushed it off, thinking he was just being paranoid, but the feeling persisted. While at a berry stand sampling the fruit and flirting with the lovely young lady who ran it, he thought he saw a familiar face out of the corner of his eye. He turned to look, but it was too late. The person had disappeared in a blink. Marius thanked the young lady, took his purchase and continued through the market.

Sebastian kept a safe distance as he pursued the dark-haired youth. Even though he hadn't seen his nephew since the last time he and Krulak had travelled home to Sighisoara, which had to have been at least ten years ago, there was no mistaking a Dragan. The boy was the spitting image of himself at sixteen.

As he followed Marius through the crowd, Sebastian could feel his entire body fill with anxious excitement. If Marius were here in Carson City, it meant Krulak was here too and probably staying at the St. Charles Hotel. Sebastian could at last confront the vampire and send him and his legion of demons back to hell! And in doing so, he would redeem his soul and win Sarah's love. Now he needed to figure out a way to destroy the vile Krulak.

Driving aimlessly through town, Sebastian found himself at St. Teresa's. He hadn't been inside a church since he was seventeen years old, but it was now time to make penance for his life and ask God for the strength he needed to bring his long nightmare to an end.

Father Daniels had seen the stranger enter the sanctuary and came up to introduce himself.

Sebastian rose from the pew and politely offered his hand to the clergyman.

"I'm Chuck Daniels," said the short, ruddy-faced priest.

"It's nice to meet you, Father. My name is Sebastian, and I would like to make my confession."

"You caught me at a good time. I just finished lunch. Please come with me. Oh, by the way, would you like to use the confessional or my office?"

"Your office would be fine. God can hear me anywhere," Sebastian replied.

Father Daniels hadn't expected such an odd but precise response.

Chapter 80

The rector of St. Teresa's motioned for Sebastian to sit in a side chair opposite the large, hand-carved rosewood desk. He removed his green stole from a desk drawer, kissed it and placed it around his neck and then pulled his leather executive chair around the desk and set it beside the newcomer. After sitting down, he made the Sign of the Cross and recited a short benediction.

Sebastian followed and said a short prayer of his own before saying, "Bless me, Father, for I have sinned. It's been twenty years since my last confession."

Father Daniels caught himself before the stunned gasp could part his lips. He cleared his throat, regrouped and politely asked, "What do you wish to confess, my son?"

"How long do you have?" Sebastian asked with a nervous chuckle.

Nothing could have prepared Father Daniels for what he heard during the next hour.

When Sebastian had finished his confession, he felt the weight lift from his shoulders and land squarely on Father Daniel's. The priest's face actually paled during the course of the confession, and when it was done he wasn't sure if he should give the man reconciliation or call paramedics and have him taken straight to the psychiatric unit of Carson-Tahoe Regional Medical Center.

In seminary Father Daniels had taken a course on demonology, but being a progressive Jesuit, he dismissed what he was taught as nothing more than archaic superstition. He thought the Church was coming out of the Dark Ages, but obviously people still believed in such creatures as demons, monsters and vampires.

"I can tell that you don't believe a word I've said," Sebastian said disheartened.

"I believe you believe what you've told me," the priest countered.

"Absolve me of my sins then, Father, and I shall trouble you no longer."

Father Daniels bowed his head and replied, "God the Father of mercies, through the death and resurrection of his Son, has reconciled the world to himself and sent the Holy Spirit among us for the forgiveness of sins; through the ministry of the Church may God give you pardon and peace, and I absolve you of your sins in the name of the Father, and of the Son, and of the Holy Spirit. Give thanks to the Lord for he is good. Now say a heartfelt Act of Contrition and go in peace to love and serve the Lord."

Sebastian muttered an angry amen and started to leave the office but was stopped by the priest's parting words.

"Before you go, there's one thing I learned in seminary that may be able to kill a vampire."

"And that is?"

"A silver dagger," Father Daniels offered, feeling somewhat foolish for even suggesting such a thing, but Sebastian was adamant that vampires existed. The priest hoped to God that the man would take comfort in this knowledge and incorporate it into his fantasy and not actually try to use such a weapon on some unsuspecting soul.

* * *

The shop bell dinged as Sebastian walked through the door of the small but elegant jewelry store. The owner, a svelte, middle-aged man with a shaved head and a burly, black mustache, greeted him.

"Good afternoon. Welcome to Coleman's. Are you looking for something in particular today?"

"I need something special," Sebastian replied.

"We have many lovely items from rings to watches."

"Can you make me a silver dagger?"

The jeweler was taken aback.

"I could, but perhaps you should check out our local pawn shops. I'm sure you could find something suitable in one of them, although I doubt any dagger you'd find would be made of silver."

"It must be a strong dagger made of steel but with a coating of silver."

"That would take some time to make, but it could be done for a price."

"Very well."

"I'll draw up some sketches and if there's one you like, I'll give you a price and we'll proceed from there," Arthur Coleman offered.

Sebastian's dark brown eyes bore into the jeweler's. "How long would that take?"

"Two or three days."

"I'll return on Friday," Sebastian said and left.

Chapter 81

"How about some coffee?" Grayson cheerfully asked his partner, although he wasn't sure if she needed any more caffeine. Sarah had been on edge for weeks, but she wouldn't tell him why. He wondered if the absent priest was the source of her irritability. She hadn't said anything about having been in touch with Father Martin. In fact, she hadn't mentioned him in some time, asleep or awake.

"Thanks!" Sarah replied, gratefully accepting the mug Grayson offered.

"Are you caught up on your paperwork yet?"

"Will I ever be?"

He laughed. "Finish one case file, and there's two more to replace it."

"So true!"

Grayson cleared his throat and then said, "You haven't been yourself lately. Do you want to talk about it?"

Sarah looked up from her coffee, her eyes wide with surprise. "What do you mean by that?"

"Come on, Baker. I've been your partner long enough to know when you're in a crappy mood. Hell! I even know when you're PMSing."

Sarah blushed furiously. "God, Grayson!"

"Don't get your panties in a twist!"

"I...I..." she stammered.

"Baker."

"Grayson."

"Talk to me."

Sarah could feel all the rage, sadness and anxiety well up inside her. She had wanted to confide in her friend for a long time, but so many things had happened over the last several months that Sarah wasn't sure where to begin. Perhaps it was unfair to burden him with everything, but he had the right to know at least as much as West did. The truth may set her free and maybe even save Grayson's life.

"If I tell you, you have to swear to God that you won't say anything to anyone. The boss knows most of what I'm going to tell you, but there's a good chunk of it he doesn't know."

"Why didn't you tell him everything?"

"Because I didn't want to get fired."

That wasn't what Grayson expected to hear. "Okay. Shoot. Tell me what you want to tell me."

"And you swear to—"

"I'll swear to anybody you want."

Satisfied, Sarah began her story from her first meeting with Patrick up until the time she collected the vampire dagger from the property room.

"That's one hell of a story!" Grayson exclaimed. "And the Dalton and Anderson crime scenes both make sense now and especially that cold case from fifteen years ago. So what did you leave out? The fact that you're in love with Father Martin."

Tears formed quicker than expected and began rolling furiously down Sarah's cheeks.

"I do love him, Grayson, and I know he loves me. That's why I can't understand why he hasn't answered my calls and texts."

"Did you ever think he might have lost his phone?"

Sarah had never considered that possibility. "Wouldn't he have gotten a new one by now?"

"Who knows? He's a priest. Maybe he had to go through some big pile of Vatican red tape to get a replacement."

"Could be," Sarah acquiesced. She was ashamed of herself for being so angry with Patrick. "I went online and tried to find a phone number for the International Association of Exorcists, but there was no listing anywhere."

"Seriously? Did you really think there'd be one?"

Now Sarah just felt stupid.

"Is there anything else?" Grayson asked sweetly. "Like why you might get fired?"

Sarah licked her lips and looked around the office, trying to find a way to tell her partner she'd broken the law. She didn't want to put him in a bad position and risk his career too.

"There was someone else. Someone I met after I met Patrick."

"So."

"It was Sebastian Dragan. I couldn't let anyone know I was involved with a man wanted for questioning in a gruesome murder. I know he didn't kill Katrina Bello. Anton Krulak did."

"And how do you know that?"

"You saw the photos. The crime scene was identical to ours."

Grayson sat back in his chair and ran his hand over his short-cropped hair. "You're right about that, but how are Dragan and Krulak connected?"

"Sebastian has been Krulak's caretaker for the past nineteen years."

Chapter 82

Grayson nearly choked on the sip of coffee he'd just taken. "Jesus Christ, Baker! You really know how to pick 'em."

"Don't be an asshat, Grayson. You wanted to know, and I told you. I didn't know anything about Sebastian's life until a couple of weeks ago."

"And you care about this guy too." It was more of a statement than a question.

"I do. Despite everything, Sebastian's a good man. You have to believe that."

Grayson blew out the breath he didn't realize he'd been holding. "You really are a hot mess, girl. But mess or not, you're my partner, and I have your back."

Sarah sniffled and wiped the tear that trickled down her cheek. "And I have yours," she replied as she rose and threw her arms around Grayson's neck and hugged him fiercely.

"Don't worry. We'll get through this."

"I know. I'm so glad you're my friend."

"Speaking of us being friends, there's something I've been meaning to ask you. This may not be the right time, but I wanted to know if you'd be my best man or should I say best woman?"

"What? You're getting married?"

"That's a 10-4. I popped the question last Saturday night, and as hard as it is to believe, Kelly accepted.

"I'm so happy for you both, and I'd be honored to be your best whatever!"

They talked the rest of the night, and Grayson told Sarah in no uncertain terms that priest or not, vampire hunter or not, she had to fight for Patrick.

Chapter 83

Sebastian stared at the black velvet bag on his lap, his fingers running across the soft material with almost pious reverence. Slowly, he pulled open the drawstring and then grabbed the dagger by its hilt. The expensive weapon glinted in the soft overhead light of Sebastian's cheap motel room, mesmerizing him with its lethal but simple beauty.

The dagger was seven inches in length and like all daggers was sharpened on both sides but with an overlay of fine silver. The quillon and pommel were devoid of detail and ornamentation, as was the blade, but the hilt was wrapped in a sturdy black and silver braid, making the dagger easy to hold in close combat situations.

The price Sebastian had paid for the dagger, as well as for Arthur Coleman's silence, was worth every penny. Had it cost him his entire fortune, he would have gladly paid it for now he possessed the instrument of his redemption and Anton Krulak's destruction.

Sebastian checked his antique pocket watch. It was almost eight a.m. He placed the dagger into its velvet bag and then left the motel room and headed downtown.

The St. Charles Hotel was one of the first hotels in Carson City. Built by George W. Remington and Albert Muller in 1862, it was initially two buildings but was later joined into one with the hotel on the top floor and the

Firkin and Fox Restaurant, a popular eatery of visiting legislators and local folks, located on the ground floor.

The hotel hadn't been open to the public for several years now, but that hadn't inconvenienced Krulak whatsoever. He paid rent year round and had a small staff on retainer to keep the property in good repair.

Sebastian looked up and down the street and then hurriedly shoved his key into the lock and pushed the brass handle. Entering the hotel, he took the stairs to the second floor. With each step the wooden floorboards creaked beneath the worn red carpeting, making him grimace. Reaching his destination, Sebastian opened the door and peered into the small, dimly lit room.

No one could be seen.

With the dagger clenched in one hand, he shoved the coffin lid open with the other. Expecting the frantic rush of demon defenders to attack upon seeing the thinnest thread of daylight, Sebastian was thunderstruck when there was only the smell of stale earth and a vacant sarcophagus.

"Were you expecting the master?" Marius asked snidely from the shadows.

Sebastian spun around and stared at his young nephew. A mean smile pulled at the youth's lips as he stared back.

"Where is he?" Sebastian demanded.

"He's safe, but as for you," Marius growled, "that's a different story!"

A thin flash of silver cut Sebastian's left cheek, but he parried and thrust before a second assault was upon him.

Marius stumbled backward, clutching his side, as a warm, scarlet rivulet oozed between his fingers. He gazed at Sebastian in stunned disbelief.

"Forgive me," Sebastian pleaded.

"Never!" Marius rasped as he fell to the floor.

Sebastian said a quick prayer over his lifeless nephew and then swiftly fled the room.

Chapter 84

"Good afternoon," Brother Ciaran said as he sauntered happily into Patrick's office.

"Don't you look like the Cheshire Cat," Patrick said. "What are you so pleased about?"

The monk said nothing as he handed Patrick a small, clear plastic box.

"Get out! Finally!" Patrick said with glee. "Crikey! I never thought it would take so long to get a cell phone! Thank you!"

"You're welcome, Father," the monk replied but made no effort to leave.

Patrick eagerly tore open the package and began assembling the phone. Realizing his friend was still in the office, he stopped what he was doing and asked, "Was there something else?"

"I thought you might like this."

Patrick glanced at the envelope in Brother Ciaran's hand.

"The postmark is from Carson City, Nevada, USA," the monk said, his smile growing wider with each word.

A dazzling smile of his own lit up Patrick's face as he gratefully accepted his mail.

"I'll leave you be now, but later I want a full report on how the girl is doing and what she's been up to in that Wild West town of hers."

Patrick carefully opened the letter. The stationary was lovely and smelled faintly of lavender and vanilla.

Sarah had beautiful handwriting, which wasn't a surprise, but it was a surprise she took the time to write a letter instead of creating a word document on her computer.

The letter was several pages long and filled with sheer desperation. Sarah detailed her encounter with the vampire, whom she believed to be Krulak, plus her odd experiences in the property room. The absolute joy Patrick felt when he learned the dagger was safe and in Sarah's hands was instantly crushed by the knowledge she had been Sebastian's lover. Priest or not Patrick was a man, and he now burned with jealousy. Sebastian being the vampire's caretaker seemed inconsequential compared to the knowledge he had been intimate with Sarah.

Patrick finished assembling his new phone and connected it to the charger. In a few hours from now, he'd call Sarah and let her know he'd be on his way to Carson City as soon as possible.

* * *

The frantic tattoo of Sebastian's heart had not ceased since he'd left the St. Charles. He was deeply saddened by Marius's death but livid Krulak had escaped.

"Damn it!" he hissed as he paced around the room, his mind swirling in frustration. How was he ever going to find the vampire now? Sebastian supposed he'd have to let Krulak find him. But how?

When no answer came to mind, he walked into the bathroom and filled the sink with warm water. The cut on his cheek wasn't too bad, but it needed cleaning nonetheless. As he washed his face, Sebastian realized he'd cut his hand. In the chaos he hadn't even noticed, although judging by the wound he must have bled quite badly. *Never mind*, he thought. A cut hand was the least of his problems.

"This is going to be so cool," Lucas whispered to his friends as the teenagers crept up the wooden staircase at the back of the St. Charles Hotel. It was nearly 2:00 a.m., and Curry Street was deserted.

The teen slipped his mom's credit card between the wooden doorframe and the lock. He jiggled the doorknob a few times, and the door opened without resistance.

"Come on! Hurry!" Justin urged, looking up and down the street.

Lucas pushed his friend through the door, and then Justin's girlfriend Zoe followed.

Zoe was having second thoughts about this ghost hunting expedition of theirs. Lucas was obsessed with all the real life ghost hunter shows on TV and had talked his two friends into exploring the St. Charles, which was supposedly haunted by several ghosts from a down and out heavyweight prizefighter to a beautiful young woman of the Victorian Era who believed the St. Charles was a mere stopover on her way to San Francisco. But what was cool on television was just plain creepy in real life.

Lucas switched on his flashlight, and the teenagers walked single file down the creaky hallway.

"All the ghosts have been seen in and around room number three," Lucas said excitedly.

"Who are we looking for tonight?" Justin asked.

"The ghost of a guy named Guy," Lucas replied and then laughed at what he'd said. "The walls of his room are painted like the Valley of the Kings in Egypt. Clint Eastwood used the room in one of his movies."

"Big deal," Zoe huffed. She wanted to leave, and the faster the better.

"This is it!" Lucas stated authoritatively.

Justin and Zoe paused at the threshold of room number three, but Lucas opened the door and walked right in as if he owned the place.

"Come on!" Lucas ordered.

Justin nodded slightly and grabbed Zoe's hand.

Standing side by side with his friends, Lucas swiped his flashlight beam around the little room but instantly stopped when he saw the coffin. "Shut the front door!" He walked around the wooden box but tripped over something in his path. "What the hell?" Lucas exclaimed as he regrouped and pointed his flashlight at the floor.

He dashed from the room, pushing his friends aside.

* * *

Sarah and Grayson met Detective Brown outside the hotel room where he was interviewing the teenagers who had discovered the dead body. Grayson tried not to smirk as he passed the kids, thinking this would be their first and last trespassing incident.

Eliot Parker was crouched over the body, making his preliminary examination.

"What's on our dance card tonight?" Grayson asked.

"Caucasian male, 16 years of age. COD: exsanguination caused by sharp force trauma."

"You're pretty specific about his age," Grayson quipped. "What do you have? A crystal ball?"

"Even better. A passport," Eliot replied, handing the document to Grayson.

"What's with the coffin?" Detective Brown asked, interrupting the two.

"Beats me," Grayson replied offhandedly, pretending he didn't know and continued to study the name and photo on the passport.

"Maybe the kid's a Dracula fan, and he's here for some kind of vampire con," Parker offered.

"You never know."

Sarah, who was lagging behind with her equipment, stopped instantly when she saw the lifeless form on the floor.

"What's his name?" she asked nervously.

"Marius Alexander Nicolescu from Sighisoara, Romania," Grayson replied.

"This boy. He looks like a young Sebastian," Sarah whispered back.

Chapter 86

Sarah hated autopsy. The stainless steel tables and cabinets, bright overhead lights and gleaming white tile walls were as harsh as death itself. She often wondered how such a sweet, sensitive soul like Eliot Parker had chosen such a depressing profession.

Parker looked up from his guest. "I appreciate you coming by this morning. I know you're tired, but I thought you'd be interested in this," he said, handing Sarah a cast of the wound tract he'd made from the body of Marius Nicolescu.

"I'm sure you're just as tired as I am," Sarah replied. "What can you tell me?"

"As you can see, the murder weapon was approximately 177 millimeters in length and double edged, which suggests a dagger. It entered the right upper quadrant of the body, nicked the seventh rib and punctured the liver."

"That will definitely kill you."

"Yes, it will, but the most interesting thing about the wound is that I discovered flecks of silver in it."

"The dagger was made of silver?"

"It looks like it, but who would use a silver dagger?" Parker asked incredulously.

Patrick was still in Rome. Could there be another vampire hunter in town? The odds of that were just too incredible.

"You got me," Sarah said as if she hadn't a clue. "But that should definitely narrow down the matches for the murder weapon if we ever find one."

"It certainly should," Eliot said as Sarah headed for the door. "Oh, before you go, there's one more thing,"

"What's that?"

"There were two blood types present on the body. Obviously, one belonged to Mr. Nicolescu, but I'll send the unknown sample over to the crime lab and see if there's a DNA match on file."

Sarah's mind was swirling as she drove home. Krulak was definitely back in Carson City, and Marius Nicolescu had to have been his caretaker. He also had to be a relation of Sebastian's, a very close one. Their looks were too close to be a coincidence, and besides, Sarah didn't believe in coincidences.

The room where Nicolescu had been killed was an active crime scene and cordoned off with the coffin inside. If Krulak wasn't resting in his coffin at the St. Charles, then where was he?

Chapter 87

"Grazie. Apprezzo il vostro aiuto," Patrick said in flawless Italian to the Vodafone representative on the other end of the line. His carrier had transferred all the data from his old phone to the new, including his contacts. As he scrolled through the text messages, his heart sank at how many there had been from Sarah. She must have been completely distraught when he hadn't responded. Her letter, as desperate as it was, seemed absolutely restrained considering the anguish she'd endured. Patrick chastised himself for having been silent. It hadn't spared her feelings, and it hadn't changed his.

It was almost 11:00 a.m. in Carson City. Sarah was probably in bed sound asleep with Bagheera, but Patrick was sure she wouldn't mind if he awakened her. *I hope she'll forgive me*, he thought as he dialed her number.

The phone rang and rang, and it seemed his call was headed into voicemail. Then he heard a groggy voice on the other end. "Baker."

"Sarah. It's Patrick."

Sarah could barely choke out a hello.

"Are you there?"

"Yes, Patrick. I'm here. It's..." she said, clearing her throat. "It's wonderful to hear your voice. I've missed you so much."

"I missed you too. Are you all right? Are you safe?"

"I'm fine, but I have even more bad news."

Patrick wondered how any news could be worse than the fact Krulak was alive and in Carson City.

"We caught a homicide the other night. The vic was a young man. A Romanian. He was discovered in a room at the St. Charles Hotel."

"A tourist?" Patrick queried.

"A tourist with a coffin in his room?"

Sarah could hear a faint gasp on the other end of the line.

"I think it was Krulak's caretaker. Our ME said the kid had been stabbed with a silver dagger. Did you send another vampire hunter to take your place who may have mistaken Marius Nicolescu for Krulak?"

"No! I didn't."

"Could there be other organizations like yours?"

"I highly doubt it," Patrick replied, almost in a panic. "But if there are, they aren't sanctioned by the Vatican."

"There's one more thing. I'm sure the vic was related to Sebastian."

"How could you possibly know that?" came the incredulous response.

"Because he looked exactly like him, only twenty years younger."

"Oh, Sarah! That must have been quite difficult for you."

"More than you know, but that's not the point. If whoever killed Marius Nicolescu isn't a sanctioned vampire hunter, but just some well-meaning idealist armed with a silver dagger and half the facts, then he or she is in extreme danger. Krulak isn't going to be very forgiving when he discovers someone has killed his servant."

"That's true. He'll be enraged and probably go on a killing spree."

"Patrick..."

"What is it?"

"When can you come back to Carson?"

"I'll be back to you by Sunday," he said and stopped short before adding the words *my love*.

Chapter 88

The vampire opened his eyes and breathed in the fresh soil Marius had added to his new coffin. This soil was high desert soil, dry and tan, and quite unlike the fragrant, rich earth of his homeland. Still, it was vaguely comforting.

Marius had paid the owner of the Autumn Funeral Home well for his master's new coffin and for a space in the business's basement to store it. Krulak would be safe here until Marius could find other accommodations for them both.

Krulak effortlessly pushed the coffin lid aside. Silence and darkness greeted him. After extracting himself from his funerary confines, he walked about the basement until he found the light switch. The overhead light was dim but allowed him enough visibility to see the extra coffins that were stored about. "A home away from home," Krulak said to himself with a chuckle.

He gathered clean clothes from the garment bag near his coffin and changed. There was no mirror in the basement, but Krulak assumed he looked fine enough to go out for dinner at a nearby café. Marius had the Escalade and would be back soon, but until then Krulak needed fresh air and a good meal.

The night was warm and the sky was thick with stars as Krulak headed toward a small shopping plaza. He chose the Mexican restaurant and was greeted by a young senõrita named Consuela.

"Buena noches," she cooed to her latest patron. "How many will be dining tonight?"

Krulak grinned and glanced around and then with a wink replied, "It looks as if it will be only me."

"Very good," the hostess replied and showed him to a small table by the window.

The meal was far better than Krulak had expected, and the fajitas were rare, almost bloody, and just as he had ordered. He hated arguing with cooks about whether or not meat should be thoroughly cooked, and he appreciated it when his meal was served as requested.

When the vampire had finished his last sip of wine, he reached into the breast pocket of his jacket to retrieve his wallet. He was shocked and incensed when his fingers brushed only an empty space inside.

"Here's your check, senôr," the waitress said as she placed a black, plastic tray with the bill in front of him.

"I have a slight problem."

"A problemo?"

"It seems I left my wallet at home. I can go get it and be right back."

The waitress looked the man over from the top of his well-coiffed head to the tip of his elegant Italian shoes. She assumed he was telling the truth, and as she was about to tell Krulak that was fine with her, the restaurant manager came up to the table.

"And how was everything this evening?" he asked politely.

"It was excellent," the vampire declared, "but it appears I have left my wallet at home. I was telling your lovely waitress that I will go and retrieve it."

"I'm afraid you'll need to pay your bill before you leave, senõr."

Krulak felt his blood pressure rising as he stared at the idiot manager. "How can I pay my bill without my wallet?"

"If you can't pay your bill, senõr, then I will have to call the sheriff."

The vampire's eyes blazed hot with anger, and he could feel the transformation about to begin. But he willed it away with all his might, not wanting to reveal himself, at least not at this particular moment.

"That is not wise," Krulak replied snidely as he threw his napkin onto the table, rose and headed for the exit. As he opened the ornate wooden door, he met a deputy sheriff coming into the restaurant for his dinner break.

"Grab him!" the restaurant manager yelled. "He's trying to leave without paying his bill!"

Krulak offered no resistance. He would remain compliant for now and then later would return and wreak havoc on the manager of Don Jose's.

Krulak was given his Miranda warning, handcuffed and then led out of the restaurant and into a squad car. After getting the man settled into the backseat, the deputy slid into the driver's side, buckled his seatbelt and adjusted his rearview mirror.

"Son-of-a-bitch! Where the hell did he go?"

Chapter 89

Patrick's entire body shook with sorrow as he read aloud the letter Brother Ciaran had given him.

> *Dear Father Martin:*
> *Sofia Pereyra was caught in a vampire ambush*
> *while investigating a derelict hotel in San Isidro.*
> *Her body is being kept in the downtown morgue*
> *and can be released to you upon your arrival at*
> *the Buenos Aires Police Department Headquarters.*
> *My deepest condolences on your loss.*
> *Yours in Christ Jesus,*
> *Father Javier Medina,*
> *Church of the Immaculate Conception,*
> *Buenos Aires, Argentina*

"Sit down, Father," Brother Ciaran said softly as he put his hand on his friend's shoulder.

Patrick dropped hard into his office chair, and as he did a torrent of tears broke from his dam of despair.

"She was so young. She should never have been a vampire hunter," Patrick said, shaking his head.

"It's what Sofia wanted; what she trained for. She knew the risks and willingly accepted them."

"I should have never allowed her to graduate. It's my fault she's dead!"

"Now, now. You know that isn't true, Paddy."

Patrick looked up at the monk.

"If there's anyone to blame, it's Satan himself and the vampires who do his bidding."

"Intellectually, I know you're right, but emotionally I feel responsible."

"We all feel responsible for the lives entrusted to us; my bees and your students. They're our children. We do the best we can, and that's all we can do."

"I know," Patrick replied, the pain palpable in his voice.

"Come to my cell after vespers. We'll have a drink and toast the memory of the dear girl. How does that sound?"

"I'd like that."

"I'll see you later then, lad."

Patrick gave a little wave as the monk ambled from the office. Now he had to call Sarah and break the news to her.

The phone rang once and Sarah answered.

"It's Patrick."

"Is everything all right?"

Patrick cleared his throat and explained what had happened to his star student. Sarah was devastated. It could have easily been someone calling about him.

"I understand. Do what you have to do."

"I'll come as soon as I can. If you discover Krulak's whereabouts, please don't try to do anything by yourself. Just keep him under surveillance without him knowing what you're doing. Promise me."

"I promise."

"Where's the dagger?"

"The same place it's been since I took it from the property room. My messenger bag."

"Good. Keep it with you always."

"I will."

"Sarah...I can't wait to see you. I—"

"Father," came a voice from behind the priest.

"I have to go now. I'll talk to you later. Bye."

"Bye."

"I have your ticket to Buenos Aires," the young deacon said, handing Patrick his ticket and flight manifest.

"Thanks."

"Godspeed, Father."

"And God be with you."

Chapter 90

Miguel Ruiz was locking up the restaurant for the night. He pulled his key from the ornate wooden door and turned to leave the little restaurant, but his path was blocked. The vampire stood before him. A scream roiled in Ruiz's throat but refused to escape his mouth.

Krulak's lips turned up into a sardonic smile.

"Chupacabra?" Miguel finally whispered.

"No," Krulak hissed as he unfurled his dragon-like wings, "but I am your worst nightmare!"

The terrified man stood paralyzed as Krulak reached out a clawed finger and slowly raked it across his chubby cheek. Ruiz could feel the blood begin to ooze, but he made no effort to move. Then the vampire lunged and grabbed his captive's neck in his razor sharp fangs. Ruiz fainted, and Krulak swept him up in his wings and flew off toward the Autumn Funeral Home.

Once inside the mortuary, Krulak headed to the embalming room instead of returning to the basement. He strapped Ruiz to the table and then removed several surgical instruments from a stainless steel cabinet.

"So glad you have awakened," Krulak sneered, hovering only inches above the man's face. "I want you to fully appreciate everything I am going to do to you."

Ruiz's eyes grew as wide and bright as a harvest moon, and he tried to scream, but once again the scream lodged in his throat.

Krulak's serpent-like tongue licked at Ruiz's neck. "You taste like fear."

The vampire took a scalpel in one hand and pried open Ruiz's mouth with the other. Slowly and smoothly, Krulak cut out the thick, pink tongue. The man's agonized screams mingled with those of the demons who circled above, delighting in his torment. Then Krulak took his thumbs and gouged out Ruiz's eyes one at a time until each glistening orb hung pathetically from its socket, held only by the optic nerve.

Thinking the man would have fainted again by now, Krulak was elated to see him still conscious. "What shall we do next? I know," the vampire said as he spotted the surgical saw. He slid the instrument across each ankle, severing the foot between the tibia and the talus. The process was repeated on the hands between the scaphoid and lunate. When Krulak was finished, he tossed Ruiz's tongue, hands and feet into a stainless steel bucket that hung from the end of the table.

Ruiz's throat was raw, and only harsh guttural noises now emerged from his tortured body.

Krulak toyed with the idea of embalming Ruiz while he was still alive, but then a better idea viciously snaked through his demented cerebral cortex. Slipping and sliding across the blood-soaked floor, Krulak dragged his captive's limp body into the next room. Laughing hysterically, he lit the crematorium.

"Ready for the ride of your life?" the vampire asked as he threw Ruiz onto the steel conveyer tray and then unceremoniously dumped the bucket of severed body parts on top of him.

Screaming louder than any soul in hell, Ruiz inched ever closer to the fire. The frenzied cacophony of Krulak and his demons joined in the excruciating song of death as Ruiz was gradually engulfed in the dancing flames.

West tapped on Sarah's office door. "May I come in?"

"Sure, boss. What's up?"

"Parker sent over the DNA results on the blood taken from the St. Charles. Would you mind running them through CODIS for me? Grayson and I caught a new case, and we're headed out now."

"Okay," Sarah replied as she took the case file from the nightshift supervisor.

"By the way, did you hear about the homicide case dayshift processed this morning?"

"No. Where was it?"

"The Autumn Funeral Home."

"What? Don't they have enough business without making their own?" Sarah asked, laughing.

"You'd think. Did you have any hits on the fingerprints from the St. Charles?"

"Not yet, but you know how long it takes to get prints into the system. The backlog is monumental."

"Tell me about it. I'll see you later."

"See ya."

Sarah's computer program systematically ran through millions of possible DNA matches, finally hitting on a match to an unknown subject. This match was linked to the homicide of Katrina Bello at the Mark Hopkins Hotel in San Francisco, California.

The crime lab in San Francisco had the DNA of two unknown subjects from that homicide. Neither sample matched anyone on record, but only one sample had been recovered from Katrina Bello's body. Sarah's detective side took over, and she wondered if the fingerprints and DNA from the St. Charles matched either of those from the Mark Hopkins. If that were the case, then perhaps Krulak could be tied to both cases and thereby eliminate Sebastian as the only suspect. Sarah desperately wanted to believe her former lover wasn't a murderer, but she needed Sebastian's DNA to prove it.

As unethical as it was Sarah decided she would take a few hairs from the brush Sebastian had left at the townhouse and send the sample to the crime lab in Reno for a mitochondrial DNA test. That would settle the matter once and for all. Until then she decided to rerun the prints from the St. Charles in hopes they were now in AFIS.

The prints taken from the St. Charles Hotel matched those from the Bello homicide, and those prints matched both scenes. Although Sarah knew Krulak had killed Katrina Bello, there was no way to prove he had killed Marius Nicolescu, and no way to definitely eliminate Sebastian as a viable murder suspect in Bello's case. Separating Sebastian from Krulak would be impossible until the mtDNA results came back.

Chapter 92

Patrick shifted uncomfortably in his seat. He didn't know which was more irritating, the ridiculously small amount of legroom on this Air Europa jet or the twenty-something year old next to him who hadn't stopped talking or flirting since their flight took off.

As the flight attendant came by, he stopped her and asked how much longer it would be until they landed. He was told they wouldn't land in Buenos Aires for another seven hours, and for Patrick it might as well have been a week.

The young woman finally tired of talking about herself and began asking a multitude of questions. "Where will you be staying in the city? Do you have friends here? Do you know any good party spots?"

Patrick complied and politely answered each question. At last she asked the question he'd been waiting for: "What do you do for a living?"

"I'm a Catholic priest."

There wasn't another word out of the young woman for the rest of the flight.

It was an uncomfortable half-hour ride from the airport to police headquarters, the ancient taxi heaving and sputtering all the way. Its meter, however, seemed to be brand new and on overdrive as the fare clicked higher and higher every few seconds.

"Aquí estamos, senõr," the taxi driver said with an ingratiating smile.

Patrick paid the fare and gave the man a decent tip then grabbed his bag and briefcase and headed into police headquarters. He met briefly with Detective Esteban Gonzales, signed for Sofia's body and arranged transportation for her remains to the airport the next day. When that was finished, he asked if he could see her. Detective Gonzales agreed, and Patrick was shown to the morgue located within the crime lab.

The morgue attendant was young and somewhat anxious as he showed the priest to where Sofia's body was stored. Even though Patrick had seen death many times over and in many forms, he was not quite prepared to see the body of his young student. He took in a deep breath as he watched the metal tray slide out from the refrigeration unit.

Sofia's pale, naked body was covered to the top of her neck with a white sheet, but the jagged red wounds slashing across her throat were more than visible. The deep claw mark across her lovely cheek made Patrick want to retch, but he did his best to remain calm and not be ill.

"Will that be all, Padre?" the young man asked in a mixture of English and Spanish.

"I just need a few more minutes," Patrick replied as he took his stole from his briefcase. He kissed it and placed it around his neck and then retrieved a small, brown wooden box filled with two vials: one holy water, the other blessed olive oil.

Patrick began the sanctification of the rite and then said the invocation. He took the holy water and made the sign of the cross on Sofia's forehead, lips and heart. Afterward, he recited a modified version of the dedication of the soul. "O Lord Jesus Christ most merciful, Lord of the earth, I ask that you receive this child into your arms." He dipped his thumb into the olive oil and made the Sign of the Cross on Sofia's forehead. Lastly, he recited a few lines from Psalm 89, crossed himself and then kissed the young woman's cheek.

The morgue attendant had never seen a priest do such a thing, but when he saw the tears streaming down Patrick's cheeks, he knew this young woman had been very special.

Chapter 93

Krulak was worried about Marius. His young caretaker
had proven to be fiercely loyal beyond the ties of blood
and had secreted him away after discovering Sebastian
had returned to Carson City and was following them.
The vampire had ordered Marius to kill Sebastian, and
the young man said it would be an honor. Marius was
ashamed his uncle had betrayed the master, thus
bringing dishonor upon the entire Dragan family. Death
was far too good for the traitor, but Marius vowed he'd
make Sebastian's death a long and painful one.

But now Marius had disappeared without a trace,
and Krulak wondered if it had to do with Sebastian or
with the vampire hunter who had been in town. One or
the other seemed a likely possibility. If Marius were dead
or had run away, this was more than a mere
inconvenience for Krulak. There were many tasks that
could only be accomplished with the help of a human;
driving was one of them. Even though Krulak could fly
as fast as the wind, he could not carry his beloved
sarcophagus or his wardrobe with him as he did so.

The vampire needed to return to the St. Charles. If
Sebastian had been there, he'd be dead and gone by
now. As for Marius, that was another matter. Perhaps
he'd been arrested or had been seen committing the
deed and had fled from the area. Without any way to
communicate, Krulak had no idea exactly what had

happened, but he feared he would never see Marius again.

Krulak emerged from his basement sanctuary shortly before midnight. He had completed the transformation prior to leaving and was headed to the St. Charles Hotel when he spied a young woman walking, presumably home from work. He flew above her for several blocks until she reached a two-story apartment complex off College Parkway. The woman had no clue she was being stalked as she walked into her building. Once inside her apartment, she turned on the lights and opened the blinds and windows.

Krulak watched the young ebony beauty, whose skin was the color of milk chocolate, strip off her clothes and discard each piece one by one on the carpeted floor. When she reached her bedroom, she was completely naked. "What a shameless little exhibitionist you are," Krulak said with a mocking laugh. He would enjoy this one. In fact, he would take his time with her.

The young woman went to the bathroom but returned to the bedroom moments later. Goose bumps raced up her slender arms, and her heart beat erratically with fear when she found the room engulfed in darkness. The bedroom lights had been on; she was sure of it. She reached for the light switch, but instead of feeling the plastic switch beneath her quivering fingers, she felt only a cold, clawed hand. As she screamed for help, another cold hand clamped down hard across her mouth.

"Be still, my beauty," Krulak hissed.

He grabbed the young woman by the throat and savagely tossed her to the bed and was upon her before she took another breath.

"No! No! This can't be real! This is a nightmare!"

The vampire raked his fangs across the smooth, flawless skin of her neck, and tiny droplets of blood followed each grazing pass. Krulak savored the exquisite taste of her life force, and her tremulous body awakened the desire of the man within him. He roughly kissed her breasts and then trailed kisses down her abdomen. Forcing her legs apart, he was about to take her when there was a loud pop.

A hellish shriek erupted from the center of Krulak's being as he grabbed his chest. The pain was excruciating. The young woman lay panting on the bed, the handgun she kept under her pillow held tightly in her hand.

"You vicious bitch!"

The vampire's demonic protectors swarmed to his defense and descended upon their master's attacker. A thousand razor sharp teeth stung at her flesh, their screams drowning out her own.

"I've never seen anything like this," Sarah said as she stared at Jessica Harrison's naked body. Anymore, that seemed to be her regular response to crime scene victims.

"What on earth do you think caused these bloody welts?" Grayson asked the medical examiner.

"At first glance I'd say insects, but something about that isn't quite right," Parker replied.

"I agree." Grayson removed his magnifying glass from his field kit. "If I didn't know any better, I'd say they're thousands of tiny bite marks, not stings."

Sarah looked at Grayson, and he stared at Parker.

"We'll know for sure when I get this lady back to the morgue. Let me know when you're done taking notes, sketching and have the photos taken. I'll be out in the hall finishing up my notes," Parker said

"Hey, guys!" Detective Brown said, greeting everyone as he entered the bedroom. He'd been interviewing the neighbors.

Everyone nodded their hellos.

"This is Miss Jessica Harrison," the detective said. "A night owl neighbor of hers said Harrison came in around midnight, but as far as she knows the girl was alone. Then around 0005 hours or thereabouts, she heard what sounded like a scream followed by a gunshot. The old lady thought it was Harrison's TV but then remembered Harrison didn't have one, so she called 911."

"Unfortunately, this was real life," Sarah said, surveying the scene, her eyes coming to rest on Jessica Harrison. "Grayson…"

"Yeah."

"This handgun was recently discharged, but I don't see a bullet hole anywhere in the walls or ceiling, and the windows aren't shattered."

Grayson looked around the room. "It had to go into something."

"Or someone."

"Ah, shit, Baker. You're right!"

Brown's phone rang with a lively tune that didn't seem to fit his personality or his profession. "Detective Brown," he stated authoritatively. "I see. I'll be there as soon as I can."

"What's going on?" Grayson asked.

"Someone found a dead guy over on Winnie Lane."

"Is that DB related to this case?" Sarah asked.

"Maybe. He's naked as the day he was born, and it seems he has a big ass gunshot wound in his chest."

"Oh, my," Parker said. "I'll get over there now. My assistant will remove Miss Harrison when you're ready."

"I'll text you the address, Baker. You and Grayson come over as soon as you finish up here," Brown directed.

"Will do," Sarah replied.

"It's going to be a long night," the detective said, shaking his head as he left for the new scene.

Chapter 95

The pain in Krulak's chest had triggered the transformation, but this time he morphed back and forth uncontrollably from vampire to human. Each faltering step he'd taken since he fled Harrison's apartment had been excruciating. By the time Krulak reached the corner of Winnie Lane and Roop, his mortal heart ceased to beat.

A street cleaner discovered him. The man had been horrified to see Krulak's naked body lying like a heap of trash at the side of the road. He tried to administer CPR, but to no avail. He then called 911 and dispatch had called Detective Brown immediately thereafter.

Eliot Parker carefully assessed the man lying before him. The initial cause of death was determined to be exsanguination due to a gunshot wound.

"Do you think this guy is from the Harrison scene?" Detective Brown asked.

"I'd say it's a good possibility. We'll know for sure when we have a ballistics match from the slug in his body to the gun belonging to the victim."

"How long will that take?" Brown asked impatiently.

"As long as it takes," Sarah said as she walked up to where the two men stood talking.

"I'll call you as soon as I extract the projectile," Parker said to Sarah, momentarily dismissing Brown.

"That would be awesome, I…" Sarah said, but stopped in mid-sentence when she saw the dead man at her feet.

"What is it?" Parker asked, somewhat alarmed. Even in the dim light of the streetlights and the flashing lights of the squad car, he could see Sarah pale to a ghostly white.

"It's nothing," she replied with a wave of her hand.

"Are you sure you're all right?" Parker asked, not believing the young woman was fine at all.

"I'm sure."

Sarah summoned all her willpower to keep from shouting, "It's Krulak!" Although the man's eyes were closed, his face was exactly the same as the portrait of the young man on the pendant Patrick carried. But how? Patrick said only the holy vampire dagger could kill Krulak, but here he was in human form and dead as dead can be. Sarah wanted to call Patrick right away, but she had to process the scene and get back to base before she could do that.

* * *

"What a night!" Grayson exclaimed as he stowed his field kit. "I think we've surpassed Reno's murder rate now. And that Harrison scene. How bizarre was that?"

Sarah didn't respond.

"Anything wrong, Baker?"

Sarah grabbed her cell phone from her pants pocket and then sat down at her desk.

"I need to call Patrick. He won't believe it."

"Believe what?"

"That DB we just processed was Anton Krulak."

"The vampire? Are you sure?"

"Quite sure."

"But I thought vampires couldn't be killed."

"Apparently, they can."

Chapter 96

"Hello, sweetheart."

"Hi, Parker," Sarah replied.

"I'm finished with the autopsy and have your projectile. Would you mind coming over before you get off shift and retrieve it?"

"Not at all. I'll see you in a few."

"Could you take Mr. Doe's prints while you're here?"

"That's something I need to talk with you about. I'm leaving now."

"All right," Parker said, hanging up the phone and wondering why Sarah wanted to talk to him about printing his latest guest.

* * *

Sarah arrived at the ME's minutes after she'd hung up the phone.

"What did you do, my girl? Fly here?"

"Don't be so dramatic."

"Me? Dramatic?"

"I know what you meant by that remark."

"You and I both know you have a lead foot. If you didn't work for the Sheriff's Department, that little yellow sports car of yours would have been impounded by now for all the speeding tickets you would've gotten."

Sarah smiled in acknowledgement, but the smile faded as she looked at the corpse on the autopsy table.

"Mr. John Doe, I'd like you to meet Ms. Sarah Baker, the finest CSI in all Nevada. She'll be fingerprinting you this morning," Parker said as he pulled the sheet down to the decedent's waist.

Sarah gazed at the pale face, broad shoulders and muscular torso. The man was perfect. She picked up Krulak's hand and studied the long, straight fingers. Perhaps these were the hands of a pianist or an artist in another lifetime. They were beautiful. How could someone so ideal become such a hideous monster? She laid his hand down on the table and turned toward Parker.

"I don't have to print him to know who he is, but obviously I'll do it for the case."

"What? You know this man?"

"His name is Anton Krulak. He's from Sighisoara, Romania, and there's no family left to claim his body."

"I'll need to notify someone before the final disposition of the remains."

"Could you notify a clergyman?"

"Yes, a priest or rabbi would do."

"Here's the number and address where you can reach Father Patrick Martin," Sarah said as she scribbled down the information on a scratch pad she'd taken from the stainless steel counter. "Let me call him first and tell him the news. Okay?"

"All right."

"I'll call you after I speak with Pat...Father Martin. I'm sure he can send you any paperwork you need to take care of Mr. Krulak."

Sarah retrieved her ink, ink roller, glass plate, coroner's spoon, and Henry ten print card from her field kit and began the fingerprinting process. These prints would definitely tie Krulak to the Katrina Bello homicide and hopefully to Marius Nicolescu's death as well.

"I'm done," Sarah said with a heavy sigh as she wiped the ink from Krulak's fingers and then her own. After washing her hands with industrial grade soap, she carefully replaced the equipment into her field kit. Grabbing the evidence bag containing the bullet taken from Krulak's body, Sarah tucked it into a pocket inside her messenger bag and headed toward the door.

"Thank you," Parker said.

Sarah turned and nodded at Parker and then gave the vampire one last look. "Anytime. By the way, cremation would be the best option," she said and walked out of autopsy without saying good-bye.

Parker shook his head, wondering how on earth Sarah knew that. "That girl is a mysterious one," he whispered to Krulak as he covered him with the sheet.

Chapter 97

"Come on, come on, come on," Sarah said impatiently into the phone. "Answer the damn phone, Patrick!"

She had called the priest several times, but the phone didn't even ring. Her elation over Krulak's death was instantly shattered and replaced with an overwhelming feeling of dread. The last time she had spoken to Patrick, he was on his way to South America to retrieve Sofia's body.

"He isn't answering his phone, and it doesn't even ring into voicemail."

"Don't worry. The last time you got so worked up about him not answering his phone, he had a very good reason. Remember?" Grayson replied.

"I remember."

"Maybe he broke his phone again. I'm sure he'll call you when he can."

"You're probably right, but he needs to know Krulak's dead."

"You'll reach him; don't worry. The main thing is Krulak is dead, and we're about to close nine current homicides and a cold case."

"That's a blessing. Now the families can have some kind of closure."

"And West can get the governor off his back too."

"That will be a relief for us all."

"What do you say I take you to Grandma Hattie's after shift?"

"I say that sounds wonderful," Sarah replied.

The last time she'd been to the restaurant was with Patrick. The poor man had nearly choked when he saw that ridiculous waitress with her phony vampire fangs.

* * *

Patrick took Sofia back to her home in San Ramon, Argentina, a mountain town six miles east of San Carlos de Bariloche. There she would rest beside her father and grandfather, both vampire hunters.

San Ramon was once suspected as the place where Adolf Hitler and Eva Braun had fled to at the end of World War II. Historians dismissed the notion that they had survived and the bodies found in the bunker were not theirs but the couple's doubles. Those who knew the truth knew the infamous dictator and his mistress, and many of those in the upper echelon of the Nazi Party, were vampires. It was very possible that Hitler and Braun still lived in the area along with many other Nazis, human and vampire alike, who had avoided prosecution for their war crimes.

Sofia had grown up hearing tales of her father and grandfather's exploits as vampire hunters, and she wanted to be just like them. Early on she had suspected that the kindly old headmaster of her school, Herr Felix Richter, was a Nazi and a vampire just like SS Hauptsturmführer Erich Priebke.

In 1946 Priebke fled Europe with the help of a bishop stationed at the Vatican, something that still embarrassed the Vatican to this day. In 1995 Priebke was discovered living under an assumed name and employed as the director of the German School of Bariloche. He was arrested and deported to Italy to stand trial for war crimes there.

While it is still unknown how and why Priebke had remained in human form, it is known that after many delays he was finally tried for his war crimes. However, he was found not guilty. Appeals followed and Priebke was eventually convicted and sentenced to seventeen years in prison. That sentence was reduced to ten years and then to house arrest due to his age. In October 2013 it was reported that Priebke had died from natural causes at the age of 100. The truth was that he had been killed at last, and by Sofia's father, in the Italian town of Albano Laziale just outside Rome.

Only Sofia's immediate family had attended her funeral Mass. Although her heroism would never be known to the townspeople of San Ramon, her life would be celebrated by her mother, brother and by the members of the International Association of Exorcists and its covert organization of vampire hunters.

Young Rafael Pereyra, age seventeen, vowed to follow in the footsteps of his sister, father and grandfather. He boldly declared that after university, he'd come to Rome and train as Patrick's new protégé.

Patrick thought the Pereyra family had sacrificed enough, but nothing he said could dissuade the young man from his ambition or his destiny. In the end Patrick acquiesced and gave the young man his blessing.

"See you in Rome, Padre," Rafael said as he saw Patrick off at the airport.

"I'll see you there."

Chapter 98

"Oh, my God, Patrick," Sarah said breathlessly as he finally answered his phone. "I'm so happy to hear your voice. You won't believe what's happened."

"And hello and how are you too," Patrick replied.

Sarah caught her breath and calmed a bit. "I'm sorry. Hello. How are you, and where are you?"

"I'm in Rome. I got in last night."

"Are you well?" she asked, her voice slowing to a normal pace.

"I'm well. Don't worry."

"How was the funeral?"

"Sad as one would expect."

"The poor family."

"Tell me what you're so excited about," Patrick said, quickly changing the subject.

"Krulak's dead!"

"What? That can't be."

"It's the honest to God's truth. I saw his body myself. He was shot while in human form and died. He's in the morgue now. We have his prints and DNA, so he can be tied to the homicides both here in Nevada and in California."

Patrick was incredulous. He had never heard of a vampire being killed by a gunshot while in human or vampire form, and he was having difficulty believing it. It went against everything he knew.

"I don't know what to say. This is unbelievable."

"Krulak was brought into the morgue as a John Doe. Parker asked me to print him so the body could possibly be identified, but I told him I could identify the corpse without any fingerprints."

"You didn't tell him about Krulak, did you?"

"No, but I did say the body wouldn't be claimed because Krulak didn't have any family."

"What's going to happen to him? He can't be buried in consecrated ground."

"I asked Parker to have the body cremated, but he needs authorization from Krulak's priest to do so."

"But he doesn't have one."

"Yes, he does."

"Who?"

"Congratulations on the newest member of your flock. I gave Parker your info, and he'll be in touch later."

"Okay, sheila. That's ace with me. I suppose it's the least I can do."

Sarah's heart skipped. Patrick hadn't called her sheila for some time. "It's over, Patrick. Isn't it wonderful?"

"Yes, but this changes everything," he replied with a slight catch in his voice.

"What do you mean?"

"With Krulak dead, I'll need to stay here in Rome and await my next assignment. I may stay here to train the next cadre of students, or I could be sent back into the field. It all depends on what the council wants. I'll send Brother Ciaran for the dagger. He can be in Carson at the end of the week."

"You're not coming back?" Sarah's voice was small and tenuous.

"There's no reason for me to return."

No reason to return? she thought. *What about me?* "I see," she finally rasped into the phone after a lengthy delay. "Don't worry about anything here, Father. I'll give Brother Ciaran the dagger, and you can wash your hands of everything," Sarah said and hung up.

"Sarah. Sarah," Patrick said to the dial tone.

Chapter 99

Mitochondrial DNA was easier and quicker to process since it was based solely on the mother's DNA. It had been a week since Sarah had sent Sebastian's hair sample to the crime lab in Reno, and the results were now in. She was ecstatic that Sebastian's mtDNA hadn't matched any evidence recovered from the Katrina Bello crime scene but absolutely devastated that it was a match to the DNA from the blood-covered body of Marius Nicolescu.

Sarah was frantic and knew her hands were tied. She had to tell West and then Detective Brown about her relationship with Sebastian. But killer or not, she prayed Sebastian had returned to Romania and hoped Romania had no extradition treaty with the US.

Since the Nicolescu homicide was still an open case, Marius remained at the morgue along with Krulak. In a perverse way, it seemed rather fitting the two should be joined together in death as they had been in life. Sarah mused that Marius would be Krulak's servant in hell for all eternity, and that allowed her to forgive Sebastian for killing the young man. Marius had not been an innocent and could have tried to kill Sebastian while defending the vampire.

Shift was almost over, and Sarah still hadn't found the courage to speak with West. She knew she'd really screwed up, and it was time to take responsibility for her actions and her heart. *When did you become such a gutless wuss? You've always been on your own, and it's no different now,* she thought. *So get it over with and get on with your life, a life without Patrick and Sebastian and most probably without a job.*

As she walked down what seemed like an endless corridor to West's office, Sarah recited her confession over and over in her mind. Turning the corner, she slammed right into her boss coming from the opposite direction.

"Are you all right?" West asked.

"Boss! I'm so sorry! I wasn't looking where I was going!"

"No kidding," he replied, laughing lightheartedly.

"I need to speak with you, and if Detective Brown is here, he'll need to join us."

"This doesn't sound good." The amusement vanished from West's voice.

"It isn't."

"Let's go to my office. Detective Brown is at lunch now, so it's just us."

Sarah nodded and walked silently to West's office. She felt like a condemned criminal on her way to the death chamber.

"Have a seat," West politely directed. He could tell this wasn't going to be a pleasant conversation.

"Thanks," Sarah managed to squeak out before falling into the aluminum chair opposite West's desk.

"Go ahead. Talk to me."

"I sent a piece of evidence to the crime lab without authorization."

"From what case?"

"The Nicolescu homicide at the St. Charles."

"Did you log in all the evidence from the hotel?"

"As always."

"Then why wouldn't this evidence be authorized to process?" West asked, confused.

"It wasn't taken from the hotel, but it is directly related to the case.

"What is it and where was it collected?"

"I sent a hair sample from a man's hairbrush. The mitochondrial DNA came back as a match to the second blood sample found on Marius Nicolescu's body, most likely the blood of his killer."

"And where did you find this hairbrush?"

"In my bathroom."

Chapter 100

West gathered his stunned thoughts before speaking. "I think you'd better start off by telling me why the hairbrush was in your bathroom. Although I have a pretty good idea, I need to hear it from you."

Sarah furrowed her brow and pursed her lips as she tried to think of a way to make the truth sound not so damning, but it was useless. "The hairbrush belongs to Sebastian Dragan. We were lovers. I wanted to eliminate him as a suspect in the Katrina Bello homicide. I sent the sample to the lab before Krulak was killed and could be linked to the murders. I had no idea it would connect Sebastian to the Nicolescu case."

If West was stunned before, he was sure his two hundred-plus pound frame could have been knocked off his chair right now by a light breeze.

"And all this time you didn't think it was prudent to tell me or the detectives from San Francisco you were involved with the number one person of interest in the Bello homicide?"

"You saw the crime scene photos Devereux brought. A man didn't kill Katrina Bello. She was killed by a vampire."

"Dragan's a vampire too?"

"No! Sebastian's a man. A good man. Anton Krulak killed Katrina Bello, and the DNA and fingerprints will prove it," Sarah replied, almost shouting.

The Bello crime scene photos were burned into West's memory. They were identical to the Dalton,

Anderson, Sandoval-Ross, and Blakely crime scenes. A man had not committed those murders, and Father Martin had confirmed as much.

"If Dragan's such a good man then why did you think he was involved in the Bello homicide, and how is he connected to Krulak?" West demanded.

"He was Krulak's manservant," came the muffled reply.

"This is too much for me, Baker. I feel like I'm in the middle of some fucking Gothic novel!" West said as he rose from his chair and furiously paced around his office. Generally, he never swore and especially not in front of a woman or a co-worker. Now he was doing both, and he was beside himself with anger and frustration.

"I didn't know Sebastian was involved with Krulak until I found his journal."

"So where's Dragan now?"

"I don't know. I threw him out. I only knew about his relationship with Krulak. I had no way of knowing he could have killed Marius Nicolescu."

"But you had your suspicions."

"No! Not at all! Like I told you. I just wanted to eliminate Sebastian as a suspect in the Bello case. He didn't deserve to be accused of a murder he didn't… couldn't commit."

West relented for a moment. No man deserved to be falsely accused.

"But what about that Nicolescu kid?"

"Come on, boss. He was killed at the St. Charles Hotel. There was a coffin in his room. The coffin belonged to Krulak."

"So you're saying that Marius Nicolescu was Krulak's manservant after Dragan."

"Yes, I am. I'm sure he didn't have a choice in the matter anymore than Sebastian."

"Everyone has a choice, Sarah."

"No. Not the firstborn sons in the Dragan family. For nearly one hundred and fifty years, a son in each generation has been indentured to the vampire. It's how the Dragan family survives. Sebastian was a sacrifice, but in the end he did the right thing. He left Krulak in San Francisco and came back here to Carson to start a new life."

"It's a sad and remarkable story, but it doesn't change things, does it?"

"No, sir."

"I should have you arrested for obstruction of justice or at the very least have you fired for conduct unbecoming an officer of the law, but—"

"But what?" Sarah asked anxiously.

"You're the best CSI I've ever known. I'm giving you a 30-day suspension without pay until I can figure out what to do about this situation."

"What about Detective Brown? Are you going to tell him what happened?"

"Do you really think Brown could wrap that thick brain of his around this situation?"

Sarah offered a timid but grateful smile to her boss.

"Now pack up and get out of here. I don't want to see you until the end of next month."

"Yes, sir," Sarah quickly replied.

"Don't make me regret this decision."

"I won't. I promise."

Chapter 101

Sarah decided to make the best of her suspension. She rarely took a vacation since work was all she really loved to do, but she thought it might be a good time to take up a hobby and maybe start hitting the gym on a regular basis. She hoped the exercise would relieve her depression, which she knew would set in hard in a matter of days when she had nowhere to go each evening. But today Sarah wouldn't think of that; she would tackle her spring cleaning. It was time to organize her house as well as her life.

She started with the kitchen cabinets. Bagheera was determined to help, especially when he discovered which cabinet held his kitty treats. He removed one bag at a time and scattered them across the floor. Then he tried his best to open one of the bags.

Sarah laughed until her stomach ached at the feline's dogged determination to remove the treats from the hermetically sealed pouch. This crushed the little black panther's feelings, as cats don't like to be laughed at, and Bagheera was no exception. In a huff he sauntered off to the living room to take his mid-morning nap.

After the kitchen cabinets were straightened, Sarah began on her dresser and chest of drawers. She had so many clothes she didn't wear because her work clothes consisted of khaki cargo pants and department logo polo shirts, not exactly trend setting but comfortable and practical in the field.

Feeling accomplished and a bit empowered after filling two bags for charity, Sarah turned to her wardrobe. The gold-framed mirrored door glided across its aluminum track, revealing a neat but packed rack of clothing and a shelf filled with boxes of various sizes.

One by one she flipped through the hangers, pulling out blouses, pants, sweaters, and jeans she hadn't worn since Barack Obama's first term. Another two bags were filled with clothing, some of which was brand new. *Maybe if you had a social life you could have worn some of these outfits.*

The wall safe was now visible between the culled out rack of clothing. Patrick's vampire dagger was stored securely inside. Brother Ciaran would arrive soon and retrieve it, and that would be the last of the dagger and definitely the last of Father Patrick Martin.

Sarah could feel her throat tighten as the burning tears welled up in her eyes. But she forced them away and scrunched several blouses in front of the safe, so she wouldn't dwell on the dagger or the priest any longer.

Instead of using a step stool to reach the storage boxes on the shelf above her clothing, Sarah stubbornly tried to remove them by standing on tiptoes with arms outstretched. As one box came off the shelf, four others followed. Odds and ends, souvenirs, gloves, scarves, and junk lay scattered at her feet. In the middle of the pile was a stack of envelopes tied with a red ribbon. *These must belong to Sebastian.*

Curious, Sarah retrieved the stack of envelopes. They weren't addressed to anyone, so she opened one and scanned the contents of the letter inside.

The words were elegant and intimate, and Sarah had never read anything more beautiful in her entire life. She could hardly believe Sebastian was writing about her instead of some lovely heroine from a Victorian novel. The depth of his feelings stunned her. No one had ever thought of her as their very breath of life or reason for being.

The tears that had threatened earlier now crested and fell down her cheeks in earnest.

Chapter 102

Orlando West dropped two case files onto Detective Brown's cluttered desk. "The first file contains the prints, DNA and the ballistic report from the perp at the Harrison scene. They match our friend in the morgue."

"Well, that nicely wraps up our case. And the second case file?"

"DNA and fingerprints from the St. Charles Hotel matched evidence taken from the Bello homicide in Frisco. We have a person of interest," he said begrudgingly.

"Anyone we know?"

The nightshift supervisor nodded. "Sebastian Dragan. Would you put out a BOLO on him and then contact Detective Devereux? Tell him about both cases."

"Will do."

Knowing what he did, West was sure there was more to Nicolescu's death than evidence from the crime scene would suggest. That, and the fact Dragan had been involved with Sarah, was enough to make him think the murder had been committed in self-defense, especially since Nicolescu had been Krulak's latest servant. West was at least comforted by the knowledge that evidence not only convicted the guilty but exonerated the innocent. But until Dragan was arrested and tried, there was no way to determine which camp the man belonged.

* * *

Trent Nelson, aged nineteen and a sophomore at the University of Nevada Reno, loved his job as night attendant at the Carson City Medical Examiner's Office. After he cleaned the autopsy, stocked supplies and swept and mopped the floors, he had the entire night to study, that is unless some unfortunate soul was brought in. Luckily, tonight had been quiet, and he was ready to buckle down and study for his Physics test.

As he started the chapter on rational dynamics, Trent heard a faint but odd noise. He stopped reading and tried to ascertain from where it had come, but then the noise stopped. He shrugged and returned to his book. But as he read, the noise manifested again. It was a high-pitched whining noise like a swarm of insects, but this area of the building had no windows, so it was impossible any insects could be present. There it was again. This time the sound was louder and much closer.

Trent gazed about the empty room. Then he looked up and saw a hideous black storm cloud of Krulak's demon protectors swirling directly above him. Suddenly, they swooped down and strafed his face like a thousand, minute fighter pilots. Trent grabbed his face and whimpered in pain. The angry demon army circled and mercilessly attacked once more before disappearing into the refrigeration unit.

It was dark and cold and pleasant. Krulak had slept well, but as he awakened he felt a strange sensation unlike anything he'd felt before in the many years he had repeated the endless dawn to dusk cycle. He ran his slender fingers over his chest and was surprised to feel the raised, ridge of skin that ran from one side to the other, tethered by some kind of filament. He followed it and discovered an adjoining ridge running the length of his abdomen.

Krulak could hear the intoxicating song of his companions humming in his ears, welcoming him to a new night. He whispered back to them as he stretched and reached out to push his coffin lid aside, but his fingers touched only cold steel. What kind of sarcophagus was this? His eyes flew open and then blazed with uncontrollable anger when he realized he was in some kind of vault and not his own safe resting place.

Krulak shrieked and kicked open the refrigerator door, and a thunderous noise enveloped the silent autopsy. Bright light assaulted him, and he cowered but then stilled. It was not daylight that greeted him. He bolted from his confines to find himself standing before a bleeding and frightened Trent Nelson. Krulak reared back and laughed maniacally, finally grasping where he was and why.

"I am not dead, you foolish creature, but you are!" Krulak hissed as he took the young man's head in his cold, delicate hands and twisted it savagely until there was a loud crunching noise.

Chapter 103

Krulak stripped the garments and shoes from Nelson's limp body, dressed in the adolescent attire and then stealthily made his way out of the morgue and into the blessed night. He followed Carson Street to Curry until he was at the back entrance of the St. Charles Hotel.

The weathered, wooden staircase groaned and squeaked in protest as the vampire made his way to the second floor. He entered the hotel and crept down the hall to his room. The door was still crisscrossed with yellow crime scene tape, but Krulak slipped easily through the vinyl restraints.

He switched on the overhead light, his eyes slowly scanning the small room. Everything was as he had left it, including his coffin. As Krulak padded softly toward his dearest possession, a large reddish-brown stain on the carpeting caught him by surprise. Though long-dried Krulak could still smell the delicious blood. He fell to his knees and lapped at the material, not thinking beyond this blissful moment or whose blood it was.

Every nerve ending in his body awakened, and the vampire reeled in near orgasmic ecstasy. He could feel the transformation was upon him. The despised mortal form shape-shifted until he was at last again the perfect creature of hell. He threw open the window and with a delighted cry took to the midnight sky.

Effortlessly, Krulak soared over the serenely lit Capitol building and State Senate and then from one end of town to the other. The freedom was exhilarating, making the vampire feel like Satan himself. Tonight he'd select difficult, high value targets, forgoing the usual dregs of society—the whores and the homeless, the drunks and the drug addicts.

In the distance Krulak spotted a Carson City Sheriff's Department SUV in the parking lot of Mills Park. The uniformed officer sat sipping his coffee, enjoying a brief break from his busy rounds. Silently, the vampire swooped down and lit next to the open window. Sensing someone near, the officer turned his head and to his horror saw a face that could only exist in someone's worst nightmare.

Krulak was upon the man in an instant, tearing out his throat with vicious abandon. Within seconds the interior of the vehicle was saturated with blood, sinew and bits of cervical vertebrae. Satisfied, the vampire regurgitated a mouthful of blood and then spat it across the vehicle's exterior, marking his kill for all to see.

Returning to the sky in triumph, Krulak circled the city, looking for his next victim. The small figure of a woman walking east on Sonoma captured his attention. He followed her until she was directly beneath a streetlight. He wanted to see the fear on her face when he attacked.

Krulak landed directly in front of the middle-aged woman with long, blonde braids. The woman's eyes grew large, but not from fright. This intrigued Krulak.

"My dark angel," she cooed, her mouth open wide.

The soft light glinted off her prosthetic fangs as she spoke.

Amused, he asked, "You know who I am?"

"Yes, my lord. I've been waiting for you all my life."

Krulak liked what he heard. "Tell me your name."

"Tippy," she replied in a small voice.

A silly name for a foolish woman, Krulak thought, but she could be of use to him.

"Would you like to join me in my world, Tippy?" he asked in his most seductive voice. "If so, I can show you wonders beyond belief."

"What would I need to do?" she asked with excitement.

"Care for me."

"I would be honored."

A sly smile gradually formed on Krulak's lips, exposing his serpentine fangs.

Thinking the vampire wished to bite her neck, Tippy bent her head to one side, closed her eyes and took a deep breath.

Krulak's cold lips were upon her skin in an instant, but he swiftly regained his composure, forcing himself away before he lost himself entirely in the glorious invitation.

"You are not ready," he said.

"I understand. But someday I will be, won't I?"

"Yes, someday."

Tippy smiled broadly.

"Come before dawn to the St. Charles Hotel. You will find me in room three."

Tippy was overcome, and her mind swirled with all the possibilities of a new life, a life of darkness and immortality. She knew the St. Charles was haunted, and now its resident vampire was asking her to be his handmaiden. No fantasy could be as sweet.

"Yes, I'll be there."

"Good," Krulak replied as he bent close to her throat and breathed in her scent, a mixture of night blooming jasmine and rose. His long, red tongue slithered across her pale white skin, tasting the fragrance.

Tippy nearly fainted with joy.

Krulak unfurled his wings, flapped them in triumph and then disappeared into the night with his demon army in tow.

Chapter 104

The afternoon sun streamed down from the heavens, gently warming the rooftop apiary. The bees seemed to buzz with sheer happiness, basking in the heat of this glorious summer day. Brother Ciaran checked each hive with the devotion of a loving parent, making sure all his charges were healthy and productive.

Bending up and down, he searched through the honey-filled combs for the perfect ones to harvest. With each movement, he felt the sweat roll from his head and trickle down into his hood. The rough, dense cloth of his habit let very little air penetrate to his skin, which was fine on winter days, but in summer it could be a bit more than uncomfortable. Yet life as a monk was not about creature comfort, and Brother Ciaran considered it a small sacrifice to be able to wear his Franciscan habit rain or shine.

As he continued to work, his breathing became labored. Huffing and puffing the monk soldiered on, taking each golden-filled comb from its hive and placing it into his wheelbarrow. When Brother Ciaran reached the far end of the apiary, his breaths were shallow and coming in rapid bursts. Then a lightning bolt of pain slashed across his broad chest, dropping him instantly to his knees. His chin came down hard on the handle of his cart, and a multitude of stars gleamed before his eyes then nothing but blackness.

* * *

Brother Ciaran gradually opened his eyes. The harsh light that greeted him was not the sun but something artificial, and he could hear a soft, rhythmic beeping sound nearby, which was definitely not being made by his bees.

"Glad to have you back in the land of the living," Patrick said in a voice that was sweet but edged with concern.

The monk's robust, pink cheeks were now as white as the fringe of hair around his head, and his pale gray eyes beckoned Patrick's green for an answer as to what had happened.

"You're all right, but you had a cardiac episode."

Brother Ciaran's brow furrowed.

"Not to worry. It wasn't a heart attack, but you do need to rest for a couple of weeks."

"What?" he tried to ask through the oxygen mask.

"Say again," Patrick asked.

"What about the dagger?" came the weak response.

"It will be fine. Sarah can keep it until I can get back to Carson."

The monk nodded in understanding.

"Sleep now," Patrick directed as he kissed the old man's head.

* * *

Bagheera had settled comfortably into Sarah's lap and was quite aggravated when her landline rang. So was she. Sarah had just turned on her favorite TV show and was ready for a relaxing evening in.

"Hello!" she barked into the phone, thinking it was a telemarketer. They routinely called at this time of night.

"Your suspension has been cancelled. You need to get to the Medical Examiner's office as soon as possible. Grayson will meet you there."

"I'll be there as soon as I can."

* * *

"Dear God!" Sarah gasped. Her bright blue eyes darkened with a raw and primitive fear as she looked at Trent Nelson's lifeless body sprawled on the white tile floor and then at the open morgue refrigerator, its door at least five feet from the unit.

Grayson came up beside Sarah and took her hand in his. "I hope to God one of Krulak's servants did this. Please tell me the vampire's still dead."

"I—" Sarah began to say when the ringing of her cell phone interrupted her. *What now? I'm so sick of ringing phones I could scream!* She grabbed her phone from one of the pockets in her khaki-colored cargo pants. "Baker."

"I need you and Grayson to split up. He needs to meet me at Mills Park. We have a situation," West said.

"What kind of situation?"

"Deputy Douglas Red Horse has been murdered."

"Do we have a suspect?"

"Yes."

"Who?"

"Anton Krulak."

Chapter 105

Sarah's knees buckled, and Grayson caught her before she could hit the floor.

"What's wrong?"

"West needs you to go to another scene. Deputy Red Horse was murdered at Mills Park. West is sure Krulak did it."

Grayson felt his own knees begin to shake and wondered how they were going to explain Red Horse's death to his new widow. It had only been two months since the young woman had been a bride.

"We're going to have to tell Detective Brown everything, or he'll be on a wild goose chase shaking down every dirt bag in town for Red Horse's killer."

"You're right about that, but he's going to have a hard time buying it. Hell! He still thinks half of what CSIs do is magic," Grayson said without a bit of humor.

"Tell me about it," Sarah replied as she retrieved her cell phone. "I need to call Patrick. He has to know what's happened and get here as fast as he can."

The phone rang and rang and finally went into voicemail. Sarah was rapidly becoming frustrated with the familiar pattern, and she nearly cursed Patrick for not answering his phone as usual. Why did he even bother having a phone if he didn't want to be reached by the outside world? Then Sarah reminded herself how aggravated she became when her phone rang incessantly.

She left a message and a text as well just to make sure Patrick got the news.

"I'll send Eliot over as soon as he's finished at his scene. Right now he's at a car wreck out on Highway 50 near the Lyon County border," Sarah offered.

"Okay. See you back at the office." Grayson took Sarah's hand in his and gave it a tender squeeze. "Don't be scared. Everything's going to be okay."

"You promise?"

"I've got your back, partner. Remember?"

"And I've got yours."

"That's ace with me."

"Learning to speak Aussie, are you?"

"Who knows? It may come in handy," Grayson replied and headed out for Mills Park.

The morgue seemed to get even chillier after Grayson's departure. Sarah realized that as many times as she'd been in here, she'd never been alone. That was enough to make her shiver, and she wrapped her arms around herself as the goose bumps furiously raced up her arms.

Trying desperately to shake off the odd sensation, Sarah began her notes. She detailed Nelson's mutilated, young face where thousands of tiny lacerations had sliced his adolescent skin to shreds. She couldn't envision a vampire's claws doing such fine damage, but if not him then who or what? And these injuries couldn't have been the cause of death. But judging by the unnatural angle of Nelson's head and the post mortem bruising that was beginning to appear, Sarah surmised Krulak had snapped the kid's neck with one clean jerk.

After her notes were completed, Sarah measured and sketched the scene. Fortunately, the morgue was small, windowless and rather easy to sketch since it and the refrigeration units and tables consisted basically of squares and rectangles.

Sarah took the obligatory photos: overall, mid-range and close-up. This was the most challenging part of the scene. The camera flash consistently bounced off the glossy white tile walls, causing a frustrating glare on each photo. She removed the flash attachment, hoping that would take care of the flaws, and finished the shots with a longer exposure.

When Sarah checked her new shots, she was astonished. Every photo had numerous orbs of light in it, and not one of those orbs had been visible on her LCD screen.

Chapter 106

The printer hummed as the colored 8" x 10" prints were ejected one by one. Silently, they fell into the tray where Sarah anxiously scooped them up. Print after print was the same. Orbs filled every photo.

She took her fingerprint loop and examined the photos carefully. Given the size of the morgue, Sarah determined that each orb was approximately 200 millimeters in diameter. She couldn't see any place where refracted light could have caused such a strange distortion, but it was clearly there. The orbs were semi-opaque, but some areas within them seemed to be translucent and shimmering with light.

"I've never seen anything like this."

"Neither have I," Grayson replied.

"It has to be some kind of defect in the camera," Sarah said, shaking her head, "or accumulated moisture inside the housing unit."

"But you've never had this trouble before, and as far as moisture goes, we're in a freaking drought. We've both been zapped by static electricity on a daily basis for the past several months, so I can't see how moisture developed inside your Minolta."

"What are you guys looking at?" Deputy Jamie Taylor asked as he placed a pile of mail on Sarah's desk.

"Some photos from the morgue," Sarah replied.

"Can I see?"

"Sure."

The young man looked briefly at the photos and then said, "These look like photos from my aunt's books."

"Your aunt's books?" Grayson queried.

"Yeah. Aunt Arlene is a writer. Her books are about real life ghost stories. She has lots of photos in her books with orbs like these. The photos have been taken all over the world."

"You're saying these orbs are ghosts?" Sarah asked.

"Well, not exactly. The more precise term would be spirits. A ghost is the manifestation of a human being after death, before it goes into the light of the world beyond."

The tiny hairs on Sarah's arms bristled.

"Spirits are something else."

"Are they good or bad?" Grayson asked with a hint of apprehension.

"They can be both."

Sarah took a deep breath and asked, "Does the color of the orb make a difference?"

"I'm not sure. Why do you ask?"

"All the orbs are white except for one. It's blue."

"I'll have to ask my aunt," Taylor replied.

"Will you? But please don't say it has to do with work. I'm afraid there a lot of folks in the department who'd think we're just nuts if they found out we were discussing such a thing," Sarah said, bluntly.

"I understand. My aunt doesn't talk about her work unless she's comfortable with the person asking questions and knows that person is a believer."

"Good to hear."

"There are more things in heaven and earth, Horatio, than are dreamt of in your philosophy," Taylor said, smiling as he left the office.

Sarah and Grayson stared at one another.

"Who would have thought the kid could quote "Hamlet," Grayson mused.

"Who would have thought you knew Shakespeare?" Sarah replied, laughing.

Chapter 107

"You look far better than you did yesterday," Patrick said to his friend as he pulled up a chair and sat down next to the monk's hospital bed.

"I'm feeling a wee bit better," Brother Ciaran replied, "but I'm worried about my bees."

"You needn't worry. They're in good hands. My new martial arts assistant is taking care of them. His father was a beekeeper in Nanchang, and Chin grew up helping him."

"What a blessing that is," the monk said softly.

"Is there anything I could get you?"

"Some honey for my porridge would be nice."

"Any particular brand?" Patrick asked with a devastating grin.

Brother Ciaran said something in Gaelic, which made Patrick laugh.

"I won't stay and tire you out. I just wanted to check on you. I'll be back this evening."

"Thank you, Paddy."

"Anytime," Patrick replied, squeezing his friend's hand.

As he left the hospital, it dawned on him that he hadn't turned on his phone since Brother Ciaran had been admitted. Like most hospitals, the Vatican hospital had strict rules governing cell phone usage, and in most areas it was prohibited.

Not surprising, Patrick had a dozen phone messages and twice as many texts. He returned the call from Cardinal Fontani as he walked back to the Association. The cardinal wanted an update on Brother Ciaran, and Patrick informed his boss of the promising news. Afterward, he called his parents and spoke briefly to each one of them, updating them on his own health and wellbeing while inquiring about theirs in return. Now that family had been taken care of, Patrick scrolled through the rest of the messages. Sarah's was the last one.

He hesitated to return the call at once, preferring to speak with her in the privacy of his office or cell. But the urgency in Sarah's voice to call her as soon as possible precluded that. Enough time had been wasted already, and his heart pounded with anxiety as he wondered what was wrong. He prayed she was safe and sound.

Sarah's voice was thick with sleep as she answered the phone.

"Sheila, it's me. Patrick. I got your message."

"Why didn't you call me sooner?" she angrily demanded.

"I forgot to turn on my phone after I got out of the hospital."

"Hospital? Oh, my God, Patrick. Are you all right?" she asked, now fully awake.

"Yes, yes. I'm fine, but my friend Brother Ciaran had a cardiac episode."

"Will he recover?"

"He's doing fine now, but he has to take it easy for a couple of weeks. We were all very worried about him. He's not a young man."

"I'm glad your friend will be okay," Sarah replied, her voice softening.

"Me too. How are you?"

"There's no time for pleasantries, Patrick," Sarah replied, the harshness returning to her voice with each word.

Patrick was taken aback by Sarah's brusqueness. "Did I do anything wrong?"

Anything? You did everything wrong! Sarah wanted to shout, but she gathered her thoughts and put aside her hurt feelings.

"Sarah? Are you there?"

"Yes! I'm here."

"Talk to me. Tell me what's going on."

"You need to come back to Carson as soon as possible."

"I'm not sure if I can get away right now."

"Well, you'll have to. I can't take care of the situation on my own!"

"Situation?"

"You were right. Bullets can't kill vampires. Krulak is alive."

"I'll be in Carson tomorrow."

Chapter 108

The last flight of the night had finally arrived, two hours late. The Reno-Tahoe airport was nearly deserted save for the few waiting friends and relatives of disembarking passengers and the handful of security, airline personnel and maintenance workers scattered about the concourse.

As weary, unfamiliar faces approached in a neat stream and then fanned out, Sarah could see dark blond curls bobbing above the throng. A smile tugged at her lips and then burst into a full grin when she saw Patrick's handsome face and outstretched arms as he raced toward her. A kiss brushed her cheek, and she was in his arms. They hugged one another a bit longer than they should have but then withdrew and exchanged hellos.

Sarah's heart ached as she gazed at the face she'd missed so much. The grief Patrick had experienced in the last few months clearly registered on his handsome features. A few shallow lines now creased the once flawless skin, and age etched at the corners of the brilliant green eyes.

"How's my favorite sheila?"

"Fine now," Sarah replied, trying desperately to hold back the tears. How's my best mate?"

"Ace," came the succinct reply, followed by another hug.

"Your hair's longer than the last time I saw you," Sarah said as she caressed a curl at his ear.

"I've been busy."

They gathered his bag from the luggage carousel and headed to the parking lot. When they got to Sarah's sports car, Patrick surprised her by asking if he could drive to Carson City.

"Aren't you tired?" Sarah asked.

"I think I've gotten my second wind now."

"Okay then," she replied, reluctantly holding out the keys to him.

Patrick winked and grabbed the keys, his fingertips briefly touching hers before withdrawing. An aching sensation lingered, not on Sarah's hand but in her heart.

Soon they were inches apart inside the tiny sports car and headed for home. It had been some time since Patrick had driven, but after a few minutes behind the Beemer's wheel, it was as if he'd never been away. It was exhilarating, and he realized how much he had missed such a simple pleasure.

After leaving the neon lights of Reno, the long stretch of US 395 to Carson City became a dark, monotonous drive, engulfed by the surrounding mountains and a sky as black as pitch. Each time Patrick hit the high beams, an oncoming car would appear, forcing him to return to normal beams. His arms tensed, and his hands gripped the steering wheel a bit firmer.

"This part of the drive always makes me nervous too," Sarah said as she reached out and gently placed her hand on his. "It's so dark and…" she began to say and then remembered her encounter with Krulak on this very highway.

Sensing her change of mood, Patrick looked at Sarah. The dashboard lights illuminated the darkened cabin enough that he could see she was scared and by more than the driving conditions. Then he realized what chilling incident had been tucked away deep inside her memory palace. He pulled the car over to the side of the road, turned on the emergency blinkers and gathered her into his arms. His fingers raked through the short, auburn locks and then slid down her cheek, wiping the tears that streamed unrelenting from her frightened eyes.

"I'm here. You're safe. I'll never let anything happen to you."

"I—" Sarah began to say when a siren's whoop, followed by flashing red and blue lights, silenced her words.

The Nevada Highway Patrol officer stepped out of his SUV and cautiously walked up to the little yellow sports car.

Patrick rolled down the window and looked up at the towering figure.

"Evening folks," he said as the beam of his Maglite flooded the car's interior. "Is everything all right here?"

Patrick shielded his eyes until the patrolman lowered his flashlight.

"Everything's fine. We just needed to pull over for a moment."

The patrolman leaned down and looked into the car. He could see Sarah had been crying. "Are you sure you're okay, miss?"

Sarah sniffled and then offered the man a slight smile. "I'm okay."

"Ah, I see. A lover's spat. You folks be careful now."

"We will," Patrick replied, taking the man's words to heart.

Chapter 109

Krulak returned to Tippy's house feeling randy and on top of the world. He'd won just enough money at the poker table that night to keep from paying the IRS, and he was ready to celebrate.

Tippy had moved all of Krulak's belongings from the St. Charles to her house, believing it was far too dangerous for him to remain at his favorite haunt. No one, including any vampire hunter, would ever look for him at her small, run of the mill duplex on Lee Street.

"Did you have a good night, my lord?"

"Exceedingly," Krulak replied as he circled her.

Tippy swooned at the nearness of him.

"I think the time has come."

The woman's heart pounded frantically with joy, thinking tonight would be her night to join the vampire in his immortality.

"Yes," Tippy whispered.

Krulak slipped a slender finger through each braid, loosening one at a time until the blonde hair fell across his servant's shoulders. Seductively, he unbuttoned her blouse and removed it, dropping it to the floor with a flick of his fingers. Then he grasped her hand and led her to the bedroom. There, he finished disrobing her and was happily surprised that both her body and breasts were still quite youthful.

As Krulak's cold hands held Tippy's pale face, he breathed in the musky scent of her perfume. The fragrance aroused him even further, and the blood coursed through his veins like fire.

Tippy pulled at the fancy, white dress shirt until it was open, exposing a smooth, muscular chest. The wounds from the bullet and the medical examiner's knife had healed completely, leaving no evidence of any trauma from the past week or the past one hundred and fifty years. Krulak had been reborn, and his mortal form was as perfect as it had ever been.

"You're so beautiful," Tippy rasped with desire. "I'm not worthy."

No, you are not, Krulak thought as his teeth bit at her neck and each breast, pulling and twisting her flesh until she cried out.

Krulak and his demons delighted in her agony. Unable to bear his own torture any longer, the vampire stripped the remaining garments from the woman's body and then his own. Roughly, he threw her to the bed and was atop her.

Tippy dragged her long, sharp nails slowly and deeply across Krulak's broad shoulders, and he reared back in unexpected ecstasy. His blue eyes blackened with passion and then burned red-hot. With each savage thrust, he took the woman to the shores of hell until they finally climaxed in a brutal orgasm of blinding pain and satisfaction.

* * *

Patrick was sleeping better than he had in weeks when a mewling sound roused him. A soft, but persistent tapping on the nose followed the sound. He waved his hand at whatever was bedeviling him, but both the sound and the tapping continued. He opened one eye and then the other to see Bagheera almost nose to nose with him. The feline patted at his nose once more.

"What do you want?"

Bagheera meowed once and jumped from the bed, beckoning the priest to follow. Patrick trailed the cat down the hallway but stopped at Sarah's bedroom door when he heard a muffled cry. He opened the door and peered inside. Like the guest room, Sarah's room was dimly lit with a nightlight. Patrick could see her curled up beneath a white satin sheet and in the throes of what must be an extremely bad dream.

Each frightened moan was like a razor cut across his heart. Without a second thought, Patrick crossed the room and slid beside Sarah and gathered her into his strong arms. Instinctively, she cuddled into him, and her breathing once again became rhythmic and deep. Patrick closed his eyes and drifted off to a deep and contented sleep.

Chapter 110

Detective Brown sat slack-jawed, staring in disbelief at his three CSIs and the priest. The story they'd told him was the most ridiculous thing he had ever heard, and he seriously thought of having each of them committed to the psych ward for evaluation.

"If you think I'm buying any of this crap, you're wrong," Brown stated flatly. "For all we know religious fanatics, frat boys or someone working for a cadaver supply company stole Krulak's body. And I'm sure as hell not going to believe this guy was a vampire. Dead men don't rise from the grave unless they're Jesus Christ, and I doubt this was the Second Coming."

Patrick winced at Brown's blasphemy but tried to keep the dialogue going. "I realize this is a great deal to take in, detective, but I assure you everything I and your forensic team has told you is true."

"But what about Trent Nelson? How can you explain his death?" Sarah piped up.

"It was an accident. He tripped and fell and broke his neck."

"Be reasonable," West pleaded.

"What the fuck do you think I'm trying to be?" Brown shot back. "Luckily, this kid had no close relatives and none who wanted to spring for a funeral. His death will be ruled an accident, and as far as Anton Krulak is concerned, he's still dead and his body was cremated. These cases are closed. End of discussion."

"But how can you ignore the facts your own CSIs and I have presented to you?" Patrick implored.

"Believe what you want, Father. That's part of your job. As for my team, I'll just chalk up this phenomenal story of theirs to fatigue from overwork. I'm not about to have them, this department or myself be made a laughing stock. I have a career that I'd like to keep, and if my nightshift would like to do the same, I suggest you and they depart my office at once," Brown said, his whole body now shaking with anger.

"We tried our best," West said as he closed Brown's office door behind them.

Patrick nodded and offered his hand to West. "I appreciate it."

"What now?" Grayson asked.

"We find Krulak on our own," West replied. "Use whatever department resources you need, but do it under the radar."

Grayson grinned.

"I pray Krulak will be found soon, and you and your city will be safe once more, and you all can get on with your lives," Patrick said.

"Do your best, Father."

"I will. You can trust me on that."

The shift had been officially over for an hour, and Grayson was hungry as usual. "Anyone up for something to eat? My treat?"

Sarah wasn't hungry, and Patrick was still tired from his trip.

"Can I take a raincheck?" Sarah asked. "I feel like going home and sleeping."

"Sure. I understand. What about you, Father?"

"I think I'm inclined to agree with Sarah. A nap sounds rather inviting at the moment."

"Another time then," Grayson said.

As he turned to leave, Patrick stopped him. "Thank you for your unwavering support. It means a lot to both Sarah and me."

"She's my partner. I'll always have her back."

A grateful smile creased Patrick's lips. "That's good to hear. And Grayson—"

"Yeah?

"I think it's about time you called me Patrick."

"Sure thing, Patrick. See you guys later. Enjoy your nap," Grayson replied with a wink.

Sarah blushed and then glanced at Patrick who was as red as an Australian King Parrot.

"Hey there, stranger," Tippy said as she pulled out her order pad. "I haven't seen you in here for a while."

"Been busy," Grayson replied as he perused the breakfast menu. "I'll have steak and eggs, cottage fries and a draft beer."

"You got it."

Grayson glanced up at the waitress and nearly gasped when he saw Tippy's fangs and the bruising on her neck and décolletage. *What a freak! You and your boyfriend are really into some kinky shit*, he thought. Then he brushed the visual aside and asked, "Have a new dentist?"

"Why do you ask?"

"Your new choppers. You didn't have them the last time I was here."

"Do you like them?"

"I'm not a fan of dental implants," Grayson replied as he pointed to the thick, pink scar that ran beneath the length of his jawline from his chin to under his right ear. "All my teeth on the bottom of this side of my jaw are implants courtesy of Uncle Sam. A Taliban IED blew out my originals."

Tippy was speechless.

"Don't worry. It doesn't hurt anymore, but it hurt like a son-of-a-bitch when it happened and after the six reconstructive surgeries."

"But you're fine now."

"I'm ace," Grayson replied.

"I'll go get your beer," Tippy said and then scampered away.

Grayson shook his head. If only she knew what he knew.

Tippy returned with his beer and disappeared as fast as she had come. Grayson had almost finished the cold brew when Deputy Diaz and Deputy Schoenfeld came into the dining room for their morning coffee break. Seeing Grayson alone at the table, they asked to join him.

"How goes it on nightshift?" Diaz asked.

"Same-o same-o," Grayson replied and then took another gulp of beer.

"Anything new with the Red Horse murder?" Schoenfeld asked as he grabbed a menu. "The funeral is next Thursday, and it'd be great if we had the bastard who killed him in custody by then."

Before Grayson could answer, Tippy was back at the table. As she scribbled down the deputies' orders, she casually asked how they all knew one another.

"Grayson's one of the best CSIs on the force," Diaz stated proudly. He's helped us close a lot of cases over the last couple of years."

"A CSI. Good for you," Tippy replied, feeling very uncomfortable all of a sudden. She wondered if he had anything to do with the murder case at the St. Charles. Krulak had told her how his young caretaker had disappeared, and she was beginning to put two and two together. Perhaps that blood in Krulak's hotel room had belonged to the young man. If he had been murdered and she could find out who had committed the deed, she would be in the vampire's good graces forever. This could be her ticket to immortality.

"She's an odd one," Schoenfeld said in a low voice as he watched Tippy return to the kitchen. "All wrapped up in that vampire shit the kids like so much."

"But she's got to be at least forty," Diaz quipped.

"True, but she believes in it. One day when I came in here after shift, we got to chatting. Those fangs had recently been implanted and were giving her pain. I recommended that she see my cousin, Marvin. He's the best implant dentist in Reno and the darling of the family. My mother always wanted me to go into dentistry like him," Schoenfeld said. "Anyway, it was a slow evening, and Tippy told me that she wanted to become a vampire. I took one look at all those tats and braids and figured she was just some old hippie whack job. But she seems harmless enough, and she's a good waitress."

"What does she think vampires do?" Grayson asked nonchalantly.

"You know. The same shit they do in the movies. They sparkle, drink animal blood to remain immortal, fight werewolves, and fall in love with beautiful human women."

Both Diaz and Grayson roared with laughter. Diaz from how ridiculous it all was and Grayson from knowing how far from the truth Tippy's ideas about vampires actually were.

Chapter 112

The next evening before shift began, Patrick, Sarah, Grayson, and West met to design a plan to find Anton Krulak. Sarah had reviewed all the latest murders and had mapped out the areas, dates and times where they had been committed. She also created a victimology for each homicide. West was sure there'd be a pattern in the vampire's attacks and charged Grayson with creating a computer algorithm to determine the frequency of the attacks and the possibilities of where and when another murder would occur. Patrick would go to the St. Charles Hotel in his writer's guise and see what information he could extract from the staff.

"Before we get going, I wouldn't mind if you gave us all a blessing," West said as he approached Patrick.

"I'd be honored."

Sarah and Grayson joined hands and then took West's hands in theirs.

"Heavenly Father, I ask that you protect your earthly servants Orlando West, Thomas Grayson and Sarah Baker as they venture into battle with Satan and all those who serve him, especially the vampire Anton Krulak. Protect them from all danger as they fight this evil being who has claimed so many lives and souls. And may the talents you have bestowed upon my friends be the tools of the vampire's very destruction. In the name of the Father, and of the Son and of the Holy Spirit, Amen."

The three CSIs clenched hands and then withdrew from the circle they had unconsciously formed.

"Let's meet up after shift," West said. "Hopefully, not much will be going on tonight, and we can get a lot done."

"It's up to us now," Grayson said. "Just like the Four Musketeers."

"I hope Krulak will prove to be an easier adversary for us than Cardinal Richelieu was for the Musketeers," Patrick said, knowing his French Literature all too well.

Grayson nodded in agreement.

Sarah gazed at Patrick with love and anxiety. She didn't like him going out into the night on his own, but he was now armed with the vampire dagger and that gave her some solace.

"Be safe," she said, wanting desperately to kiss him.

"No worries, sheila. I'll be fine."

Patrick arrived at the newly reopened St. Charles Hotel dressed in a snug black tee shirt that accentuated his taught, muscular chest, black jeans and black leather boots, and looking like sex on a stick. The young woman at the check-in desk didn't have a chance against his good looks or his Aussie charm.

"Evening," he said with a wink and a dazzling smile. "What's a pretty girl like you working on a Saturday night instead out dancing?"

"Hello," the clerk said, giggling. Plain and plump, she couldn't be more than twenty-one and was unaccustomed to handsome men flirting with her.

"My name's Patrick Mars. What's yours?"

"I'm, ah...my name's Allison."

"Nice to make your acquaintance, Allison."

"Do you want a room?" she asked with another giggle. "Are you here on vacation?"

"No. I don't need a room. I'm staying with a friend here in Carson while I research my new book."

"You're a writer?"

"Yes, and a right good one at that," Patrick said, laying on his accent nice and thick. "Maybe you could be a character in my new story."

"Ooh, I'd like that. What kind of stories do you write?"

"Murder mysteries."

"Cool!"

"I hear a lot has happened over the years at this hotel. Do you know anything about any residents or guests who have met with foul play?" Patrick asked as he reached for his pad and pen. As he pulled the notepad from his pants pocket, the small porcelain pendant with Krulak's portrait came out with it.

Allison instantly scooped it up. "I know this man!" she said excitedly.

"You do?"

"Yes! His name is Anthony Krulle. He's been a guest on and off since the hotel was officially closed, and for several years he's rented out the entire hotel just for himself and a friend. Last week the St. Charles was officially reopened to the public. Anyway, I've only seen a glimpse of him over the couple of years I've worked here. He's a real night owl. He comes here to gamble."

"Really. Tell me more."

"I..." Allison began to say, but then stopped and looked at the pendant and then at Patrick. "This pendant looks really old, so it couldn't be Mr. Krulle, could it? Where did you get it?"

Patrick's mind raced as he tried to come up with a plausible answer. "I found it in an antique shop over on Curry Street. The proprietor said it was a portrait of a young man who lived here many years ago. Perhaps your guest is a relative of his and that explains the strong resemblance."

"Wouldn't that be interesting if they were long lost relatives? What a great story, huh?"

Patrick nodded.

"Did you know the young man living with him died in one of their rooms?" Allison asked, almost in a whisper.

"No, I didn't," Patrick, replied as the fine blond hairs on the back of his neck and his arms bristled.

"The dayshift clerk told me that Mr. Krulle's friend was found by some kids who had broken into the hotel late one night. It looked like he'd been stabbed. I really don't know much more than that. Maybe you can get more information at the Sheriff's Department."

"I'll try that. By the way, do you know where Mr. Krulle is now?"

"No. He moved out before his companion died. I don't think he left a forwarding address."

The bright spark of hope that had just been ignited was instantly snuffed out. "I see. Well, thank you for your help anyway, Allison."

"You're welcome, Patrick."

"You have a good evening," he said and turned to leave.

"Do you have a number where I can reach you in case—"

"In case of what?"

"In case his friend comes back."

Chapter 113

"What friend?" Patrick asked.

"The lady who moved everything from Mr. Krulle's hotel rooms said she was a friend of his."

"What was her name?"

"I don't know. I actually didn't see her. My supervisor told me that she called and made arrangements over the phone. One of the young men she hired left an envelope full of cash to pay the rent and a nice tip for Jackie too. He had the room key, and he and another young man moved out all the stuff. I heard they moved a coffin too. I wonder why Mr. Krulle had a coffin in his room. Probably for that kinky sex those kind of guys are into," she said, thinking Anthony Krulle and his friend had been lovers.

"Could your supervisor tell me who these young men were and where the items were moved?"

"I'm not sure, but you can call her," Allison replied as she jotted down a phone number on a Post-it note and then handed it to Patrick.

"You're a sweetheart."

Allison giggled again.

Patrick held his breath and dialed the number Allison had given him. After a couple of rings, Jackie Malone answered. Patrick gave her the same story he'd given Allison, and Jackie was more than eager to help an author who was writing about the St. Charles.

"Thank you so much for the information, Jackie. I'll be sure to add a note of thanks to you in the forward of my new book," Patrick said, carrying on the writer's guise.

"That would be wonderful! If you need any more help, you know how to reach me."

"I do," Patrick said and hung up.

Seconds later he was calling a woman named Tara. The phone rang a dozen times but then terminated without going into voicemail. *No worries*, Patrick thought as he hurriedly walked around the block from Carson Street to West 3rd where he had parked Sarah's sports car. The important thing was he had a name and number and could keep trying.

Although the Sheriff's Department was only a few minutes away from the St. Charles Hotel, Patrick felt like it had taken an hour to get there. As he drove the short distance, he had a peculiar feeling of being watched but shrugged it off as nervous excitement. He parked the car in Sarah's assigned spot and nearly ran into the building.

Krulak circled overhead, watching with angry, apprehensive eyes as the blond man disappeared into the red brick building. He knew at once who it was. It was the priest—the vampire hunter! And he was driving the same bright yellow sports car Krulak had followed out on US 395 some months ago. Were the vampire hunter and the young woman who owned this car in league with one another? Who was she? His sister? His friend?

Perhaps the priest was a fallen one like himself and the woman was his lover. Krulak needed to know more.

Descending from the evening sky, he could feel the transformation taking place. By the time Krulak lit to the ground, his mortal form had taken shape. Swiftly, he entered his small sanctuary on Lee Street and emerged minutes later dressed in the plaid shirt and blue jeans Tippy had bought him.

Although Krulak preferred flying, enjoying the freedom and excitement of it, he used his ability to dematerialize and rematerialize at times such as this and within seconds found himself a block from the Sheriff's Department. Several patrol SUV's passed him by, but he walked down the street with complete anonymity. After all, Mr. Krulle hadn't killed Deputy Red Horse.

Krulak casually sauntered into the parking lot and found the yellow sports car in space number ten. The door was unlocked, and he chuckled at the absurdity of how easy everything was for him. He grabbed the documents from the glove compartment and scanned them beneath the overhead beam of the streetlight a few feet in front of her car. According to the Nevada DMV paperwork, Sarah Baker was the registered owner, and she lived on East Fifth Street in Carson City.

"Well, Miss Baker. I am definitely coming for a visit," Krulak said as he carefully returned the document to the glove compartment. "And very soon too."

Chapter 114

"Hey, Patrick," Grayson said as the priest came into the office. "You're back earlier than I expected. Is that good or bad?"

"Actually, it's great, and I couldn't wait until after shift to tell you what I've learned," he said excitedly like a little kid keyed up on too much sugar.

"Is everything all right?" Sarah asked as she stood at the office threshold, a cup of coffee in each hand.

"I've got a lead on Krulak," Patrick replied, taking one of the cups from her hand. "Do you mind?"

"Be my guest," Sarah said as she handed Grayson the other cup.

Patrick took a sip of the coffee before speaking. "I've confirmed that Krulak was at the St. Charles with Marius Nicolescu."

"Was?" Sarah asked, defeat tingeing her voice.

"Yes, was. I don't know where Krulak is now, but I do have the name and phone number of the woman who helped move his belongings out of the hotel. Perhaps she can give us a forwarding address for him. I also know the name he's going by."

Sarah's face visibly brightened. "What's he calling himself?"

"Anthony Krulle."

"That's rich," Grayson groaned. He would have laughed at the irony if it hadn't been such a serious situation.

"It is rather, isn't it?" Patrick conceded.

"I don't give a damn what the bastard is calling himself. All I want to call him is *dead*!" Sarah snapped.

Patrick and Grayson turned in unison and looked at Sarah.

"Take it easy, partner. Patrick's doing everything he can. I'm sure it's only a matter of time until Krulak meets his boss down below."

Patrick smiled a bit.

"What's so funny?" Sarah snapped again.

"For a moment, I thought Grayson was going to say Down Under instead of down below."

"It gets that hot in Australia?" Grayson asked.

"I imagine the Devil himself takes his holiday in the Outback during February; it's that bloody hot."

Grayson laughed and so did Patrick. Sarah couldn't help herself and began laughing too, and the tension in the room slowly but steadily faded.

For the next hour, the three tried to formulate a plan of attack on Krulak. They narrowed down his recent killing areas and were confident they would be able to predict the general time and area where the next killing would take place. However, they hoped to prevent that by finding Krulak and killing him before he had the chance to kill again.

"Hey, guys," West said as he came halfway into the office.

"What's up, boss?" Grayson asked.

"I knew my good mood from Patrick's promising news wouldn't last long."

"What changed it?" Sarah queried.

"We have a 407 combined with a 426 at the AM/PM minimart on North Carson."

"A robbery/rape at a convenience store? That's a new one on me," Sarah said, disgustedly.

"Maybe the store surveillance cameras caught the crime. Sarah, get over to the medical center and do a rape kit, and Grayson, you process the scene," West directed.

"On it, boss," he replied with a salute.

"I don't know how long I'll be," Sarah said to Patrick.

"I'll just stay here and work. Be careful, the both of you."

The CSIs nodded and were on their way.

As they gathered their gear from their lockers, Grayson turned to Sarah and said, "You're really lucky, Baker. Patrick has the patience of a saint."

"I was thinking the very same thing."

Chapter 115

Shelby Lynn Ford sat on the edge of the examination table dressed in an obligatory examination gown. Her face was smeared with tears, old and new, and the bruising under her eye, on her cheek and around her neck was just beginning to show.

"Shelby. I'm CSI Sarah Baker from the Carson City Sheriff's Department. I'm here to do a rape kit."

When the young woman heard the word *rape*, she burst into tears again. Sarah's heart went out to her. She tenderly placed her hand on Shelby's shoulder and looked her in the eyes. "It won't hurt. I promise. The nurse will help me."

Shelby sniffled a couple of times and then mumbled, "Okay."

The attending nurse prepped the patient and then Sarah gently took a semen sample and secured it in an evidence bag. Afterward, she carefully scraped beneath each of Shelby's fingernails and put the scrapings in another evidence bag. She then combed Shelby's her hair for any trace evidence. When the hairs and minute debris were secure, Sarah shot a series of photos, making sure to capture every detail of the young woman's injuries.

As she was finishing up, Detective Brown announced himself on the other side of the curtain.

"In a minute," Sarah called out. "Detective Brown will ask you a few questions now. I'll stay with you if you'd like."

"Yes, please stay," Shelby replied, desperately grabbing Sarah's hand like it was a lifeline.

"You can come in, detective," Sarah directed.

The big man was nervous; he hated interviewing rape victims. Making them relive an attack just added insult to injury, but it was part of the job.

"This won't take long, Miss Ford," he said in a kindly voice. "Can you tell me what happened and if possible describe your attacker?"

"I was working behind the counter like I always do," she began, her eyes darting to Sarah for support.

Sarah squeezed Shelby's hand and nodded for her to continue.

"A man came into the store..."

"What did he look like?" Detective Brown coaxed.

"He was tall, slender and very handsome. He had black hair and his eyes were blue, but his skin was pale like he'd never been out in the sun."

Sarah's attention was instantly piqued.

"It...it's hard to describe what happened," Shelby said as new tears rolled down her cheeks. Time seemed warped. One minute he was in front of the counter, and the next he was on top of me. I was fighting. I really was, but he was so strong!"

"There, there," Brown soothed.

Sarah shot the detective an annoyed look. *There, there. Are you fucking serious?*

"You did all you could. It's not your fault, you know. Can you tell us anything else that would help us capture the man who did this to you?" Sarah asked.

"That's just it. I don't think it was a man!"

Sarah and Detective Brown stared at Shelby and then at each other.

"If I tell you what I saw, you'll think I'm delusional."

"I promise I...we won't think any such thing," Sarah replied softly.

"When he was on top of me, I had my eyes shut tight, willing it to be over. But just for a moment I opened them, and he was the man I saw in the store. Maybe I hit my head when I fell to the floor, but all of a sudden..."

Shelby's shallow breaths came in rapid succession, and her chest heaved up and down just as rapidly. Sarah feared the young woman was going to faint before she could finish her sentence.

"Go on, if you can," Sarah coaxed.

"All of a sudden he wasn't a man. I know this sounds crazy, but you have to believe me. He was some kind of hideous winged creature with blazing red eyes and fangs. His nails were like claws, and he...he...when he came inside me it was like fire. Then he became a man again. I think that's when I passed out. When I came to, he was gone and so was all the cash in the register."

"I believe you, Shelby. You've been very brave telling us what happened to you," Sarah said. "We'll leave you alone now so you can rest. Here's my card. Please call me if you need anything."

Shelby looked at Sarah's business card and then at her. "I will."

Sarah and Detective Brown turned to leave the exam room but were stopped at the striped, multicolored curtain cordoning off the room from the rest of the emergency ward.

"When you find who did this to me, don't arrest him, Detective Brown."

Brown gazed at the woman, his eyes beckoning for clarification.

"Kill him."

Chapter 116

"Now do you believe me?" Sarah growled at Brown when they'd reached his unmarked, black sedan.

"What am I supposed to say? That girl just went through hell, but you want me to believe she was raped by a vampire?"

"She told you as much!"

"By her own admission, Ford hit her head. It's a wonder she didn't see Santa Claus doing the deed, and that makes about as much sense as a vampire."

"God, Brown! How the hell did you ever make detective with such a closed mind?"

"I've got a description of the perp, the real perp. And when he's found, I'll prove to you that he's only a man."

"You don't need to prove anything to me. I know what's real and what isn't, and I know the truth. Shelby Lynn Ford does too. Just do your job, and I'll do mine," Sarah spat and stomped off to the Crime Scene Unit SUV.

There was no way Brown was ever going to believe the truth no matter how hard it hit him squarely in the face. After Sarah had calmed down, she decided that might be a good thing after all. His stubbornness might keep him out of harm's way and out of hers.

* * *

An IT tech traced the number Patrick had for Tara back to a disconnected burner phone. Sarah thought she could literally spit nails she was so mad.

"We'll find the woman and whoever moved Krulak some other way," Patrick said, trying to calm the angry young woman standing before him.

"How? When?" Sarah demanded.

He was afraid to tell her he didn't know.

"Why don't you go home and get some rest, Patrick," Grayson suggested.

"I think that's a good idea. I'll see you all later," he replied and left the office without saying good-bye.

Sarah grabbed a handful of case files from off the filing cabinet and sat down at her desk with a huff.

"You know I love you like a sister, Baker, but honestly, you can be a real bitch sometimes."

Sarah looked at Grayson like he'd just sprouted horns.

"Don't give me that look. You know it's true. Patrick's doing the best he can, so give the man a break."

"I'm doing the best I can too!"

"No one said you weren't."

Humbled, Sarah grabbed her cell phone and dialed Patrick's number. "I'm sorry," she said as soon as he answered.

"No worries, mate."

"So we're still mates?"

"You bet," came the forgiving response.

"Patrick..."

"Yes."

"When all this is behind us, we need to talk."

"I know."

Chapter 117

Tippy rolled over and looked at the clock on the nightstand next to her bed. It was almost three a.m., and she wondered where her dark angel was on this moonlit night. She longed to be with him, but she knew she had to remain patient. *All in good time*, she told herself. *You'll have all eternity with him, so be patient. Be patient.*

Tossing and turning for another hour, Tippy decided she might as well get up and be ready to welcome Krulak home. She grabbed her robe from the end of the bed and slipped it over her naked body. Padding softly down the hall, she stopped at his bedroom door and looked in. The blackout curtains were drawn tightly, and the coffin lid was ajar. The shiny mahogany glinted in the light that filtered from the hallway, beckoning Tippy as she gazed at the holy vessel. She wondered how it would feel to lay in it as her lord and master did each dawn to dusk. A smile tweaked the corners of her mouth, and her eyes twinkled with delight at the very thought.

Tippy pushed the heavy lid aside. The pungent earth called to her. She slipped from her robe and lay down in the coffin. The earth was cool and comforting as she closed her eyes and imagined what it would feel like to be immortal.

"Is my sarcophagus to your liking?" Krulak demanded.

Tippy's eyes flew open to find the vampire and his demons hovering above her. He glared mercilessly down at her, enjoying the fear and remorse shining in her eyes. Before her heart could beat again, he descended upon her. His claws viciously raked her plump, white breasts, and his fangs sank into the soft, pale skin of her throat. Tippy howled in agony. The vampire tasted her life force and was exhilarated beyond imagining, but he restrained himself, knowing the servant must only be punished and not killed. She was far too valuable to mortally wound.

His wings unfurled and formed a satanic canopy over the open coffin. Then he brutally took his handmaiden, stabbing her with his scalding shaft until she felt like she would split in two. Again and again the vampire rammed into her dry vault, savagely tearing at the delicate skin of her inner walls, until they bled.

With each vicious thrust, sobbing moans erupted from Tippy's gaped mouth. The demons shrieked hysterically as they circled above, reeling in each agonizing movement as if the vampire were violating them as well. Then Krulak screamed like a banshee and spent himself deep within his lover's quivering flesh, the burning essence calming his body and his soul. He suckled at her throat once more, savoring the delicious, warm scarlet fluid before withdrawing his still angry shaft. Tippy's entire body shook in painful gratitude upon her master's retreat.

As the dawn broke outside, the light of hell was extinguished for another day.

Chapter 118

Deputy Red Horse's funeral on the Pyramid Lake Indian Reservation was traditional, vibrant and befitting a noble warrior. His widow, family, friends, the Mayor of Carson City, all off-duty deputies and detectives in the department, as well as hundreds of officers from Northern California and Nevada, and the nightshift crime scene unit attended.

After the service West spoke briefly with Adrian Red Horse, the deputy's widow, and assured her that he, his team and the department were doing everything in their power to find her husband's killer. West desperately wanted to tell the young woman the perp would be dead in the near future, but he wondered if he believed that anymore. Each time they got close to Krulak, it seemed like he was one step ahead. Now he had vanished completely—again.

"Native Americans have many similar traditions to the Aborigines of Australia," Patrick said with admiration as he, Sarah and Grayson headed to their cars.

"Is that so?" Grayson replied.

"Hmm," was all Patrick could think of to say. More than the pall of the funeral had descended upon them.

Sarah was glad it was her RDO. The last thing she wanted to do tonight was go to work. Suddenly, it all seemed so futile.

"Why don't we go out and do something fun tonight," Patrick offered.

"Fun? What's that?" she shot back.

"Be nice," Grayson piped up.

"What do you and Kelly do when you have the same night off," Patrick asked.

"We're lucky to both work the night shift. Our off days don't always coincide, but we make the most of it when they do. Kelly's a movie buff, so we try to see the latest releases. A couple of weeks ago we went dancing at the Aura Ultra Lounge. We had a great time."

"How about that, sheila?"

"How about a movie instead?" Sarah countered.

"Deal."

"You kids have fun," Grayson said, laughing as he opened his car door.

"Hold down the fort tonight," Sarah called out as he drove off.

Grayson waved out the window, acknowledging the directive.

"Do you want me to drive?" Patrick asked.

"Yes, you can drive," Sarah said, handing him the keys.

Patrick jumped into the driver's seat before Sarah could change her mind. As she opened the passenger side door, she thought she heard someone call her name. She turned around but no one was there. *It must be the wind*, she thought and got inside the tiny car.

It was a beautiful day, and Sarah enjoyed the scenery as they drove back to Carson City. But soon the warm sun beating into the cabin and the road vibration lulled her to sleep. Patrick smiled and slipped his hand over hers, reassuring her that he'd see them safely home.

They hadn't travelled more than a few miles when he spotted a gray-colored sedan in the review mirror. It was a couple of car lengths behind them, but Patrick thought it looked like the same car parked outside the townhouse that morning. It and that car had black tinted windows and a busted out left front headlight. He changed lanes, and the car mirrored the movement. Again he changed lanes, and again the sedan followed suit. When Patrick sped up, it sped up. When he slowed, it slowed. This was far too much of a coincidence for his liking. He took the next exit ramp, hoping to evade his unknown pursuer.

Sarah woke as the car reached the surface street. "Where are we?" she asked, her voice thick with sleep.

"I thought I'd fill up the tank for you," Patrick replied, hoping to sound credible.

"That's nice."

A moment of silence followed as Patrick searched for a gas station. He saw a Chevron a block down and headed toward it. Although the tank was still half full, he didn't want Sarah to worry and continued with the charade.

As he pulled the hose from the car, he glanced out to the street. The gray-colored sedan drove by at an even pace. Patrick couldn't see the driver, but he was sure the driver had seen him and knew who he was. When they reached the highway again, the car was gone, but the strange feeling Patrick had of being followed remained.

Chapter 119

"Admit it. You loved the movie," Sarah sweetly demanded as she and Patrick walked up the brick path to her townhouse.

"I'll admit it was better than a sharp stick in the eye," he replied, chuckling and giving her a playful elbow in the side.

They were almost to the door when a cat ran up behind them and began yowling. Sarah immediately turned and was shocked to see Bagheera at her feet.

"How did you get out, you little booger?" she asked, sweeping the cat into her arms.

"He probably slipped out when we left. That will teach him," Patrick said as he grabbed the doorknob. The door cracked open. "I'm sure we locked this door."

"Yes! I double checked it."

"Stay here," he ordered. Cautiously, Patrick swung open the door and switched on the light. He couldn't believe the chaos that greeted him. All the furniture was on its side with the upholstery slashed and the stuffing yanked out; the framed prints that hung on the walls now lay smashed on the floor, along with the flat screen TV and every knickknack. The walls were smeared with what looked like blood, and huge spots on the carpeting reeked of urine.

"What is it?"

"Don't come in, Sarah. Call Detective Brown and Grayson. Now! Someone's vandalized your home."

In less than five minutes, a patrol deputy, Detective Brown and Grayson were at the townhouse. The deputy ordered Sarah to remain outside until he secured the premises.

Begrudgingly, she obeyed the order and waited on the grass with Patrick, Grayson and Brown.

"All clear," the deputy said as he came out of the townhouse and secured his weapon. "I have to warn you, it's not a pretty sight in there."

"Come on. Let's get it over with," Brown said as he led the way into the living room.

Sarah hadn't gotten but three feet into the townhouse before she retched and then violently vomited popcorn and soda across the floor. "Shit! Shit! Shit!" she wailed. "I just contaminated the crime scene."

"It's okay, Sarah," Grayson said softly, using her Christian name. "We can eliminate you as a suspect."

"Who would do this and why?"

"Have you had any run-ins with anyone lately? At a scene maybe?" Detective Brown asked.

"No. No one."

"No threats? Comments? Harassment of any kind?"

Sarah shook her head and carefully stepped around the disaster that used to be her home.

"There is something..." Patrick said and then stopped.

"What's that, Father?" Brown asked.

"On the way home from the funeral, I thought someone was following us."

"Why didn't you say anything to me about it?" Sarah asked, looking incredulously at Patrick.

"I didn't want you to worry. You have enough giving you bad dreams at night as it is."

The detective raised an eyebrow at the comment.

"After I pulled over for gas, the car passed us by, and I didn't see it again."

"Sounds like a coincidence to me," Brown stated authoritatively, but give me the description and the plate number if you have it just in case."

Patrick described the car, but much to his dismay had forgotten to get the license plate number.

"Well," the detective said, aggravated, "at least we have something to go on." He advised Sarah to pack a bag and spend the night elsewhere while Grayson processed the latest home invasion in Carson City, Nevada.

Chapter 120

It had been a fitful night for everyone. Sarah tossed and turned. Patrick barely slept as he kept watch over her, and Bagheera jumped from one queen-sized bed to the other, trying to figure out which Holiday Inn bed he should sleep in and with whom.

By dawn Sarah was up, showered and dressed. Patrick had finally fallen asleep with Bagheera cuddled in his arms, so she tried to be as quiet as possible. It would be a full day meeting with her insurance agent to fill out claim forms and then finding someone to clean up the mess in her house.

All Sarah's possessions downstairs were ruined and would have to be hauled away. The carpeting needed to be replaced and the walls cleaned and repainted. Luckily, the perp hadn't touched the upstairs, which was a surprise, but she was grateful nonetheless.

"Hey, sleepyhead," Sarah said as Patrick awakened and stretched lazily.

"G'day," came the happy response.

As soon as Bagheera heard them talking, he was up and meowing for his breakfast.

"You'll have to wait a bit, mate," Patrick said. "Your mum needs to go out and buy you some food."

"Damn!" Sarah spat. She'd packed a few things so quickly last night that she didn't even think to bring Bagheera's food and bowls.

Sarah went to the bathroom and turned on the cold water. Bagheera was right behind her. He jumped on the counter and put his head under the tap and drank and drank and drank, making her feel even guiltier than she already did.

"Want me to run down to Walmart and get some food? I should pick up a box and some litter too."

"I'm already dressed. I'll go," Sarah replied.

"Okay. Be careful."

Sarah grabbed her car keys and was out the door. It was already warm and sunny, and the day looked brighter in more respects than just the weather. Then the heavens opened up and a torrential downpour of despair washed over her. Her beautiful sports cars sat in ruins. The headlights, windshield and side windows had been smashed out. The convertible top was shredded to pieces, and all the tires were flat. Long, deep scratches ran the length of the car on both sides, and the hood looked as if some kind of acid had been thrown across it.

For the second time in less than twelve hours, Sarah was calling 911. She dialed their room and told Patrick what had happened and then waited for him and the sheriff to arrive.

"Oh, Sarah," Patrick said as he put his arm around her.

"What's happening? I don't understand."

"I don't understand it either, but you'll get through it. We'll get through it. Everything will be all right."

Patrick thought they should move to a different hotel. After arranging for a rental car, they moved into a room at a Bed and Breakfast Inn near the Governor's mansion. He prayed that whoever was terrorizing Sarah wouldn't have followed them, and she could get some rest there.

The woman who ran the B & B was a friend of West's, and a cat lover, so Sarah felt a bit more secure with these living arrangements than she had with the hotel they'd chosen out of desperation late last night.

After surveying the townhouse, the insurance agent estimated the amount of damage to Sarah's home and possessions was almost $17,000. He also wrote off her car. The price to repair the little roadster far exceeded the vehicle's worth.

"I guess I won't complain about paying for insurance anymore," Sarah said as she signed the paperwork.

"I hear that all the time," the insurance agent said. "If you need anything else, please don't hesitate to call me." He packed his briefcase, shook Sarah's hand and was off to see another client.

As he went out the door, the men from 1-800 Got Junk? arrived.

"What do you need hauled away?" a young Hispanic man with a heavy accent asked.

"Everything on the first floor plus the carpeting needs to be ripped up and removed," Sarah replied as she looked about the living room and dining area."

"Okay, senora."

Senora? In my dreams.

Two other Hispanic men joined him, and they began loading the dumpster that now sat in front of the townhouse. Sarah put up a brave front as she watched her possessions, now trash, being tossed piece-by-piece into the large metal bin.

"They're just things," Patrick said as he came up beside her and took her hand in his.

"I know, but they were *my* things."

Chapter 121

It was late afternoon when the men finished cleaning out the first floor of the townhouse. By then Sarah was ready for something to eat, a hot shower and a good night's sleep.

While she locked the front door, Patrick took a few of their things to his car. As he closed the trunk lid, he noticed a gray colored-sedan parked a few houses down the street. Like an Olympic sprinter he bolted for the car, yanked open the door and grabbed the man by the throat.

"Who are you?" he demanded. "And why are you following us?"

The man pushed Patrick's arm away and bailed out of the car with fists ready, but Patrick beat him to the punch. He knocked the big man to the ground and was about to land a devastating blow to his face when Sarah yelled at him.

"No, Patrick! Stop!"

He spun around all the while keeping the man at bay.

"I know him!"

"You know this man?"

"Yes," came the faint answer. "What are you doing here, Sebastian?"

"Sebastian?" Patrick echoed, staring first at the man and then at Sarah. He unclenched his fist, lowered his arm and stood up.

"I've been watching over you, Sarah. Krulak is in town."

"I know, but you shouldn't be here. There's a warrant out for your arrest."

"Believe me, Sarah, I never meant to kill Marius, but I do mean to kill Krulak."

"That's impossible," Patrick interrupted. "A vampire can only be killed in a certain manner."

"Then are you going to kill him, Father?"

"Yes, I am. But we have to find him first."

"He's no longer at the St. Charles Hotel," Sebastian stated. "I went there, but all his things were gone."

"We know," Sarah said as she gazed at her former lover, her heart sinking.

Sebastian had lost weight, at least twenty pounds. His hair was now dull and shaggy, and his face was covered in a thick, dark beard flecked with gray. His warm brown eyes held the sadness and fear of a man who'd been on the run.

"He has a new servant," Sebastian said.

"You know this for sure?" Patrick asked.

"Yes, and the woman is clever. She eluded me when I followed her home one night, but I know where she works."

"Where?" Sarah nearly shouted.

"She works at a restaurant where you and the priest eat sometimes."

"My name is Patrick."

Sebastian looked the priest over with a wary eye and then hesitantly held out his hand. "I'm Sebastian."

They shook hands, acknowledging their common goal.

"We need to get out of the street," Sarah said. "Are you hungry? Why don't you come with us and get something to eat?"

"You can't be seen with me."

"Tell us where you're staying. I'll bring you some food, and we'll talk."

"No. I'm all right."

"Tell me where you're staying."

"I'm staying at the Pussycat Ranch Motel," he said, embarrassed.

Sarah laughed, breaking the tension. "Well, it's not like anyone would look for you at a whorehouse. We'll come by later and bring you some food."

"No, I—"

"I insist. Now go."

Sebastian nodded in gratitude and withdrew, but Sarah grabbed him and hugged him fiercely.

Patrick felt a painful twinge in his chest.

Chapter 122

Sarah and Patrick met Sebastian shortly after 8:00 p.m. The Pussycat Ranch was located off Highway 50 in Dayton. Unless one was frequenting the business, people drove past the establishment in a steady stream, not caring any more about it than they did a convenience store or a church.

"Please come in," Sebastian said as he opened the door and welcomed his friend and new ally into his makeshift home. "We have a great deal to discuss."

Sarah unpacked the bag of groceries and deli sandwiches she'd brought and then joined Sebastian and Patrick at the small table in the corner of the room.

"I suppose we shouldn't waste any time and get down to brass tacks," Patrick said.

Sebastian looked blankly at the priest, not understanding the idiom.

"We need to discuss Krulak and the woman who now protects him," Sarah interjected.

"Ah, yes."

"What's the name of Krulak's new servant?" Sarah asked.

"I don't know, but I can describe her to you. She's a very strange woman."

Patrick immediately knew who Sebastian was speaking about, and the words tumbled from his mouth. "It's that waitress with the phony vampire fangs!"

"Yes! Yes! That's the one."

"Holy crap!" Sarah whispered through gritted teeth.

* * *

Krulak awoke feeling refreshed. The last few nights had been glorious. He had gone into the mountains and fed with abandon on deer and Big Horn sheep, something he had done in Romania when he first became a vampire. When he was sated, he came back to town and followed Sarah, watching her every move. He had delighted in trashing her home and car. Soon she would be at the breaking point and even the priest would be unable to comfort her—or rescue her.

"My lord, did you rest well?" Tippy asked as she gazed with desire at the vampire. His naked body was beautiful and whole and perfect.

"I did."

Krulak had slashed his hand and used his blood to swipe across Sarah's walls, marking her home and her as his own. Soon he would take her as he had the woman who now served him. When his lust for her flesh had been sated and the fire in his groin had been extinguished, the vampire would satisfy his lust for her blood. Slowly, he would tear her apart, piece-by-piece. And if he had his way, this splendid torture would be done as the priest watched on in helpless agony.

* * *

"The waitress doesn't think I know who she is," Sebastian said. "I overheard her talking with a co-worker at the restaurant. They all think she's crazy, and they laugh at her when she's not around."

"I imagine so," Sarah said, remembering the first time she had seen the woman sporting vampire fangs.

"She spoke at great length about the man who now employs her. She didn't reveal the man was a vampire, and who would believe her. However, she bragged he was from a noble family in Sighisoara, Romania. That couldn't be a coincidence. She is a foolish woman, enamored by the vampires. She has no idea the danger she's in."

"Amen to that," Patrick declared.

"It's my hope she will lead me to Krulak. Tomorrow afternoon, I will follow her when she gets off work."

"Do you have a phone?" Sarah asked.

"Here's my number. As soon as I know where she lives, I'll call you."

"Thank you, Sebastian," Sarah said as she reached out and took his hand.

"I would do anything for you, Sarah."

"We should go now," Patrick suggested as he rose from the table. He nodded at Sebastian and headed toward the door. Sarah followed closely behind.

"Before you go, Patrick, may I speak to you alone?"

"I'll be out in the car," Sarah said, her fingertips touching Patrick's arm with reassurance.

When she was out of earshot, Sebastian said, "Please take care of Sarah. I love her."

"I do too. I'll guard her with my life."

Chapter 123

"What day is it?" the restaurant manager asked.

"Payday," Tippy said as she grabbed her check from his hand.

"Mama's bringing home the bacon," Sally, Tippy's co-worker, said. "So what are you and that fine new man of yours doing tonight?"

"Something special."

"You go, girl," the manager said and returned to the kitchen.

Tippy nearly ran the entire three miles home. She didn't know if her heart was beating wildly from the exercise or the excitement of what the night would bring.

"Now you understand what to do," Krulak said.

"I understand perfectly."

"Good. You will be well rewarded, my faithful handmaiden."

"Thank you, my lord."

The vampire smiled, reared back and then struck Tippy hard across the face. Several brutal blows followed. He rent her blouse with little effort and then ran his serpent-like tongue across both breasts before biting down on one of the hard, pink nipples.

Tippy gasped in ecstasy.

"That should do nicely for now," Krulak said, withdrawing.

"Yes, I think so," Tippy replied as she gathered her senses and wiped the blood from her mouth. Then with unsteady fingers she picked up the phone and dialed 911.

* * *

Sarah studied the lab report. The test result on the blood sample taken from her house was definitely human. *What kind of sick son-of-a-bitch uses human blood to vandalize someone's home?* she thought. Then it hit her like a proverbial ton of bricks. Krulak! She compared the DNA markers from the blood at her townhouse to the vampire's DNA. It was a perfect match.

Grayson looked up from his paperwork just in time to see Sarah fall heavily into her desk chair. Her face was as white as death, and her entire body shook uncontrollably.

"What's wrong?"

"The blood from my house…it was Krulak's."

Grayson felt like he'd been sucker punched.

"You can't go back home. It's not safe."

"No place is safe as long as Krulak's alive."

"You're right. Why don't you and Patrick move in with me? I have plenty of room."

"That's all you need, us and Bagheera as houseguests. We'll stay where we are for now. Hopefully, it won't be for long."

"Are you sure?"

"Yes, but thanks for the offer."

"Anytime."

The phone rang and Grayson answered. "Uh, huh. Got it. I'll let her know. Okay. You caught a case. A home invasion and a possible 415. Here's the address."

"You're not coming with me?"

"I'm going in the opposite direction. I have a 406 out in Carson Valley."

"I guess I'll see you when I see you," Sarah said as she grabbed her messenger bag and was out the door before having the chance to call Patrick and tell him about the lab results.

* * *

The neighborhood was dark and quiet when Sarah pulled up to the duplex on Lee Street. All the residents were home for the night, so she had to park the Crime Scene Unit SUV a block from the vic's house.

As Sarah unloaded her field kit from the back of the vehicle, she felt a hand lightly tap her shoulder. She jumped and turned, thinking it was a nosey neighbor come to ask her questions about what was going on. But no one was there. *God, Baker, you're really losing it.* Sarah continued unpacking her gear but turned around again when she felt another soft tap on her shoulder. The vampire's face was mere inches from hers, his hot breath burning her skin. Krulak swept her into his arms and then took flight.

Chapter 124

Two hours into shift, West was only a third of the way through his end of month reports. When the phone rang, he was glad to have an excuse to take a brief break.

"Crime Scene Unit. Dr. West."

"Sorry to bother you, Dr. West. This is Deputy Mike Runyon. I'm at a home invasion with assault on Lee Street. I've been waiting for one of your CSIs to arrive, but so far no one's showed."

"What? I sent Baker over there an hour ago."

"Maybe she went to the wrong address."

"That's highly unlikely. I'll call her as soon as I hang up."

"By the way, the vic doesn't want to go to the hospital, but I'd like the scene secured and processed for prints and trace before I leave."

"I understand. I'll call you back in just a few and let you know Baker's ETA." West hung up and immediately called Sarah's cell phone. The call went straight into voicemail. An uneasy feeling roiled in his gut. Sarah was never late, and she always answered her phone. He redialed the deputy.

"Runyon."

"Runyon. West here. I'll be at your scene in ten minutes."

"10-4," the deputy replied.

West called Detective Brown and apprised him of the situation.

"I don't have a good feeling about this," the detective declared. "I'm going with you. I'll meet you at my car."

West didn't waste time with pleasantries and hung up without another word. A few minutes later he was in Brown's Crown Vic, lights flashing and siren wailing. As Brown turned on Lee Street, he could see the department SUV parked at the curb. "She's here," he said with relief.

"I don't think so," West said as he jumped from the vehicle before it had rolled to a complete stop. He ran to the SUV and found its back door open, but Sarah wasn't inside. Her field kit sat undisturbed on the ground.

Checking the house numbers, West found the duplex and knocked on the door, announcing himself as he came in.

"Dr. West," Runyon said, "this is Tara Tipton—"

"Ma'am," West said politely, cutting off the deputy. "I'll be right with you, but I first need to speak to Deputy Runyon in private."

The deputy shot West a curious look.

"Come outside for a minute."

Runyon nodded and obediently followed West out to the front porch where they met Detective Brown.

"We have a situation. Baker arrived on scene, but I believe she's been abducted."

"Abducted?"

West grimaced. "Detective, would you call for back up while I go speak with Ms. Tipton."

"Sure thing."

"Miss Tipton, I apologize for the interruption," West said as he came into the duplex. "What the hell is going on?"

Tara Tipton was nowhere to be found.

Chapter 125

The night was perfect, and Krulak was nearly delirious as he flew toward St. Teresa's with Sarah tucked securely under his arm. She'd fainted when he had swept her into his embrace, and it made him laugh hysterically.

The outside of the church was well lit, and the elegant brown brick sanctuary with its multicolored, modern stained glass windows was like a welcoming beacon, guiding the weary travelers in from the night.

Krulak lit down at the front door and pulled the handle but met only resistance. His temper flared. He kicked in the massive glass door without a second thought, and thousands of diamond-like fragments crashed to the ground.

Storming into the narthex, Krulak looked about for the priest or sexton. The church was empty. Sarah started to come around. Quickly, he carried her into the sanctuary where he bound her to the heavy, wrought iron rack of flickering devotional candles with the rope from around his waist. As he tightened the last knot, Sarah's eyes flew open. Krulak's blazing black eyes stared back into hers.

"Good evening, dear Sarah."

"Krulak!" she spat back.

"So you know who I am. Silly me. And here I thought we would need a proper introduction."

"You and your crimes are well known to me, my partner and—"

"Speaking of partners, where is yours tonight?"

"Grayson will be looking for me, and so will every available deputy in the Carson City Sheriff's Department."

"Come now, Sarah. I am talking about your priest."

Sarah caught herself just as she was about to cry out Patrick's name.

"Is he as useless a lover as he is a vampire hunter?" Krulak asked with a sneer.

The blood chilled in her veins.

"Not to worry. Your fair knight will be joining us shortly, and then I will put an end to him forever," Krulak pledged.

Sarah was silent.

"Now, now. Vampire got your tongue? I—"

"What in heaven's name is going on in here?" Father Daniels shouted as he ran toward the bowed figure.

Krulak twisted around, his fangs bared, saliva dripping from the open maw. His legion of demons swarmed around him, protecting him from the holy man. Father Daniels crossed himself, and the action instantly incensed the vampire. He was upon the priest before the man could say, "Amen." Gnashing and growling, Krulak tore open Father Daniels's throat. Seconds later the priest slumped to the floor, his eyes vacant as his life and soul seeped from his body.

Sarah mumbled a frantic prayer for Father Daniels and then one for herself.

"Save your prayers for a god who cares," the vampire hissed. He bent close to Sarah's face and breathed in deeply. He could smell the thick scent of fear as it erupted from her delicate skin. Yet she did not beg for mercy. "Do you remember when we first met? You were quite brave that night. Much more so than the old man I killed afterward."

Sarah refused to answer.

"Since you are not in the mood to talk, whatever shall we do to pass the time until the priest arrives?" Krulak asked as he brushed a clawed finger across Sarah's breast.

She spat her answer into his face.

The vampire chuckled lightly and then wiped his face with a lick of his tongue.

Chapter 126

"Sherriff's dispatch. What is the nature of your emergency?"

"I'm not sure if this is an emergency, but I was driving down Lompa Lane and noticed the front door of St. Teresa's was open. It looked damaged, so I thought I'd better report it," said the caller.

"I'll send a patrol over to St. Teresa's right away."

The dispatcher disconnected the call and then directed any units in the vicinity of St. Teresa's to investigate.

* * *

"Patrick! Thank God I got a hold of you," West blurted as the priest answered his phone.

"What's wrong?"

West could barely choke out the words. But when he did, they shot out of his mouth in rapid succession like bullets from his Glock on qualifying day at the range. "Sarah's been abducted. Detective Brown and a dozen deputies are searching for her now."

"I have to help."

"Meet me at—"

"Hold on," Patrick directed. "Grayson's beeping in. Hello, Grayson."

"I'm finished with my scene and wanted to relay some important info to you—"

"I need to tell you something first," Patrick interrupted. "Sarah's gone missing. West thinks she's been abducted."

"Jesus Christ! It's Krulak. He took her."

"How could you possibly know that?"

"He's the one who trashed her house and probably her car. It was his blood at Sarah's house."

Silence.

"Patrick. Are you there?"

"I'm here. West is on the other line. Let me finish with him, and I'll call you right back."

"Call me as soon as you can."

"I will. I promise."

* * *

A patrol SUV pulled up to the front of St. Teresa's. Veteran officer Eddie Myers hopped out with his Maglite in hand and walked to the church entrance. He flashed a beam across the shattered glass door and then into the narthex. He immediately called base and reported his location and disposition of the scene. Assuming vandalism, he continued into the church expecting to see graffiti covered walls but instead found a scene straight out of a horror movie.

Father Daniels's naked body lay prostrate across the altar in a pool of blood, an upside down crucifix stuffed into his anus. Krulak had taken great delight in desecrating the priest and the altar with this abhorrent act.

To the right of the altar Sarah sat tethered, shaking her head, her eyes wide with fear. Meyers moved toward her, but Krulak caught him from behind, snapping the deputy's neck in two before he could take another step.

"That was far too easy. I promise I will take my time with the priest," Krulak vowed.

* * *

West hurriedly took photos of the Crime Scene Unit SUV, Sarah's field kit, the street in both directions, and the surrounding houses. Then he secured the equipment and the SUV and met up with Detective Brown.

"Did any of the neighbors see or hear anything at all?" he asked Brown.

"No. Everyone was either watching TV, in the shower or sleeping.

West ran his hand over his mouth and sighed. He had never felt so helpless in his entire life.

As he and Brown drove back to the department to meet Patrick, West heard the call coming over the scanner regarding an unresponsive officer. He called dispatch and asked what was going on.

"Turn around." West demanded. "I know where Baker is. Hit the damn gas and head for St. Teresa's."

The Crown Vic's tires squealed like a cat in heat as Brown whipped a U-turn in the middle of North Roop.

"Patrick. West here. We're five minutes out from St. Teresa's. Krulak has Sarah there. I'm sure of it."

"I'm leaving now."

"See you—"

The sickening crunch of tons of metal colliding with one another cut off West's words, and his cell phone went sailing to the floorboard as the vehicle helplessly spun out in the middle of the intersection.

"Oh, shit!" Brown growled as he held the steering wheel tightly in his beefy hands.

When the Crown Vic finally came to a stop, the men bolted out of it; Brown to confront the driver of the truck that had hit them and West to inspect the damage. The front right quarter panel and wheel were crushed into the engine block. They wouldn't be going any farther tonight in this vehicle.

West retrieved his cell phone and called Patrick and advised him of the situation.

"I'll call for backup now."

"No! Don't do that!" Patrick shouted. "If Krulak sees an army heading for him, he might kill Sarah right off. I'll take care of him."

"Are you sure you want to go it alone?"

"Your bullets are useless against Krulak. I'm the only one who can kill him," Patrick replied without bravado.

"We'll stand down. God be with you, Patrick."

"And with you."

Chapter 127

"You truly are beautiful, Sarah," Krulak crooned as he leaned close to her face, breathing in her scent once more.

Sarah retreated as much as she was able within her biting restraints.

The vampire's blazing black eyes searched her face and then slowly scanned her breasts, his gaze coming to rest at the spot where her legs came together.

"Do you taste as delicious as you look?"

Sarah's scream echoed throughout the quiet sanctuary.

"At last, you have found your voice." Krulak loosened the rope from around Sarah's ankles and began tearing at the cargo pants she wore.

She thrashed frantically, trying with all her might to fight him.

"Krulak!" Patrick shouted as he ran toward the vampire, the dagger clenched in his fist.

The demon legion swarmed down upon the priest, biting and clawing his hand as he closed in on their master. But Patrick held steadfastly onto the weapon, and the holy blade sunk deep into Krulak's chest, missing his heart by an inch.

The vampire reared back, a blood-chilling screech erupting from his throat. Then from his right side another silver dagger dug viciously into his flesh, and he reeled in surprise.

Sebastian stood glaring at his former master, his soft brown eyes hardened with hate.

"My old friend," Krulak said in a weakened voice as he pulled the dagger from his chest and then the one from his side.

Sebastian stood firm.

"Your dagger, although not quite as pretty as the priest's, cannot kill me."

Before Sebastian could respond, a sharp, burning pain tore through him. He stared in helpless disbelief at the dagger now lodged firmly in his abdomen.

"Sebastian!" Sarah cried.

"Forgive me, my love," he whispered and fell dead upon the cold, stone floor.

As Krulak returned his attention to Sarah, Patrick lunged at him. He knocked the holy dagger from the vampire's hand, seized it and thrust at him again. But Krulak's reflexes were like lightning, and his clawed fist swiped the priest's hand away before the dagger found its mark.

The weapon flew through the air, landing several feet away next to where Sarah sat still bound. An angry blow came down hard and loud across the side of Patrick's face and stars instantly burst across his field of vision. Then everything blurred, and the world went black.

Menacingly, the vampire advanced on Sarah. She was all his now, and she would die a beautiful death, crying out to God and all the saints as he brutally raped her before slowly tearing her apart. He was only a foot away when Sarah startled him by leaping to her feet. She scrambled from where she'd been tied and grabbed the heavy dagger.

The silver blade glinted in the soft light of the sanctuary as Sarah waved the dagger back and forth. Krulak found the young woman's resolve amusing and watched until he grew tired of her silly heroics. Unfurling his wings like a giant bird of prey, he flapped them furiously and flew into the vaulted ceilings. His legion of demons followed.

Sarah watched with anxious eyes, trying to gage when the vampire would attack. There was nowhere to hide, so she had to stand and fight.

The demons shrieked wildly, urging Krulak on. When Sarah's arm dropped slightly from fatigue, the vampire made his move. He dove straight for her throat, but halfway to his mark he was knocked off course.

Krulak circled the sanctuary, looking for what had impeded his descent. Seeing nothing, he attacked again. This time from the corner of his eye he saw the heavens open, and Michael the Archangel appeared above him, brandishing his golden sword.

Krulak's demons abandoned him en masse.

Michael's sword raked across the vampire's wing, and Krulak tumbled through the air. Disoriented and unable to regain his equilibrium, he crashed to the floor. Michael gazed lovingly down at Sarah, filling her trembling body with strength and her soul with courage.

She nodded, obeying the silent command, and raised the dagger high into the air and then plunged it into Krulak's heart.

The creature gasped and frantically clawed at the dagger, but Sarah pulled it from its resting place before the vampire's fingers could find purchase. Jerking back Krulak's head, Sarah ran the dagger's blade hard and fast across his throat until the grotesque head was severed from its body. It fell to the floor and rolled until it came to rest near Sebastian's feet.

Sarah pushed the vampire's body aside and ran stumbling to where Patrick lay. Scooping him into her arms, she rocked him back and forth, chanting, "*1 Corinthians 13, 1 Corinthians 13, 1 Corinthians 13.*"

Patrick groaned and opened his eyes. His injured hand touched the side of his face, and he winced in pain. Blood still streamed steadily from the wound at his temple. As his vision cleared, he could see the tears running down Sarah's cheeks, collecting on her lips. He smiled, reached up and tenderly cupped the tear-stained face. Pulling her close until their lips brushed ever so slightly, Patrick tasted her tears and then claimed her mouth.

As they desperately held on to one another, the sanctuary floor began rumbling. A thunderous roar followed, and the entire church shook violently. Flames shot from the earth deep below the foundation, and stone tiles exploded all around. Sarah instinctively covered Patrick with her small body, keeping him from further injury as the stone fragments rained down upon them.

A billowing black cloud rose from the flames, and a hideous creature, his body aflame and viler than any vampire, hovered above them. With a keening howl, he reached down and grasped Krulak's skull in his fiery hand and pressed it close to his breast. As the creature descended into the bowels of the earth, a blinding flash consumed Krulak's body.

All evidence of the vampire vanished.

"How are you feeling today?" Dr. Mayes asked her new patient.

"I couldn't be better," the woman replied in an excited voice.

"Are you ready to see what your baby looks like?" the doctor said as she pulled the sonogram equipment close to the examination table.

"I can't wait."

Dr. Mayes squirted a generous portion of KY Jelly onto the woman's belly and then took the sonogram wand in her hand and ran the instrument gently over the baby bump. "Congratulations! It's a boy! The heartbeat is strong, and he looks perfect," the doctor said as a rhythmic whooshing noise filled the air.

Moving the wand to and fro, she showed the mother-to-be the outline of the baby's head and body and then its beating heart.

"As you can see, he's absolutely beautiful, and—" Dr. Mayes yanked off her glasses and rubbed her eyes, barely able to comprehend what her eyes were telling her brain.

"What is it, doctor?"

"I think the equipment needs recalibrating," she replied. "Nothing to worry about. It's obviously just a shadow."

"A shadow? A shadow of what?"

"A wing!"

Tippy smiled.

About the Author

Brette O'Connell lives in Northern Nevada.

Ms. O'Connell's short stories and poetry
have been published in
Chamber Cameos and *Mask: Tales from the Underground 2.*

Ms. O'Connell holds a degree in
Administration of Justice/Forensic Science Technology
and is a member of the
American Criminal Justice Association.

One of her crime scene diagrams
was published in *Crime Scene Investigation:
The Forensic Technician's Field Manual.*

Other Brette O'Connell Titles

The Measure of a Man
Changing Terms
Wishes and Wings

All titles are available online at Amazon.com,
Createspace.com and Barnes and Nobel.com.

Quotes

"The dead cannot cry out for justice. It is a duty of the living to do so for them."

Lois McMaster Bujold

"Once you eliminate the impossible, whatever remains, no matter how improbable, must be the truth."

Arthur Conan Doyle

31560415R00239

Made in the USA
San Bernardino, CA
13 March 2016